Dervogilla

Dervogilla

Bríd Mahon

POOLBEG

Published in 1994 by
Poolbeg,
A division of Poolbeg Enterprises Ltd,
Knocksedan House,
123 Baldoyle Industrial Estate,
Dublin 13, Ireland

© Bríd Mahon 1994

The moral right of the author has been asserted.

A catalogue record for this book is available from the British Library.

ISBN 1 85371 352 X

Cover illustration by Alex Callaway
Cover design by Poolbeg Group Services Ltd/Red Dog Graphics
Set by Poolbeg Group Services Ltd in Goudy 10.5/13
Printed by Cox & Wyman Ltd, Reading, Berks.

To my sister, Brenda

Acknowledgement

I am deeply grateful to my friend, Mary Semple, for her invaluable help and encouragement in tracing records.

Author's Note

Dervogilla, Princess of Meath, is one of the most fascinating and enigmatic women in Irish history. Yet little is known of her life. She was a renowned beauty. Early writers refer to her as Ireland's Helen of Troy. Like her lover Dermot McMurrough, she was a patron of the Irish church, and gave lavish gifts of gold and cattle to the new Cistercian Monastery at Mellifont as well as rebuilding the exquisite Nuns' Chapel at Clonmacnois, the ruins of which still stand.

She was the wife of Tiernan O'Rourke, Prince of Breifne, who came of an aristocratic and ancient lineage. From the dark strands of history we learn that he was a man of violent temper and that he abused Dervogilla. She eloped with Dermot McMurrough while her husband was on pilgrimage to Lough Derg, and lived with the Leinster king in his castle at Ferns for two years. Tiernan O'Rourke forgave neither his wife nor his rival and set out to destroy Dermot McMurrough but in so doing destroyed himself and hastened the invasion of his country.

The Irish annalists have surprisingly little to say about Dervogilla. It is as if they decided to write her out of history. Together with Dermot McMurrough she has been reviled as the cause of the Norman invasion, though it is likely that Henry II of England was only biding his time. According to some of the Norman historians and to popular folklore, she accompanied Dermot McMurrough on his flight to England, Wales and France, seeking help.

She outlived Dermot McMurrough and Tiernan O'Rourke by many years.

In a brief entry in the *Annals of the Four Masters*, it is recorded that she died in the Abbey of Mellifont in the year of Our Lord, 1193.

The ancient kingdom of Breifne embraced the modern counties of Leitrim, Cavan and part of Roscommon. At one time, Tiernan O'Rourke, hereditary Prince of Breifne, ruled over territory extending across Ireland from the mouth of the Erne to the mouth of the Boyne.

The ancient kingdom of Meath included the present counties of Meath, Westmeath, Longford and parts of Offaly.

IRELAND
IN THE XIITH CENTURY
Immediately prior to the coming of the Normans

English Miles

Boundaries of Separate Kingdoms
Boundaries of Subordinate Kingdoms
& Groups of Tribes

Prologue

Mellifont, 1170

Dawn had barely broken when the horseman made his way along the bridle path running through the Greenwoods. As he left the shadow of trees and undergrowth to emerge into a clearing, the sun rose out of a bank of crimson clouds filling the sky with light. All around was the promise of a halcyon day but the rider paid no heed to the beauty of beech and oak, the heady perfume of wild flowers clustered in bank and hedge, the chorus of blackbirds and linnets or the far-off song of the lark, clear in the morning air.

Strange that he, Robert Balmais, tonsured clerk, secretary to the Archbishop of Canterbury, should be so obsessed with the story of a scandalous lady, now past her prime. He had first heard of the Princess Dervogilla from a monk, one of Malachy's order, out of Armagh. He was a strange, austere man who fasted and scourged his body for the sins of his fellow clerics and his wayward people. His voice had been harsh when he spoke of the Meath Princess.

"Dervogilla with her wanton ways," he said. "A woman who brought disaster on her country. False wife of Tiernan O'Rourke, Lord of Breifne, whore of Dermot McMurrough. Oh, but O'Rourke made McMurrough pay in the end though it took him many years." The monk ended his tirade on a strangely satisfied note, for so holy a man.

Since coming to Ireland, Robert Balmais had heard many different accounts of Dermot McMurrough. Some described him as a cowardly traitor, a king who sold his people to greedy Norman adventurers for gain. Others saw him as a man of vision, looking to Europe to bring a civilising peace

3

on his war-torn land. His bitterest enemies wrote him off as a cuckolding fool whose carnal appetites were such that he deflowered even the Abbess of Kildare, saintly successor to St Brigid herself. All were agreed that his downfall dated from the day he abducted the Lady Dervogilla from her husband's castle in Breifne. O'Rourke nourished his anger for years and eventually was avenged. Dermot McMurrough was driven from Ferns, his stone palace razed to the ground, the town burnt and his followers put to the sword. Harried and hunted, the once proud Leinster king took ship to Bristol to seek help from his Norman friends, thus setting in motion a train of events that ended in the conquest of his country. What magic had certain women, Robert Balmais wondered, that for their sakes, men threw away kingdoms, honour, even life itself?

The horseman had reached the river Boyne. His eyes raked the waters in vain for a place he could safely ford. Here the currents ran deep and swift. Away on the far bank he spied a boat, but there was no sign of the ferryman. He let out an almighty shout, startling a sleeping fox and causing a pair of swans to stop in their stately progress and rise with an irate flutter of wings. They were followed by a line of raucous gulls, making for the sea, four or five miles to the east. A couple of ragged urchins came out of the ferryman's hut, followed by a small squat man, who stood with his eyes squinting into the sun. The rider waved and the ferryman came down to the boat, crossing swiftly, skilfully nosing the barge into the bank, swinging it around with the current so that it steadied sufficiently for the horseman to lead his reluctant mare on board, the animal nervously pawing the wooden bottom.

At the far side of the river, the Norman cleric swung himself up on his horse, tossing the ferryman a handful of coins for his passage. "Am I on the right road for Mellifont?" he called down.

The ferryman puckered his lips. Then his face cleared and he pointed. "Aye. Droicheat Átha. Take the road north."

The horseman recalled that the natives referred to the monastery by the old Irish name of the townland. It was a poor enough place, though beginning to show signs of improvement, thanks to the Norman baron who had helped himself to broad acres and built a castle to defend his land. Already the village boasted a decent forge, a tanner, a bakery, a silversmith, a few freshly thatched houses, even an inn.

It was very quiet in the valley. Somewhere around was the sound of running water. The rider ran a tongue around dry lips, turned his horse, found the river and, cupping his hands, drank thirstily, then ducked his face and head. Now that he was so near journey's end, he felt a sudden reluctance to meet the lady he had travelled so far to see. When the archbishop had given him the opportunity to visit Ireland and to write an account of how the Irish church was facing up to the new disciplines from Rome, he jumped at the chance. Dervogilla's story had fascinated him since his meeting with that gaunt Irish monk. In Dublin he enquired for her whereabouts and was directed to Mellifont on the borders of Meath. She was known as patroness of the

5

Cistercian Abbey. He wondered how the years had treated her since the days of her wildness. Irishmen and women who hated her name, Norman barons and lords who admired her style were all agreed that she possessed rare beauty. They spoke of her great green eyes flecked with amber, her hair, dark as the raven's wing. Charming, fascinating, voluptuous, generous, graceful, all the well-worn adjectives had been used to describe her. In her youth she had been likened to the legendary Helen of Troy and to Eleanor of Aquitaine, King Henry's Queen, for whom the troubadours of France had made songs of love:

If she whom I desire should stoop to love me
I would look down on Jove

Innocent breasts, when I have looked up on them
Would that my hands were there.

The seductiveness of the song made his blood race. He felt himself harden and, swearing irritably under his breath, swung himself up on his horse. No matter what legendary Helen he might meet in Ireland, he had no intention of breaking his vows of celibacy. He was a professional churchman. One day he would receive the oils of ordination on his brow, perhaps the bishop's crozier between his hands. He felt a surge of pride at the thought. Yet there was something about Ireland, the soft air, the ever-changing colours of sea, sky and mountains, that could put a man astray. Ireland was the enchantress, casting her spell on inhabitants and visitors alike. Even the hard-bitten Norman soldiers had been seduced since coming to Ireland.

The track the horseman was following led across ploughlands, then dipped into a valley that housed a cluster of cottages, little more than hovels thatched and with holes in the roofs for smoke to escape. Pigs rooted in the dust and a gaggle of geese marched in procession down to the village pond where hens and ducks were scrabbling for food. Women, petticoats tied around their waists, slapped and pounded clothes in a running stream. Babies and dogs tumbled together and older children fought, screaming and laughing. There were no men around; ploughing or lambing or working within the Abbey precincts, the horseman guessed. Carefully he guided his mount along a path that led through a small copse. Then grace and symmetry took charge. Beyond the cluster of trees rose the outlines of a magnificent church. He clattered up to the gate and was admitted to a courtyard by a small dark monk speaking voluble French. He recalled that Malachy, Abbot of Armagh, had visited Abbot Bernard, the holiest man in Christendom. Malachy was worried about the state of the Irish church and had asked for help, and Bernard had responded generously, sending ten of his monks to found the first Cistercian house in these islands. Now Malachy and Bernard were dead, buried in the one grave in Clairvaux and already the French and Irish brothers were at daggers drawn.

A tree-lined avenue led to the church. The rider swung down and tied his horse to a hitching post, then decided to offer a prayer for safe arrival. The entrance to the chancel was by way of a wrought archway. Sun poured through the wide windows illuminating the gold of the high altar, the wooden pews and the great ornamental cross studded with jewels. Bernard had sent over a French architect to design the church, the first great basilica built of stone.

On his way out of the church, the horseman found himself faced with a procession of monks coming in the opposite direction, chanting psalms. He side-stepped into a garden where a grey-haired monk was plucking herbs.

The old monk looked up and saw a tall stranger, by his dress Norman, by his tonsure a cleric. He tittered foolishly. "I decided to miss Lauds. I have patients in the alm house in sore need of help. You will find food and drink in the hospice." The voice wavered. Somehow this well set-up cleric with the arrogant eyes didn't give the impression of need of any kind.

"I have come here in the hope of meeting the Lady Dervogilla," the stranger said impatiently. He had feared that the Abbot might refuse his request, but this ancient could be handled.

The old monk looked slyly from under red-rimmed lashes. "You are a scribe. Come to write our history. Like so many more. You Normans believe in writing things down, we Irish keep stories in our heads."

"The Lady Dervogilla," the visitor insisted. "Where can I see her? Is she about?"

"Oh, indeed she is." Painfully, the old monk got to his feet. "You are in luck." He winced. "Helping a fellow Christian will atone for my lack."

Moving quickly in a kind of shambling gait he led the visitor across a broad lawn. Beyond were the peasant quarters, stables, a mill, granaries, cellars, a river. They skirted the cloister and saw a figure in grey robes coming in the opposite direction, carrying an armful of flowers.

"A visitor to see you, Princess," the monk called out.

Robert Balmais drew in a deep breath. Under the robes her figure was shapely. The face was oval, the skin luminous, the mouth made for laughter and love. She had so fixed her wimple that one side fell seductively over her left shoulder, covering part of her face. "The face that launched a thousand ships," he thought, only this Irish Helen had launched two thousand Norman archers and men in mail on her island home. And they were here to stay.

He shook himself free of such thoughts and bowed stiffly. "I am Robert Balmais, monk of Canterbury. You are the Princess Dervogilla?"

She inclined her head. "Your business with me, sir?" She had an enchanting voice, deep and warm, with a hint of laughter.

He decided to be frank. He guessed she was a lady who would demand the truth. "I am in Ireland to write a history of the Irish people and of the part played by Dermot McMurrough, the Leinster king, in recent events. I am on my way to Armagh, and have made a detour to meet you. I should be glad of an hour of your time."

She paused as if to gather her thoughts, then handed the flowers to the elderly monk. "If you will be so good, Brother, as to take these to Our Lady's altar."

The monk bobbed and scurried away, and she led

9

the young Norman along a leafy path to a wooden bench beside the river. She seated herself, beckoning him to join her. "Fr Abbot told me you were expected." She had lapsed from Latin into impeccable Norman French. "News travels fast, even in this backwater. Lepers and other children of God's homeless come and go and bring us news of the outside world. Little happens that the monks do not know."

He nodded. "You have made Mellifont your home, Princess?"

"Not yet. Perhaps some day. Gardening is my joy. Brother Herbalist allows me help him concoct brews for the sick. He is skilled."

Robert Balmais reminded himself he had not travelled all those extra miles to talk of cures. "If you could tell me a little of your early life," he said briskly. "When did you first get to know Dermot McMurrough? What was he like, as a king, a man, a lover?"

"You are asking a great deal. Some things are best forgotten."

"For the sake of the records. Already the scribes have damned him." Robert Balmais rooted in his pocket and produced a parchment. "An annalist in the *Book of Leinster* has this to say." He cleared his throat and read:

Dermot McMurrough, King of Leinster, by whom a trembling sod was made of all Ireland – after having done extensive injuries to the Irish, after plundering and burning many churches – died of an insufferable and unknown disease, for he became putrid while living through the miracles of God's saints . . .

Her face twisted in pain. "I have heard what they say. Dermot died of a broken heart. He loved children, animals."

The same could be said of some of the greatest scoundrels in history, Robert Balmais thought, but he considered it wise to hold his peace. Passing through Tara on the way to Mellifont, he had seen the gaunt pile that had once been Maolseachlain's fort. He dismounted to examine the burnt-out ruins though little remained standing except scorched walls. "Strongbow and his men destroyed the castle where you were born," he said. "It must have been impressive in the days of its glory."

She gazed into the distance. "It was all so long ago. Bronwyn, my nurse, talked about the castle so often, I could paint a picture for you if I had the skill." Her voice had a dreamy quality. "The winter evenings, the huge logs burning in the open fire, sending up spirals of smoke that clung to the rafters; the tapestries and rugs and drinking horns and plates of gold. Maolseachlain seated in his carved chair surrounded by soldiers, retainers, and his priest and druid. I was born on a night of storm and high wind. The banshee, that faery woman who cries of death, was abroad that night and a star fell through the heavens. Crom Dorcha, the dark druid, foretold what would happen. Like Deirdre in the old story, I would bring ruin and desolation on the men of Ireland."

"And who was this Deirdre?"

"Deirdre," she echoed. "They tell her story in the *Táin*, the great Ulster saga. She too was born on a night of storm. She fell in love with Naoise, but Conor MacNessa, High King of Ireland, lusted after her. Because of his jealousy, the sons of Usna were killed and Ulster destroyed."

Her eyes were bright with unshed tears. She was looking back down the years at Ferns, flames crackling and rising, women and children weeping, men wounded and dying. She saw once again the pale triumphant face of her husband, Tiernan O'Rourke. Dermot setting sail for Bristol, and afterwards the long columns of Norman knights in armour marching on the Norse cities of Wexford and Waterford and Dublin. She shivered. "We were pawns in games of war, Deirdre and I."

When she spoke again her voice was controlled. "Maolseachlain wanted to kill me, but his hand was stayed by the druid. When he disowned me, my grandmother, the Lady Deborah, took me to Dublin to live. She insisted that I be known as the Princess of Meath. She believed in my star."

"Had your grandmother second sight?"

Dervogilla smiled. "There was never a woman as down to earth as the Lady Deborah. She taught me to fence and ride and swim, to recognise flowers and plants, to play chess and backgammon. She believed in exercise for mind and body. Other than that, she left me to my own devices."

"Your father, Prince Maolseachlain, was her son?"

"By her second marriage. She was only fifteen years old, walking the strand at Anglesea when she was captured by a band of young Dubliners on a raiding expedition to Wales. Ragnor, great grandson of Sitric Silkenbeard, claimed her as his prize. A year later she gave birth to twin boys and he married her in St Mary's Abbey. It was a love match. Life was good until the morning Ragnor took the two-year-old twins sailing in the bay. The sea holds no terrors for anyone with a drop of Norse blood in his veins. But they never came back, nor was the boat ever found. She was only nineteen years old and had lost husband and sons. After that she didn't much care what happened to her."

Balmais was strangely moved by the Lady Deborah's story. "How did she come to marry into the kingdom of Meath?"

"The old prince needed a son and heir. The marriage was arranged in the Thingmote by the leading Ostmen. They had a treaty with Meath. They were relieved when she made no protest. She was a prize to be bartered, young, beautiful, wealthy. Ragnor had left her a comb factory, a row of houses, ships. She wasn't happy in her second marriage, but she kept her part of the bargain, she gave the Prince a son. He was sent to be fostered. It is the custom."

"You have spoken of your grandmother. What of your mother?"

"She died giving me birth."

"Why did Dermot McMurrough invite my fellow Normans to invade your country? What drove him?"

She bent down and picked a rose. "Dermot longed for peace. He would have made a good High King, but there was no time." She tossed the petals into the water and they floated downstream in the shape of a crown. "Leinster flourished under his rule, but Tiernan O'Rourke destroyed him in the end."

"Did you drive him to it? After all, you eloped with McMurrough. You betrayed your husband when he was on pilgrimage to Lough Derg."

"You speak of matters of which you know nothing." Now there was winter in her voice.

He had the grace to look ashamed. "Forgive me, Lady Dervogilla. There is so much hearsay, gossip. I want the truth."

She made a moue of distaste. "Was it Pilate who asked, 'What is truth?' Each day I ask God to help me forgive Tiernan O'Rourke."

"What did he do that made you so bitter? Can you not forgive him? They say he is a sick man."

She stood up, tossing back her head. Then he saw what the veil had concealed, a jagged weal that slashed one perfect cheek from eye to chin. He was so shocked that he could scarcely bring out the words. "He branded you. In God's name, why?"

"Jealousy," she said and turned away. In the distance the church bell was ringing for Terce. "Nine o'clock," she said in a matter-of-fact tone. "Time I was on my way. I have a distance to travel."

He put out a hand to detain her. "Shall we meet again? There is so much more you could tell me."

She shook her head. "There is no time."

He said in frustration, "If only women were lettered, I would ask you to write your story."

Her dimple flashed. "Unlike our Norman sisters, we are taught to read and write. The Brehon Laws give us equal rights."

"Will you do as I ask?" As he stood there with pleading hazel eyes and tousled curls, she was reminded of the young Dermot McMurrough.

"Some day I may be tempted."

"Will you let me read what you have written?"

"I make no promises." She allowed him kiss her

14

hand, then she was gone, moving swiftly down the river path.

Later he watched as, booted and kilted, she rode out through the gates of the Abbey surrounded by her entourage. "God speed you, Princess," he called after her and she raised her hand in a final salute, before disappearing down the country lane in a cloud of dust. He was destined never to see her again.

Part I

Dublin, 1135

Dervogilla's Story

Chapter 1

I have returned to the house on the strand, the
house where my grandmother took me to live as a
child. I have always loved Dublin, her streets, her
people, the wide reaches of sandy beach where
Dermot and I walked on a sunlit day hand in hand.
Mostly the sea rolls gently in, scarcely causing a
ripple but on days of high wind it is possible to see
high-tipped foam riding the waves far out where sea
and sky meet. White sea horses, carrying Oisín across
illimitable oceans to a country called Tír na nÓg, the
Land of Youth. Dermot used tell me the myths and
legends he learned as a child. He pointed out Howth,
on the other side of the bay, where the lovers
Diarmuid and Gráinne made their bed, and ended
their story with Diarmuid's death.

My Dermot had been schooled by the monks of
Clonmacnois, had cut his teeth on legends of valour
and high deeds, set down in the *Book of Leinster*, the
Speckled Book and in the *Book of the Dun Cow*. His
favourite story told of Cuchulainn holding the Pass of
Ulster against an invading force. It is something I
still cannot understand – why Dermot, who longed to
unite his people, to become their High King, did

what he did. Had he counted the cost when he coaxed and bribed the marcher lords of Wales to invade Ireland? Richard de Clare, with his grandiose title of Strongbow, the sons and grandsons of the notorious Welsh princess, Nesta Fitzgerald, selling her favours to the Norman conquerors. He even offered his daughter Aoife in marriage to Strongbow as a reward. The girl was distraught. I was in the Castle of Ferns when he broke the news, in Waterford when Strongbow and Aoife were married while the city still smoked.

What demon rode his back? Ambition, a thirst for revenge? Or did he really think reaching out to Europe would set us all on a path of peace and prosperity? He had the backing of the Church all the way. Laurence O'Toole, Bishop of Dublin, was his lodestar with talk of reform and renewal. I saw it all. I was with Dermot in Bristol, in London, in Aquitaine when he bargained and pleaded. I tried to intervene, grant me that, advising him it was folly to invite the Normans in. "Once let them get the taste of our cities, see our rich pastures, our rivers teeming with fish, our forests of wild deer and game, and they will settle for good." But my words fell on deaf ears.

Dermot laughed at my fears, ran a teasing finger across my mouth, kissed the pulse in my neck, and I was so much in love with him that I gave in, held my tongue. In those days nothing mattered except his arms around me, his mouth on mine, his body in mine, the thrust, the rhythm, the climax of love. We fitted together. We could not have enough of each other. Oh yes, in my own way I was as great a traitor as Dermot McMurrough. My sin was loving a man who was never mine, whose mind I could never fathom. I never truly knew what went on behind that wide brow, never learnt to read his eyes.

Dermot, teller of tales, visionary, warrior, the ruthless leader, the tender lover. He was all of these things. Handsome too, with golden hair and hazel eyes; speckled, limpid, trout-stream eyes. And he was generous, loading me with jewels, gold, silks, though I had no need of such. He called me beautiful, likened me to Deirdre, to Helen of Troy, kissing the love spot under my breast. And yet he could not be prised away from his red-headed wife. He said she was the legendary queen, Maeve of Connaught who invaded Ulster through jealousy, come to life. All this was by way of a joke. I besought him to divorce Mor, even to take me as his second wife, though it would have been demeaning for me, a Princess of Meath, but no, Mor would not agree. To keep the peace with her warrior clan, he betrayed our love. He stood aside while I married Tiernan O'Rourke of Breifne. He was to regret it in the end when my husband's jealousy destroyed him, left Ferns in flames, a blackened ruin so that he was forced to take shelter in a woodsman's hut.

With no allies, no friends, even Mor had deserted him, beggared and beaten, he sent for me and I came. Why would I refuse? I was the cause. I set out with him on that fatal journey to Bristol, saw him humble himself to base-born men, adventurers, mercenaries. Dermot, whose princely line went back more than a thousand years, to the days when Balor and Aengus and Lugh were gods and the Celts were great. Yes, and I would do it again for love. He still is and always

21

will be entwined in the labyrinth of my mind and heart.

It was meeting Robert Balmais that unsettled me. A young Norman cleric, green in judgement, with his plan to write the history of Ireland, to explain the hows and the whens and the wherefores of our misfortunes. Cause and effect. He sought me out, questioned me, thought to set the record straight, to tell the truth of what happened, to explain our story to the world. As if any foreigner can ever fathom the Irish mind. Like the spirals and whorls carved on our burial stones, painted on our manuscripts, worked into our jewellery, so are we twisted and coiled.

We are a complex people, we Celts. We hide our thoughts, we tell strangers what they wish to hear, and let them make what they will of our stories. Yet maybe it is right that this once I should set down the truth. Perhaps the Norman historians will deal more kindly with Dermot and me than our own. Already the Irish annalists have had their say.

"*Dermot McMurrough, king of Leinstermen and the Foreigners, the disturber of Banba and destroyer of Erin,*" they have written. "*Dermot McMurrough by whom a trembling sod was made of all Ireland, who brought over the Saxons . . .*" And they haven't spared me, either. I am remembered as the faithless wife, the great whore of Babylon who helped encompass Ireland's ruin. And yet there were other bright strands woven into the fabric of our love story. A wish to bring peace after centuries of turmoil to a land held dear, a love of the common people, a respect for the traditions of our past. He was a great teller of tales, was Dermot. He patronised bards, scribes, artists, workers in gold and silver, wood and stone, collected illuminated manuscripts, wore his gold brooches and collars and finger rings with pride. His favourite character in history was the Gobán Saor, the master craftsman. Oh yes, let no one deny that Dermot McMurrough was the quintessential Celtic prince.

I was on the threshold of womanhood, my fifteenth birthday, when I first set eyes on Dermot McMurrough. We had been standing for hours, my nurse Bronwyn and I, in the narrow crowded streets of Dublin waiting to see the Leinster army march in through the city gates. They were grim – disappointed that there hadn't been a sack. Dermot rode at their head, his purple cloak caught by a great gold Tara brooch, a golden torque at his throat.

Like most Dubliners I was scared by the stories that had circulated about the Leinster King. They told of how he fought the Ossorymen, blinding their leaders and taking no prisoners. It was whispered that he believed in the right of a king to bed any woman who took his fancy. More horrendous still were the rumours of the rape of Kildare. I marvelled that so handsome a man could be guilty of such terrible crimes.

Yet clearer than anything else in my mind is the gaiety of that day. Flags flew from the Thingmote, fluttered from St Mary's Abbey on Hogges Green; pennants swung from the battlements and children perched on the city walls to wave and cheer. We had been nerved for trouble, ready to flee, our portables packed and ready, ships waiting to take us to Bristol, to the Isle of Man, to the Orkneys, and the relief was so great when we heard of the truce that we turned a defeat into a fiesta.

For weeks we had charted every step Dermot McMurrough had taken. Magnus MacTorcail, King of Dublin, had his network of spies who sent him word when the Leinster army set out from Ferns, where the Hy Kinsellas had their stronghold and marked the army's passage through Tír Dubh, the black country.

Since the day when the young Dermot McMurrough had been crowned King of Leinster, Dublin had been waiting for trouble. The dogs in the street knew that he had sworn to take his revenge on the Ostmen of Dublin for the death of his father, six years before. After Brian Boru's success at Clontarf, the Viking king was deposed and one of the McMurrough clan crowned in his stead. It was a bitter blow to the Dubliners. Of all the Hy Kinsellas who had ruled over them in the intervening century, none was more hated than Dermot's father. He was a proud and overbearing man who sealed his own death warrant when he gave judgement against an Ostman who had been grievously wronged. Some of the City Fathers stabbed McMurrough on the spot, and buried his body under the flagstones of the Great Chair with the carcass of a mad dog.

Magnus MacTorcail, a descendant of Sitric Silkenbeard, was crowned in his stead. When the moment came for Dermot to avenge his father, the Ostmen, knowing they could not withstand a siege, sent out a diplomat to parley with Leinster. After two days of negotiations, and a wildcat killing, an agreement was reached. Dublin was declared an open city, there would be no sacking, no rapes, no looting.

The ships in the quays would be allowed go about their lawful business. In return, MacTorcail would acknowledge Dermot as his Overlord, give him tribute of one thousand gold pieces and appoint his kinsman, Abbot Laurence O'Toole of Glendalough, Archbishop of Dublin.

That evening the civic leaders with their wives and daughters were invited to the Thingmote to pay their respects to the Leinster King. As the wealthiest and most influential woman in Dublin, my grandmother, the Lady Deborah, was invited too.

I sat on the side of her bed and watched her dress, fingering the small gold balls she used to tie the ends of her plaits while she told her maid to lay out her black gown, scarlet cloak and river pearls.

"I neither like nor trust Dermot McMurrough," she murmured. She wasn't really paying any attention to me; she had a habit of speaking to herself. "The whole affair stinks. The Leinster King will use the city as he sees fit. Sometimes I think I should go back to Wales, or even London – though they have their own troubles there with the war between King Stephen and the Empress Matilda."

I sighed. "I'd like to go with you."

"To London?"

"No," I said patiently, "I'd like to go with you to the Thingmote, to the reception."

She looked at me in amazement. "Whatever for? It will be boring. There will be interminable delays while the leading citizens pledge their fealty and there will be speeches and entertainment. As you know I enjoy good music, but it will be impossible to hear anything above the din. I grant you the food

will be good. Magnus MacTorcail will see to that."
She was determined to be fair, at all costs. "Not that
it matters, I am on a diet." She held onto a post while
her maid pulled the strings binding her waist. I took
up her bronze mirror and made a face at myself. She
took the mirror away. "Don't do that. You will stretch
your skin and spoil your looks."

"Please, Grandmother, I never get to go
anywhere." I could hear my voice turn to a whine.
She hated that and I arranged my face in a coaxing
smile. "Millany the comb maker's daughter is going,
and Birgitta, she is only a year older than me." I
wouldn't admit to my grandmother, would hardly
admit to myself, that I wanted to see King Dermot
again and maybe even speak to him. Such a wicked
man and so handsome. It would be something to tell
my friends.

With a practised flick the Lady Deborah arranged
her bracelets. "Maybe you are right. And today is
your birthday, poor darling. Perhaps it's time you met
people of your own class. You spend too much time
with Bronwyn's son. Not that I have anything against
Cormac, personally, but his father was a common
soldier in Maolseachlain's service, and not a very
dependable man at that. He died in a brawl."

"Bronwyn told me he died in a sortie, defending
the castle, not that it matters to me. I like Cormac," I
said.

She ignored my remark. She hated arguments.
"Wear your yellow gown and do get Bronwyn to help
you."

I rolled the golden balls around in my hand, they
were hollow and weighed very little. "May I borrow

26

these for the reception? Millany has six."

To my surprise she gave in. "Oh very well. Get Bronwyn to dress your hair in plaits. And now be off and leave me in peace."

As I went out of the room I could hear her ordering her maid, "Greta, bring me a plate of those figs from the Saracens' ship. They will take the edge off my appetite." She looked at herself unhappily in the long mirror. "I really must lose some weight."

When we reached the City Hall, the place was thronged with merchants and shopkeepers and tavern owners in hide jerkins, beards combed, wearing earrings and bracelets, and women dolled up in furs and fine wool. A platform had been set up at one end of the Great Hall and Dermot sat on a dais with MacTorcail and other Norse nobles. We stayed at the back of the room while a long line of Ostmen shuffled their way to kiss the hand of the Leinster King and offer him tribute. Already the floor around him was heaped with gold and skins, combs and brooches, caskets of wine and ale. A chill air from the underground river seeped through the floor and walls and I sneezed.

"It is all your own fault," Grandmother said crossly. "Such vanity. Showing off your figure."

"My cloak is too old and my shawls the wrong colour," I muttered. I might catch my death, but it would be worth it if Dermot was impressed with my yellow silk gown. I tossed my head to get the effect of the golden balls. Despite Bronwyn's grumbling I had insisted on curls. I shivered and sneezed again, moving nearer one of the fires. Light from the candles in sconces and lamps combined with wood smoke from the fires gave the Hall a mysterious glow. I was reminded of Bronwyn's story of the enchanted fairy palace of the Quicken Tree.

It seemed to take hours before the line dwindled away. Dermot and Magnus MacTorcail were deep in conversation. The noise in the Hall was rising to a crescendo. Leinster soldiers were exchanging bawdy stories with their Dublin counterparts. Women were squealing, flirting with the Norse nobility. Well-padded matrons swapped gossip with merchants and bishops. I couldn't see any sign of my friends and yawned behind my hand. I hoped supper would be served soon. I remembered I had eaten nothing all day. Servants were bearing in food and drink. Grandmother was right. Magnus MacTorcail was a good host. I edged nearer to one of the tables.

"Dublin bay cockles and mussels and fine fat oysters caught fresh this morning," a voice in my ear remarked. I was about to help myself to a plate of beef and pork sausages, or even the hard black bread and cheese which the Ostmen loved, but the man beside me was talking again.

"Before you make your choice, cast your eye over the jellies and syllabubs, and of course there are cheese cakes and honey cakes and wine to bring a blush to a maiden's cheek." He was becoming a bit of a nuisance. I tore my gluttonous eyes away from the table to watch Dermot.

My companion was nudging me and for a moment I gave him my attention. He wasn't at all bad looking. He might have been worth flirting with if I hadn't had better fish to fry. I knew by his yellow hands that he was a brewer. No matter how much they washed they could never rid themselves of the grain or heather or whatever it was they used to colour their ale. As if he could read my thoughts he said, "The purest of golden ale and potent too, with the taste of honey heather. You should sample my brew."

"I prefer Burgundy," I said haughtily, though to tell the truth the apple cider our cook made was my favourite drink.

The brewer sighed. "My family brought the secret of the heather ale with them when they first came to Dublin, sweeping down the North Sea and around the Irish coast in their scarlet and silver crafts, putting their dragon ships into the black pool we call Dubh Linn. Did you notice I am by way of being a poet?"

"Tell me more," I encouraged him. I wasn't really paying any attention to his nonsense, but out of the corner of my eye I could see Grandmother approach.

"Down the years we have been offered bribes by the envious Irish to give them the secret of the heather ale," he continued, clutching my hand. "Gold and thoroughbred horses, the fleetest of wolfhounds, even our choice of nubile young maidens, though none half as fair as you." He circled my waist. "My family would sooner die than betray the secret, but if you gave me a kiss I might be tempted."

I laughed loudly. I wanted Dermot to notice I had an admirer.

He looked up at the sound, passed his hand across his mouth and pushing the men around him aside jumped down from the dais and made his way to where we were standing. I almost died with excitement, but managed to bat my eyelashes and toss my gold balls. He didn't even notice I lived. Instead he grasped the brewer by the hand, greeting him like a long lost brother.

"The one Dubliner it is a pleasure to meet," he shouted. "Would you have a mind to come to Ferns and be my cellarer?"

The brewer actually punched the king's arm. "You are my best customer!" he grinned, "but not even for our new Overlord will I leave Dublin."

I coughed to let them know I existed. "I was just about to give away the secret of the heather ale to this young lady," the brewer said, pulling me close. "You interrupted us just in time, my lord."

Dermot laughed and touched my cheek. "A pretty wench," he said carelessly and on an impulse I blurted out:

"I understand you are an expert on such matters, so unfortunate for the Abbess of Kildare."

The brewer let out a low whistle and Grandmother who had joined us put a hand to her mouth. "You will forgive the child, my lord," she turned an imploring face on Dermot. "Today is her fifteenth birthday." She looked at me sharply. "What have you been drinking?"

I shrugged and Dermot said, "Much is forgiven a good-looking wench. What is your name, girl?"

"Dervogilla, Princess of Meath," I said defiantly. I never used the title. He wagged a finger under my nose. I felt like biting it off. He didn't look much older than me. He couldn't have been more than twenty-three or twenty-four at the most.

"Some day you will learn the true story of Kildare, Dervogilla of Meath," he said. "The mother Abbess that was has just given birth to a son. She and my captain are overjoyed. Nuala O'Faolain has been heard to pity her former companions walled up in their convent in Kildare. But enough of this nonsense." He swung around and took the brewer's arm. "I have a thirst would sink a ship. I will try a bumper of your heather ale and if I like what I drink you may send a hogshead to my castle in Ferns."

At the last moment he turned back to me. "What do you think of this affair, Dervogilla of Meath?" He waved his hand at the room.

"Pillars of gold and silver, a ceiling of swans' feathers and a company of fair men and women with a handsome king presiding over all," I said recklessly.

He laughed. "Who taught you that?"

"Nobody. It's in a story called 'The Fairy Palace of the Quicken Tree'."

"One of the Fenian tales," he said delightedly. "Someday I must invite you to Kinsealy to meet my favourite *seanachaí*."

"I'll remind you of that," I said boldly.

The brewer laughed and Grandmother took hold of my arm. "All this excitement has been too much for you," she said crossly. "It is high time you went home."

I didn't care. I was heady with excitement. I had spoken to King Dermot McMurrough and he had invited me to his castle at Ferns. I would get there somehow, someday, soon.

Chapter 2

It was to be two years before I met Dermot McMurrough again. Summer came early that year and with it a heat wave that turned the city into a sweat house. Water was scarce, the Liffey at a low ebb. In the Shambles, the alleyways and the narrow streets, drains and cesspools gave off an overpowering stench of refuse and excrement. Fever broke out, hundreds fell ill and burial carts were piled high with the corpses of those who had died of the fever and had to be cremated at once. Though we lived outside the walls and within sight of the sea, there was danger all around. When one of our maids fell ill, Grandmother decided it was high time we left for a healthier spot.

"My house in the Boyne Valley," she said. "The river is cool."

I pulled a face at the news. Mia, the innkeeper's daughter, had just got herself betrothed to my old admirer the brewer. I was to be one of her bridesmaids. Already I was planning my gown, cut lace over ivory silk, with flowing sleeves and a train. Bronwyn grumbled that I was going too far, I wasn't the bride, but I didn't care. Magnus MacTorcail's grandson had fallen in love with me. He wasn't my choice, but he was handsome and considered a catch. I protested and Grandmother relented and said we would leave the day after Mia's wedding.

"I shall take Greta, and Bronwyn, and of course Cormac," she said, ticking them off on her fingers. "Bronwyn will not move a step without her son and you need her to take care of you."

I pointed out that I wasn't a child. I hated fuss but I might as well have saved my breath.

"Bronwyn and Greta can help with the cooking," she said. "Of course they will squabble, but I have decided to ignore any unpleasantness." She always did. "We must take a good supply of blankets, pillows and cushions, a couple of sheepskin rugs for the floors which are stone, there are pots and pans in the cottage. We must remember our silver knives and linen napkins. It is so important to keep up standards. Our nearest neighbour, the miller, will supply us with flour and his brother the farmer with all the milk and meat we may need. Cormac can fish." She looked at me: "I entertain the hope that he will soon enter a monastery. Clonmacnois, perhaps. His lordship, the Abbot, is a friend of mine. He tells me the monks could use Cormac's talents. We both feel it is what God wants of him."

I wasn't fooled. Grandmother had no interest in what the Almighty might or might not want. Too many of Ragnor's pagan beliefs had rubbed off on her. She would be glad to see the back of Cormac. We were too great for her liking.

Here I must explain about my foster brother, for that is how I shall always think of Cormac. Bronwyn had been a scullion employed in the castle when Maolseachlain brought my mother Emer there as his young and unwilling bride. She looked after my mother, they liked each other, needed each other in that grim household where everyone went in fear of the lord and master. When Bronwyn discovered she was pregnant, mother arranged that the soldier responsible would marry her, but before the wedding could take place he was killed in a skirmish, or so Bronwyn always maintained.

After my mother's death Bronwyn came with Grandmother and me to Dublin. Cormac and I were much of an age and she nursed us both, taking turns at her breasts. From the first day I could walk I was Cormac's slave, handing over my balls and bats, not even whimpering when he sent the toy ship, carved by an Ostman friend of my grandmother, out to sea. He said it was bound for foreign parts. He even buried my doll in the garden. We were playing at funerals and he had appointed himself as gravedigger. I loved that doll but it was never the same after Bronwyn scrubbed away the painted wooden face. I truly believe I would have given Cormac my eyes if I thought he had need of them.

That summer in the Boyne Valley was idyllic. The house was a long low building, two cottages built into one, with a well thatched roof, an orchard, an herb garden, and a rose bower. In a sun room overlooking the river we played chess and Cormac strummed his guitar while I sang. Cormac and I fished the Boyne for trout and salmon, swam naked in water so cold we screamed, raced our horses across open land, jumping hedges and walls with reckless abandon, laughing and pelting each other with gorse when we tumbled and fell. We picked wild mushrooms in a wood behind the cottage for Bronwyn to cook with bacon and the black puddings she made to her secret recipe.

Nothing I would ever eat again would taste as delicious as these early morning meals, eaten outdoors in a small paved courtyard with the hot sun beating down on bare arms and legs. When June came around we made pigs of ourselves with wild raspberries and strawberries covered with thick cream.

One evening a blind beggar man called and, in exchange for a meal and cup of mead, related a Fiannacht tale. No one could guess his age, he had a long grey beard, white hair, a sparse frame and a voice that put you in mind of a running brook. His words spun a tapestry of the ageing Finn MacCool, the beautiful Princess Gráinne and the handsome Diarmuid Ó Duibhne, charmer of women. We listened enthralled while he related how Diarmuid and Gráinne crossed the Shannon and built a house of yew wood in a sheltered spot. But pursued by Finn they were forced to make their escape under darkness. Breathlessly we followed their flight across Ireland until they came at length to the Hill of Howth. And there they were discovered by Finn.

The story ends on a note of high drama when Diarmuid, who has been mortally wounded by a wild boar, begs Finn, who has the gift of healing, to bring him a drink of water. Twice Finn goes to a nearby well and each time, remembering how Diarmuid stole Gráinne away, spills the precious water. The third time he relents, but too late. Diarmuid is dead.

For years afterwards I was haunted by that story, even though I could not know then with what bitterness and jealousy my husband Tiernan O'Rourke would pursue Dermot McMurrough and me across Ireland. Well, it is over now, finished and done with. I ride no more tormented. Dermot is dead and in that sense I am free. Yet even still I can sometimes hear his voice in the winter wind, or in the lonely cry of the curlew, and again in the glad song of a lark, the music of water dancing and I know that in time we forget so much that has happened. Faces, places, names, fade from our minds, but the memory of a beloved voice can live forever.

Early in June we paid a visit to the castle where I was born. I had seen nothing of my father since the day I was carried away in the arms of my nurse. Prince Maolseachlain lay gaunt and haggard. The stench of illness filled the chamber, and, as Bronwyn said, "Death was waiting in the corner." He didn't seem to recognise us even when Grandmother whispered our names.

"I do not think he is long for this world," she observed, and I wondered how much she cared for this man to whom she had given birth. He had inherited power and a princely name, and had been a hard taskmaster, sometimes cruel. My mother had been his third wife and he had married her by force, though she was betrothed to her cousin with whom Bronwyn said she was deeply in love. From the day grandmother took me to Dublin he ceased to recognise my existence, yet as he lay there scarcely breathing, I was overwhelmed with sadness.

To my surprise, grandmother insisted on staying near at hand to help nurse him. Maybe it wasn't so strange after all. Grandmother had a strong sense of duty and always put family first. She wouldn't let me help, sending me off instead to another part of the castle to amuse myself. I hated the whole atmosphere and spent as much time as I could walking the dogs or riding for miles across the lanes and fields. It wasn't only the gloom of the castle that oppressed me but the fact that my half-brothers could not wait for their father's end. They were a motley crew. Cinit, the youngest and kindest, dressed outlandishly in magnificent laced boots, a richly embroidered trousers of fine linen bound below the knee with scarlet cross garters, and an embroidered linen shirt bought from a Norman freebooter. Cinit with his girlish voice and mincing walk didn't bother me, unlike MacDara the handsome, who was tall and strong and attempted to fondle me whenever he got the chance. Once I slapped his face and Donnchadh, the eldest, consoled me by promising that when his father, the Prince, was dead, he would make a match for me with a worthy suitor. I was sure he had his friend and ally Tiernan O'Rourke in mind.

If I disliked MacDara the handsome, I loathed O'Rourke, who was more than double my age. He had a long patrician face and the black patch he wore over one eye gave him distinction of a kind. It was whispered in the kitchens that he had lost his right eye in a fight with his twin brother when they were small. Afterwards the brother was found drowned in a shallow pool. They said it was no accident, that Tiernan O'Rourke was responsible. I could well believe it of the man. He seemed to spend all his time plotting revenge on his enemies.

When Maolseachlain was buried, O'Rourke made war on Conor O'Brien, King of Thomond, with the help of the man who would one day become his mortal enemy, Dermot McMurrough.

I had plenty of opportunity to observe Tiernan O'Rourke during the month I spent in his company. The hounds bared their teeth whenever he appeared in the Great Hall, and though he deferred to my grandmother when he was in her presence, he mocked her behind her back. He had a habit of questioning me about the Brehon Laws, Magna Carta, the names of English kings and so on. Boring subjects. Then he would smile and whisper the answers in my ear, his face close to mine.

It is a mercy that we cannot see into the future. That summer when I was seventeen years old, it seemed to me that I was free as a bird, that I could do what I pleased. Bronwyn's stories of my birth and the druid's warning were now no more real to me than the fairy tales I had heard as a child. I can only say that we live and learn.

On St John's Eve, MacDara and Cinit took me to the Midsummer bonfire near the Hill of Tara. I was wary of MacDara, but we would not be alone, half the county was going. The custom of lighting a bonfire on a hilltop on summer's eve is very old. By the time we reached Tara, dark clouds were scudding across a sky lit by a handful of stars and a thin crescent of moon. Around the bonfire the crowds of the world had gathered. Many were drinking a mixture of mead and the fairy herb we call wort.

Cinit warned me against the drink, it was a powerful aphrodisiac and could have a curious effect. Youths clapped their hands and called out ribald remarks as scarlet-skirted girls whirled and turned cartwheels to the music of horn and pipe. Older men and women joined hands to leap over the flames of the bonfire and before I knew it MacDara had caught me up in a fertility dance. Cinit and our bodyguard, a young man with a look in his eyes that boded no good, had vanished. Like a writhing snake, the line of dancers wriggled down the hill. I struggled to free myself and was rescued by a girl with long red hair and wild eyes who pulled me away and kissed me on the mouth. MacDara grabbed hold of her and together they disappeared into the oak wood, shedding their clothes as they went.

I felt suddenly cold and frightened and hurriedly climbed back up the hill to where the flames of the bonfire licked the sky. An old man was telling a group of children the story of Deirdre and the sons of Usna. As I sat crouched in the shadows, the past overpowered me again as it had done in the nursery, when Bronwyn described Crom Dorcha the druid and the future he had seen for me in the stars. I saw again in the leaping flames of the fire, shadows that turned into men falling in battle. I think that was the moment I made up my mind to marry Dermot McMurrough. He was strong, he had handled the Ostmen of Dublin, no mean task, he would save me from my fate. I hugged the thought of him to myself, and felt his arms around me, his mouth on mine, then scolded myself that I was bewitched by the night and the bonfire. Soon after I found my horse and rode home alone in the dark. Back to the castle where there was no sex magic, no coupling, no beginnings of life, only a man fighting his last battle with death.

When they had waked the Prince, when the funeral games were over and the corpse was buried under a cairn of stones, Grandmother sent me back to her house in the Boyne Valley. She remained behind. There were matters to which she must attend; cattle and gold to be claimed as part of my inheritance. She was rich and I was her heiress but to her money spelt security and she said that some day I might need all the protection I could buy. Was she thinking of Crom Dorcha's words? Maybe so.

That was the summer that Leinster prepared for the Fair of Tailteann, an event which took place every four years. The Fair would be opened on Lá Lughnasa, the first of August, and would last a month. On the opening day the chief men of Leinster would first meet in assembly under Dermot McMurrough. Then, business done, they, like their subjects, would give themselves over to pleasure; feasting, horse racing, games, music, dancing and love-making. There was even a Marriage Mound.

We were sitting in the kitchen after supper, Cormac and I, roasting chestnuts, Bronwyn stitching a petticoat and telling us how the first Tailteann Fair began.

"Lugh of the Silver Arm decided to hold a fair to honour his foster-mother Tailtiu." She bit the end of a thread and went on. "Lugh decreed that the fair should be held every four years. If the Leinstermen failed they would be cursed with baldness, toothlessness and a fool of a king."

"And what reward did Lugh promise to those who attended the fair?" Cormac demanded, winking at me. We had laid our plans.

Bronwyn sniffed and said nothing.

"Tell the truth," Cormac challenged her.

"Corn in the fields, milk in the byre and a fruitful marriage with fine sons and daughters," she said, ruffling his hair. "I know you are going. I shall make you a picnic. You can take the black horse. Dervogilla can ride the mare."

"We must visit the Marriage Mound," Cormac shouted as we trotted along the road to Tailteann the following morning. His hair was bleached by the sun, his freckles stood out and his voice was a bellow. I often thought he had Viking blood in his veins.

"I heard something from Grandmother about you entering a monastery," I teased.

"I heard something from mother about you wanting to marry Dermot McMurrough," he shot back.

Bronwyn could never keep any confidences to herself. I knew what he would say next.

"If you marry Dermot McMurrough, there's nothing left for me but the celibate life," he yodelled.

"Don't let that put you off taking the cowl," I said coldly. "The Abbot of Glendalough has decided to pass his crosier to his first born son."

He was so surprised he forgot to shout. "You mean Laurence O'Toole?"

"Laurence O'Toole is a saintly man," I said impatiently. "He's now Archbishop of Dublin or had you forgotten? I believe his successor in Glendalough has a way with women."

Cormac hooted with laughter. "You're right as usual. The new Abbot down there is one of the O'Tooles of Wicklow. A wild bawdy crowd, the same O'Tooles. Dermot McMurrough has just got himself betrothed to the chieftain's daughter, Mor."

I kept my eyes on the road, my voice even, giving nothing away. "What's she like?"

"Red hair and a temper to match. The Hy Kinsellas and the O'Tooles have made peace after years of fighting each other. Mor is part of the bargain. She wants to be High Queen of Ireland."

I prodded my horse and she broke into a gallop. "Damn Mor O'Toole, and damn Dermot McMurrough," I raged silently.

"Hey, wait for me," Cormac shouted. He hit his horse with an ash plant and the animal shot forward, so that we were racing neck and neck. Down the road, parallel with the river, we thundered, startling a bird out of the weeds. With an angry squawk it flew across the fields and a couple of badgers and hares fled for shelter. In a bush a blackbird, feathers puffed out, jigged up and down on the back of his mate. I felt emotional, near to tears as if nature was playing ducks and drakes with my body. In a spirit of recklessness I threw my leg over the mare and urged her on.

Cormac chortled with joy. "The hell with riding side saddle. Are you hot for a man or what?"

I could have killed him on the spot.

We had reached the outskirts of the fair. Booths had been set up around Tailtiu's burial mound. Men who had travelled from France were carefully arranging chessmen made of ivory, exotic fruits, silks, creamy parchments and parrots in gaudy cages. Small dark men who had come over from Wales with pack mules were unloading wool fleeces and sheepskins. Traders from Dublin were setting out silver bracelets and furs which they had shipped in from the Norse lands. Rosy cheeked farmers' wives were bartering lengths of the wool which they had dyed scarlet and brown and green with shellfish, lichen, bracken and wild flowers, for the famous Dublin combs and for gloves which they would never wear. Children and dogs fought each other for hot sausages, gingerbread and anything else they could steal or beg.

Cormac tied our horses to a hitching post, promising an urchin a silver penny if he would keep an eye on them until we returned. A dark-eyed man with a hooked nose was tumbling out heaps of jewels, garnets and Kerry diamonds, amethysts and Irish river pearls. I picked up a silver ring set with a dragon's eye and tried it on. I wished Cormac could give it to me, but he was poor as a church mouse.

"Queen Maeve of Connacht was given a ring like this by her husband," I said turning it around on my finger. "It was set with two dragon stones the size of her eyes."

"You and your old wives' tales," Cormac scoffed. He dragged me over to where a group of jockeys were waiting for the first race to begin. A crowd had gathered and young men and women and not so young spinsters and bachelors were pushing their way through to the Marriage Mound.

"Will you marry me, Cormac?" I asked suddenly. I

43

was sick with jealousy of Mor O'Toole.

"The Lady Deborah has my passage booked to Clonmacnois," he said blithely. "I have high hopes of becoming Abbot one day. Which reminds me, a certain black mare is running in the next race. I fancy a bet."

"They'll put a stop to your gallop when you get to Clonmacnois," I snapped and marched away. He made no attempt to follow me.

A colourful tent, bearing the royal flag of Leinster, had been set up in a hollow, near the race course. Chieftains and petty princes were streaming out of the tent, anxious to be in time for the first race. I stood at the door craning to catch a glimpse of Dermot. A runt of a servant attempted to push me away. I pushed him back. In the struggle that followed I lost my footing and tumbled onto the race track. All around me people were screaming. A riderless horse was bearing down on me. Cormac came zig-zagging across the field, to hurl himself at the horse, attempting to mount her. She kicked him in the head.

I stood in the path of the maddened horse, unable to move with shock. Then two arms reached out, tossing me out of the way like a doll. Dermot, purple cloak swinging, didn't wait to see was I dead or alive but ran to where Cormac lay crumpled, blood pumping from mouth and nose. Jockeys were running the length of the field, a soldier had skewered the maddened horse, and a couple of men came bearing a stretcher. When they picked Cormac up he was dead.

I do not remember what happened after that. I do not want to remember. I lay in shock while

Grandmother hurried back from the castle and helped Bronwyn wake and bury her son.

Grandmother was arranging a bunch of wild flowers which gave off a heady perfume, while I lay listlessly on a couch. Sun poured through the open window and a blackbird flew into the room and flew out again in a hurry.

Bronwyn had brushed my hair till it shone, Grandmother had loaned me her bedgown of ivory silk which had been a wedding gift from her beloved Ragnor.

"You must look your best," she said, eyeing me critically. "King Dermot is calling to pay his respects before he returns to Ferns."

Tears started to my eyes and I turned my head away. I didn't care any more about Dermot. Cormac my childhood companion was dead and my heart was broken. "It's all my fault," I sobbed. "If I hadn't wandered away it would never have happened."

"You were not Cormac's keeper nor was he yours," Grandmother said in her no-nonsense voice. "Accidents will happen."

"Cormac died trying to save me," I wept.

"From what I have heard from onlookers the King did that. You would do well to remember and thank him."

From outside the window came the clatter of horses' hooves. Grandmother hurried out to greet the King. Then Dermot was in my room, alone.

He sat on the end of the couch and held my hand. "You are making a good recovery," he said. "I am glad." His voice was strong yet musical, used to command and yet somehow caressing.

I swallowed and stole another glance. He was even more handsome than I had remembered. The difference between him and dead Cormac with his shaggy blond curls, his grin, his freckles, his very ordinariness, struck me with such force that I burst into tears.

Dermot took me in his arms. "Try not to grieve. No one was at fault. The horse bolted."

"I know," I sobbed into his shoulder. "Cormac was going to enter Clonmacnois." Somehow this made it all seem worse.

"He will have earned as much grace as if he had devoted all his manhood to God," Dermot said sadly, and I thought if Tiernan O'Rourke had said the same I would have spat in his face.

"What will Bronwyn do?" I asked wretchedly.

Dermot rubbed my face with his. It was wonderfully comforting. "I have given her gold; the fair is my responsibility. She is resigned to God's will. She intends to make her home in the convent in Kildare. My kinswoman Mother Dymphna will welcome her."

I wiped my eyes. "I shall miss her. She was always a second mother to me. She helped Grandmother rear me."

He smiled. "And filled your head with fairy tales. You were to be another Deirdre of the Sorrows."

"You don't believe it." I was a little indignant.

"I believe we are masters of our own fate. In your case, mistress," he smiled though his eyes were grave, "the Lady Deborah tells me she intends to take you away on a visit to London."

"I don't want to go," I wailed. All I wanted at that

moment was for him to sit beside me, hold my hand, talk to me. He made me feel safe. "You promised someday to invite me to Ferns." And suddenly, like a douche of cold water, I remembered Mor O'Toole. "You are to be married," I whispered.

"Yes, it is time I married," his voice was brisk.

"I hoped you would marry me," I said recklessly. I was forward and ill-bred but I didn't care. I loved him with all my soul.

Part II

London, 1137

Chapter 3

We rode along by the Thames and over the bridge and there before us the city stretched out, different to anything I had imagined. The streets, the lanes, the alleys of Dublin were old familiar faces, but London was new and exciting. I had never seen anything to equal the shops, tanners, shoe-makers, glovers, candle-makers, money-makers, silversmiths, goldsmiths, even a cook shop. And what a cook shop! My mouth watered, and for the first time in weeks I realised I was hungry. I had been too upset after Cormac's death to bother with food, and too seasick on the gale-blown crossing from Dublin to Bristol. It was a relief to feel I was on *terra firma* again.

Grandmother had hired a well-sprung wagon to take us from Bristol to London, but the once great Roman highway had fallen into disrepair, and many of the minor roads were little more than dirt tracks, pitted with pot holes. We put up in convents and hostels along the way, but they were poorly run places, offering badly cooked food, lumpy beds, cockroaches and mice scarpering around the room. For years England had been caught up in a civil war, and people were too worried to care about comfort or even the ordinary civilities of life. I found it impossible to get a can of hot water to wash. All the talk was of how King Stephen and the Empress Matilda had divided England into two warring camps. People changed sides as often as they changed their coats, it was as bad as at home.

I had little interest in what went on though I heard talk of Matilda's son, known as Henry FitzEmpress. There was also much gossip about the Duchess Eleanor of Aquitaine, the girl who would one day be Queen of England. Eleanor was considered the most scandalous woman of her age. She had gone off on the Second Crusade with her husband, Louis of France, dressed in man's garb, riding a destrier, no less. It was said that she was fast turning into a whore, sleeping with anyone who took her fancy along the way, even her uncle Raymond, the Prince of Antioch. Louis had been forced to drag his wife from her uncle's bed. I never thought that I would meet the fabulous Eleanor face to face, but a day came when I did and she was kind. Even after all those years I can still see her in the gardens in Poitiers, floating by on a cloud of oriental perfume, trailing laces and silks, her golden head turned to one side listening to her favourite troubadour, the great sapphire eyes missing nothing. Whatever about her love affairs, and they were many, she was undoubtedly the most fascinating woman I ever met. But that was in the future. Meanwhile here was I, just seventeen years old, driving through one of the most exciting cities in the world.

I missed Bronwyn and wondered how she was settling down in the Convent in Kildare. Grandmother had been generous, settling her in, giving her gifts; money, gowns, a warm cloak, boots, hose, while I had donated gloves, a chest of blankets, a patchwork quilt and a pillow decorated with cut lace, in addition to the gold Dermot had sent. The horse, the unwitting cause of Cormac's death, had belonged to the royal stables, and the King had paid more than double the compensation laid down by the Brehon Laws. Oh yes, our Bronwyn had gone off in some style.

Grandmother settled a cushion at the small of her back and sighed. "This is such a tedious journey. I hope Gwyneth has soft beds."

"Tell me about Kildare," I prompted. "What is the place like?"

"Very impressive. St Brigid chose her site well, on the rich plains of the Curragh. I am glad to say that the nuns keep up the tradition of hospitality. The kitchens, refectory and parlours are the finest I've seen. And of course the church is magnificent. Kildare people are very generous. I met the Abbot, a greying man, but with little taste for power, unlike the present Abbess. Mother Dymphna is a Hy Kinsella by birth. Breeding is so important."

"And what of Nuala, the former Abbess, who was torn away from the convent in the middle of the night by Dermot McMurrough and raped?" I asked nastily. I would never forgive him for marrying Mor O'Toole.

Grandmother raised an eyebrow. "People will gossip. Dymphna told me the whole story. Nuala was most unsuitable, squandering money, upsetting the workers, always a mistake. One of them put a curse on her, not that one believes in such nonsense." She threw me a sharp look and continued. "There was never a rape, merely a marriage of convenience. Nuala was not cut out to be a nun, much less an abbess. Even the monks didn't like it and they usually keep out of convent politics."

"And what does Bronwyn think of all this?"

"Bronwyn settled down very nicely. Everyone made her most welcome. She might yet take the veil. She has a rich dowry, thanks to Dermot. The more I hear of that man, the more I like him. As I remarked to Dymphna, we're lucky to have him as King of Dublin."

I didn't want to talk about Dermot, didn't want to remember our last meeting. "Do you think London a good place to shop?" I asked.

Grandmother loved nothing better than talk of fashion. "Traders put into the port of London from every corner of the world. Cousin Gwyneth tells me you can get silk from Florence and linen from Genoa. She described a magnificent cloak of sable she bought from a Norse trader. What you need, Dervogilla, is a really good dressmaker, the cut of a garment is so important. I must have a word with Gwyneth. She is bound to know who is the best."

Compared to the city, the garden suburb through which we were passing and where Gwyneth lived, could have belonged to a different country, another time. Even the incessant pealing of church bells in the streets of London had died away, to be replaced by bird song, and the rippling of the river in full flow. Sun dappled the trees, which shaded the avenue of handsome yellow stone villas, each with its own long garden leading down to the river where boats and barges were moored.

Gwyneth came out to the courtyard to welcome us with hugs and kisses. Her husband, Rupert de Luci, a pompous little man, made a speech, telling us what an honour it was to welcome the Lady Deborah of Dublin and the Lady Dervogilla of Meath to his humble abode. By the tone of his voice it was evident he considered his home anything but humble and indeed it was handsomely built in the Roman style with piped water from an aqueduct and the latest in glass window panes. He took us on a tour of the gardens, pointing out the playing fountains, the urns and statues scattered around the courtyard, the rare shrubs and the various exotic flowers. Inside, the villa was even more magnificent, boasting a splendid hall, a sun-room, bedrooms furnished with carpets and tapestries, hangings and lamps. Grandmother tested the beds and pronounced them comfortable and to her liking. Even the fireplaces were up to date, with chimney breasts built into the recesses of walls so that the smoke could find an outlet, an innovation from France. On the spur of the moment Grandmother determined that when she went back to Dublin she would have new fireplaces installed in her house on the strand.

"So much cleaner than the fires in the centre of rooms with the smoke spiralling in all directions," she said, "so hard on old eyes."

Rupert de Luci preened.

That evening in hall at supper I was put sitting beside the De Lucis' nephew, Gilbert de Breton, a young man with an earnest expression, eyes of an indeterminate colour, and a monotonous voice. "I consider myself a knight in the service of King Stephen of Blois," he whispered confidentially.

I was saved a reply by our host leaning across the table, demanding to know what his wife had chosen for supper. He could have held his tongue for at that moment the servants were carrying in steaming dishes and platters of food.

Gwyneth who was round and rosy and motherly laughed. "What's for supper husband? Why, chicken boiled with marrowbone to give it flavour, salt beef, salads, a meat pie from the best cook shop in London, followed by apple cakes and almond tarts, and then figs, dates and cheese for desert. And of course wine from the vineyards of France."

Rupert de Luci patted his stomach.

"I was just telling the Lady Dervogilla about the over-weening pride of the Empress," his nephew said testily.

Rupert de Luci frowned. "I support Stephen myself. Not that we barons of London take much interest in wars. Trade and commerce are more to our liking." He sniffed the wine. "What does the Lady Deborah think of the bouquet?"

The Lady Deborah was too busy eating to reply, she liked to masticate every bite ten times; she said it was good for the digestion.

At that moment I was overwhelmed with homesickness for Dublin, for the wide stretches of her beaches with the blue grey mountains looking down, for my own people. At times like this I wished Dermot could sweep into this hall and show them all what a king should be like. He could teach their Empress Matilda, or their Stephen of Blois how to rule.

We celebrated the twelve days of Christmas in style, visited by mummers, troops of jesters and even a company of actors who performed a morality play on the steps of London's cathedral, featuring Everyman and the Devil who wore a red costume with long horns and a tail and terrified the adults, though the children squealed with delight.

By the month of January winter had set in with a vengeance, snow and sleet were followed by a great frost. Rupert de Luci and his nephew Gilbert took us on a visit to London Bridge. The Thames had frozen over and the City Fathers held an ice fair. Booths and stalls had been set up along the riverbanks and were doing a roaring trade in mulled wine, mince pies and barbecued ribs. Boys with the shin-bones of animals tied to their feet pushed themselves out on the ice with staffs, skimming and looping and darting like birds, and when they grew tired their place was taken by young men playing ice hockey. Strolling musicians strummed guitars, jesters in parti-coloured hose and tunics juggled silver balls, and dark foreign men told fortunes. I had to admit it was fun and exciting.

"I think I have fallen in love with you," Gilbert de Breton whispered in my ear. It was a daring speech for a solemn young man, but he had been trying his best to please me all day, praising Ireland, agreeing that we were more civilised than the English. I tossed my head. I was wearing my new scarlet wool cloak and hood trimmed with fur and I knew I looked pretty. I allowed him squeeze my waist, then he spoiled it all by announcing that he intended to ask Rupert de Luci for my hand in marriage. De Luci was little more than a stranger to me. What right had he over my future? I pulled away and didn't speak to him for the remainder of the day but that didn't deter him. After supper he spent an hour closeted with Uncle Rupert. When they emerged De Luci was rubbing his hands and Gilbert was looking pink about the gills. I went to bed early, pleading a headache.

"You could do worse, you know." It was the following morning and Grandmother was seated at a tapestry frame in the sun room, drawing red and blue threads through the hunting scene she was embroidering. "Not that I shall influence you, Dervogilla. The decision is yours alone."

Sun flooded the solar and light blinded my eyes. I felt confused. All night I had been dreaming of Deirdre of the Sorrows, and I had awoken to the crash of helmets, the crackle of burning buildings and the screams of women and children. Dermot was somewhere in my dream, but I couldn't find him in all the confusion.

Gwyneth bit on a thread. "Our nephew Gilbert is a well set up young man and comes of a good family. He is also my husband's heir. As you know, all our children died in infancy." She smiled wistfully at her loss. "His father is a flourishing clothier."

As if I didn't know. I had been forced to spend one interminable day with Gilbert being shown over the family business. He took me to the sorting house where men and women in clogs washed wool in tubs of cold water before sending it to another building to be oiled, spun and woven. I dutifully followed him to the tenter fields where the fullers stretched the cloth. After that we visited the dyeing vats and he pressed me to know my favourite colour. I was almost in tears of fatigue and boredom by the time we reached the warehouses where bales of cloth were stored on shelves. He insisted on giving me the scarlet wool for my cloak, which I had to admit was most becoming.

The trouble was I couldn't see myself as a merchant's wife, even if Gilbert considered himself King Stephen's knight. I would infinitely prefer the intrigue and excitement of power at home, yet my destiny hung over me like a funeral pall.

"I'm not in the least in love with him," I said mulishly, sticking the needle through my finger and drawing blood. I sucked my thumb, tasting salt, and was reminded of Cormac's brains like a crown of roses spilling out on the field at the Tailteann Fair.

I drew in a deep breath. "I have decided to marry Gilbert de Breton and settle down here." When all was said and done London wasn't a bad place to be, there was always something happening. Besides, the further away from Ireland I kept, the better for all concerned.

"I don't think you will regret it," Gwyneth said tranquilly. "My husband's nephew is well-meaning but none too bright. But then who needs intelligence in a husband?"

By the month of April I was Madame de Breton. Afterwards it seemed as if I married Gilbert in a dream. To this day I cannot remember the ceremony. Cormac was dead, Dermot was married and I was saving my country from ruin and desolation. I saw myself as something of a heroine. Looking back, I was young and foolish, but I was also beginning to enjoy my time in London and it pleased my vanity to have a doting husband who pandered to my every wish. I spent most of my time shopping with Gwyneth. Grandmother had given me jewels and a chest of light wood, painted vermilion on a background of deep blue. I couldn't wait to fill it with silks and silver belts, tooled leather purses and coloured gloves.

Our house, which was outside the city, near the Palace of Westminster, was, if anything, more splendid than De Luci's villa. It had vaulted chambers, fine fireplaces, large bedrooms, and even a closet. With my new husband I visited the slave market. Men and women from Spain, Africa, Constantinople, Cyprus, Crete and the shores of the Black Sea were manacled together. I hated to see them looking so unhappy and picked out a young Jewish girl who had been brought back by some traders from Jerusalem and who had learnt a smattering of Norman French. I christened her Rachel. In the years to come, when I badly needed a friend, she would become my closest confidante and help.

Looking back on that summer we seemed to spend our time in a round of entertainments. Each day we had guests, and they returned the compliment by inviting us to their homes where we ate delicious dinners and suppers, followed by musical evenings and games. That year, acting was all the rage. Every Guild had its own patron saint and celebrated the feast day with a play to which the public were invited. My husband, knowing how much I enjoyed the theatre, made sure that we had the best seats.

Spring drew to a close and on May Day Gilbert and I with our friends went on a picnic to Windsor, the ladies travelling by barge, the men riding along the riverbank, shouting compliments, telling jokes. I thought life would be perfect but for my husband's clumsy love-making which I was forced to endure each night.

Then on Midsummer's Eve everything changed. Earlier in the year King Stephen had been captured by the Empress and put into chains, after which Matilda sent word to London that she would receive the crown at Westminster on St John's feast, according to ancient custom.

From the end of our garden we could see all that was happening. In the early afternoon the Empress arrived, flanked by her brother the Earl of Gloucester, her Uncle David, King of the Scots, and her guards and retinue.

"She means trouble." My husband's face was long and his voice was drear.

"At least there was no fighting," I consoled him, craning to catch a better glimpse of the gardens, the old Palace of Westminster and the church around which silken tents were being hastily erected. It looked a festive scene, the gardens at their flowering best, the river sparkling and the Empress walking around dressed in gold as if presiding at a garden party. I thought I wouldn't mind being there.

"She'll put a price on our heads. She'll squeeze us dry. She'll leave us without a rag to our backs," my husband muttered, shaking his head. I closed my ears to his moans, wishing he wouldn't trot out all the old fears.

Midsummer's Day dawned perfect with a blue sky decorated with a soft nimbus of clouds, like airy cherubs. I watched from our courtyard as my husband and Rupert de Luci, together with the mayor of the city and some aldermen with their clerks and standard bearers, rode at a walk to the Palace where the Empress received them in the great cavern that was Rufus Hall. Later, my husband related all that had happened.

Her Imperial Highness was greedy, no doubt about that. She demanded the coffers of London and ordered every baron and freeman of the city to hand over gold, silver and jewels. She would not bargain, she would not barter, she gave them twenty-four hours to gather the loot and if they failed she would set her soldiers loose to sack the city and put the leading inhabitants to the sword.

"We're ruined," my husband said that night. His head was buried in his pillow and I knew he was weeping. For the first time in our marriage I felt sorry for him and put my hand on his shoulder. I was even willing to submit to his love-making, but he was too bound up in his misery to notice. To give him his due, he had always been loyal to King Stephen, but more than anything else, he feared ruin and poverty.

"We can go home," I promised. "Dublin is pleasant. I am Grandmother's heiress and I own cattle and land in Meath."

"To Ireland?" he squeaked.

You would think I was asking him to come with me to the jungle or the Moors in Outremer . . .

"Oh, very well, have it your own way," I said huffily and turned my back.

We were almost thrown out of bed by the loud jangle of bells.

"They're sounding the tocsin, it's an attack of some sort," Gilbert shouted, jumping onto the floor, hunting around for his clothes. I climbed out with more dignity and went to the window. The morning was fine and bright and I could see right across to Westminster where people were running around like ants. By now the alarm was taken up by every church in London: St Trinity's mournful toll, the sweet peals of St Mary Colechurch, the brassy bells of St Mary Magdalene, and the deep boom of St Paul's. With that the door burst open and Rupert de Luci catapulted himself into the room.

"Stephen's army is marching on London," he shouted.

"Has the king escaped?" My husband's voice was muffled, he was pulling on a shirt and trews in a hurry.

De Luci ran to the window to see how things were in the palace.

"The King is still held in chains," he said over his shoulder, but during the night his queen arrived with an army from Rochester.

He wheeled around and made for the door. "Will you hurry, for God's sake, nephew, the men of London are gathering at the bridge to welcome the Queen and lend their support."

My husband didn't even wait to kiss me goodbye. The last I saw of him was racing across the courtyard to where a couple of servants were waiting to mount him and his uncle. I waved goodbye from the window. He didn't bother to look up.

The Empress Matilda was eating her breakfast in her silken tent when news was brought to her that Stephen's queen was entering the town by London Bridge and the men of London had rallied at Ludgate and were marching on Westminster, accompanied by a howling mob. With her brother Gloucester, her uncle Scotland and her retinue, she mounted her swiftest horse and the whole court was gone, leaving not only their possessions, but the maids, butchers, butlers, larderers, cooks, ushers, even the priests, to fend for themselves. Quickly enough they followed suit, taking their heels to the Oxford road.

As the last straggler melted into the countryside, the mob entered Westminster and proceeded to ransack the sumptuous tents. My law-abiding husband tried to put a stop to their plundering and was picked up by a giant Londoner and tossed over his shoulder. When they picked Gilbert up, they found his neck was broken.

"If only our nephew had died in battle, but to be killed by some looting Saxon rascal . . . " Rupert de Luci sighed.

"If only our nephew had died in battle," Gwyneth echoed.

"It's all my fault," I wept.

"But you weren't there," Gwyneth opened her eyes in amazement. "How can you blame yourself, Dervogilla?"

"It's written in my stars," I said crossly. "I cause the death of every man I happen to know. First Cormac, next my husband, soon it will be a prince or king and after that, who knows?"

"Pull yourself together, Dervogilla," Grandmother said sharply. "Don't play the part of Godfather Death. I buried my first husband, and my two sons, but I didn't blame myself. It was an act of God."

Rupert de Luci plucked nervously on his beard. "Maybe you should take your granddaughter back to Ireland now that the funeral is over, Lady Deborah." Like hard-nosed merchants everywhere he was given to superstition.

I was sick of London, sick of Gwyneth and Rupert de Luci and of my failure at marriage. Things couldn't be worse at home. I knew by the gleam in Grandmother's eyes that she was thinking the same.

"Call your maid Rachel and get her to pack your boxes," she said in a voice that brooked no opposition. "The sooner we leave for Dublin, the better for all concerned."

Part III

Dublin

Chapter 4

It was good to see Dublin again, the High Street, Smock Alley, Fishamble Street, Winetavern Street, crowded with the traders and merchants, who make up the pulsating heart of a city.

It was easy to identify people by the clothes they wore: the knights templar in white, their surcoats marked with a red cross, a sign that they had been on crusade. Doctors and surgeons were sober in red, while Brehons and law clerks flaunted scarlet gowns and flat white caps. Noisy young men with eager, hungry faces in shabby black cloaks and tabards, en route to the great monasteries of Glendalough, Armagh and Clonmacnois, swung by arm in arm. In Hoggs Green a group was gathered, re-hashing the story that had scandalised Christendom almost a decade before, when Peter Abelard, the stunningly good-looking Breton cleric who had filled the Schools of Paris had fallen in love with Heloise, the young niece and ward of a Canon at Notre Dame. A child was born, and the story ended badly. Abelard was castrated by a drunken doctor in the Canon's pay and left for dead. He recovered but was accused of heresy and banished to St Denis, the most forbidding monastery in France. On that bright summer morning listening to the young voices, I marvelled at how the story was still as fresh as the day the scandal rocked the cloisters of Paris. Why was it that all the great love stories of the world ended badly? Did the answer lie in ourselves or were the gods jealous of something they could never experience themselves?

Autumn had come and I left my bed before dawn to walk the strand in the direction of the Black Rock. Outside the mist was so thick that it caught at my throat. The sea sighed away, and the mist melted before the sun coming up out of the east. The tide had left small puddles and tufts of gorse and seaweed amongst the boulders. On the edge of the sea a boat was slowly making its way down into the Liffey basin.

I sat on a rock and watched a fat-bellied crab imprison itself in a thin channel of water, feeble claws waving. Then it appeared to give up and lay like a stone. In a nearby pool oyster-catchers and herons were busy searching for food and a gull stood motionless for so long that I felt sure it had injured a wing.

Something was niggling at the back of my mind and gave me no peace until I took it out, examined it and saw the face of my grandmother, wrinkled and frail. She had been different since our return to Dublin, her independent way of looking at life muted, her sparkle dimmed. It hit me that she was in failing health. I caught my breath in a sob. She was all the family I had ever known.

That evening as we sat in the solar she broke the news I half expected and yet dreaded to hear.

"I have decided to enter the convent at Kildare,"

she said, peering at me over her tapestry frame. "I think it time."

I hugged her tight and she laughed.

"Don't break my bones, Dervogilla, I still have need of them. I have written to Mother Dymphna, the Abbess. She will be glad to have me and then there is Bronwyn. She will see to my needs."

"I would do that," I protested. "You looked after me all those years."

"I know, darling, but you must have your youth." She leaned across and gave me a peck with cold lips. I saw the black spots on the back of her hands, grave marks, and swallowed a hurting lump in my throat.

She said in her matter-of-fact voice, "I was never a religious woman, as you know, but now I think the time has come to make my soul."

I knew by her tone that her mind was made up, and that nothing I could say or do would change her.

"I shall miss you, darling," she said, "you have always been a joy to me, from the first moment I took you in my arms."

I felt the wild treacherous tears welling up and fought them back.

"It is not the worst way to end one's days," she said tranquilly. "To be within easy reach of the church, to walk the cloisters, to listen to the bells summoning the community to prayer, to put the cares of this world behind."

"What will I do without you?" The words were wrenched from me. I was nineteen years of age, had been married and widowed, yet here I was behaving like a lost child.

She rooted in her scrap box under a heap of

threads and took out a letter. "I have had word from Meath," she said peering at the writing. "Your brother Donnchadh writes to tell me he would like to have you on a visit. MacDara has married a girl from Munster and has gone to live in the south."

I smiled sourly. "I wish her joy of MacDara."

"He will settle down and take enjoyment in his sons and daughters," Grandmother said placidly. Remembering the red-haired girl at the St John's Eve bonfire I had my doubts. I only hoped that MacDara's new bride was a full-blooded woman who enjoyed a romp and didn't expect fidelity in a husband. Otherwise the marriage might be of short duration. Yet MacDara had charm when he pleased.

"I hope Donnchadh has abandoned the idea of marrying me off to that friend of his, Tiernan O'Rourke," I said gloomily. The thought of spending the winter in the castle depressed me. "I don't trust him."

Grandmother moved impatiently. "You are your own mistress, Dervogilla, as I never tire of telling you. I must admit I would like to see you safely married. It is not easy for a young woman and especially one of your class to remain widowed. There is always the danger of abduction."

She was right in this. If a prince, a chieftain or even an outlaw decided to take a woman by force, there was little anyone could do. The girl would be lucky if marriage was mooted. Her family might demand compensation, even in extreme cases resort to force to get her back, but in any event her fate was sealed. She might end her days in a convent, if she had a dowry, tainted, looked down on by the other nuns. She would never be appointed to a position of power or trust.

"There is no need for you to wrinkle your forehead." Grandmother leaned forward to smooth out the worry lines between my eyes. "Don't frown, Dervogilla, it leaves ugly marks." She held me close which was unusual, she was not a demonstrative woman. "You will know what is right for you to do. Otherwise," she smiled, "I have failed miserably in bringing you up." Then she said, "Donnchadh is expecting a Christmas visit from King Dermot. He would like you to act as his hostess."

My traitorous heart leaped at the mention of Dermot's name. I didn't dare pursue that line of thought. Instead I said, "It's a wonder Donnchadh never married. He should, now that he is Prince of Meath."

"I have no doubt he will," Grandmother said vaguely. "There is some talk of an alliance with an Ulster princess." She got up from her chair, and put a hand to her back. The small gesture pierced my heart. "That maid of mine is a long time gone. I sent her to fetch a night-cap."

Petulantly she rang her bell. Almost immediately Greta came running in, excusing herself that she had been heating a brick to warm the bed and that the night-cap of milk and honey was waiting. Between us we brought Grandmother to her room and settled her down.

A month later I closed up the stone house on the strand and with the help of my maid, Rachel, on whom I had come to depend more and more, saw Grandmother safely to Kildare, where she would spend the remainder of her twilight years.

Bronwyn was there, looking well and rested. She greeted Grandmother with all the familiarity of a retainer and said it would give her something to do, be like old times to look after one of the family again. She told me sharply that I was much too thin and instructed Rachel to make me a posset of marigold juice, purlane and garlic which she swore would give even a stone an appetite. She refused to listen when I told her I was trying to slim. Bronwyn would always think of me as a youngster in need of care.

I was pleasantly surprised by the prosperity of the town of Kildare, which had spread itself around the original foundations. Even more impressive were the convent and the monastery inside the walls. All the buildings looked sturdy and well cared-for: refectories, dormitories, kitchens, the vaulted church, the small oratory, the cloisters; even the fountains were carved and gilded.

Behind the convent and monastery two fine hospices catered for the poor and were tended by nuns and monks.

I was put up in one of the lavishly furnished guest houses. The Abbess boasted of the quality of previous guests who had come to visit the holy shrine of St Brigid in search of favours. She pointed to the gold and jewels they had left behind. Before the Battle of Hastings, Harold, the Saxon King, had visited Kildare and had taken away the saint's cloak as a relic and shield. More than a century had elapsed since then but pilgrims still came from across the water and were provided with every luxury by the nuns.

As Grandmother was quick to point out, it wasn't

only piety that brought them but the cuisine. The monk who was chief cook had gone on the Second Crusade with King Louis of France. On his return he had ordered wall ovens and imported rare spices. He had even introduced wine glasses and forks to the dinner table. Grandmother of course was enchanted with all this. She said that the table appointments in Kildare had no equal in Ireland. I was relieved that the beds were soft, and the bugs few and far between.

By the time I was ready to leave, Grandmother was ordering the Abbess to install the modern fireplaces. I could see that Dymphna was impressed. I felt sure that before a month had passed, Grandmother would be running the convent. The Lady Deborah was used to ordering people about.

Part IV

Meath, 1139

Chapter 5

I arrived at the Maolseachlain stronghold in November. In the mist the towers and walls of the castle loomed up ghostly and unreal. A torn flag fluttered from a standard twisted with ivy, and as I rode up the cobbled zig-zagging road flanked by towers, it seemed I was entering a prison from which there would be no escape.

Donnchadh and a richly-dressed Cinit welcomed me warmly. I was relieved that there was no sign of Tiernan O'Rourke.

On first inspection of the place my heart failed me. There was an air of decay about the castle, even the servants were sluttish and down-at-heel. It was clear to me that there had been no chatelaine for a very long time, not even a housekeeper to keep watch. With Rachel's help I set about ordering the small army of maids to clean the Great Hall and principal rooms. If it was true that the King of Leinster was expected for Christmas, it was only right that he should be received in some state.

Rachel had brought recipes from the kitchens of Kildare, but when she attempted to instruct the cook, a fat slob of a woman who seldom moved from her chair, she was met with rebellious murmurings. Master Donnchadh didn't care what he ate so long as it was bacon and cabbage, Master Cinit was happy to stuff himself with honey cakes and mead. Rachel, who was bright and enthusiastic, listened impatiently to the litany of all that was wrong in the castle: the fires smoked, the maids wouldn't do as they were bid, the well in the corner of the kitchen was rusty, the spit was broken, the cook needed new pots and pans. She came to me with the bad news and in desperation I enlisted Cinit's help. I told him bluntly that the food he was eating would ruin his figure and that for the sake of his complexion and appetites – I didn't specify which – he should eat a balanced diet. He agreed without demur, visited the kitchens, and after that we had no more trouble.

Dermot arrived on Christmas Eve with a retinue of servants and men-at-arms. To my chagrin Tiernan O'Rourke was amongst the company.

During the year that was ending, Dermot had formed an uneasy alliance with Conor O'Brien of Thomond and together they had besieged Waterford. After that Dermot sailed up to Breifne and made peace with Tiernan O'Rourke, inviting him to spend Christmas in the Maolseachlain stronghold in Meath. The Prince from Breifne seemed subdued, but Dermot, though battle weary, was in high spirits. Rachel and I had festooned the Great Hall with holly and ivy and fires of apple logs blazed in every room. Cinit laid on a succession of entertainments: jesters; ballad singers; harpists; Mummers; Wren boys. There were even choristers to sing Christmas hymns.

On the Twelfth Day of Christmas a hunt was

arranged in Dermot's honour. I had had little opportunity of speaking to him privately and I was determined that I would take part in the hunt, even though snow had been forecast by a shepherd who was our weather expert. MacDara had arrived with his wife, a blowsy red-head with a loud manner. I was glad to see she was well able to handle her uxorious husband. They couldn't keep their hands off each other.

The day was crisp and clear. From the start Dermot was in the lead, closely dogged by Tiernan O'Rourke. It was a beautiful morning, with that brightness that comes before snow. I had never felt so alive, so carefree, as I galloped over the flatlands of Meath, the stag in sight, hounds in full cry. We took hedges and ditches with breath-taking speed and cornered the stag, antlers thrust forward for the last ditch stand, while the hounds wheeled and whinnied and circled and the huntsmen closed in for the kill.

"He was a noble animal. I was tempted to spare him," Dermot said on the homeward run. "But the hounds would have torn me asunder."

I thought this a strange remark coming from a huntsman and king who had a reputation for ruthlessness. Later, when I knew Dermot better, I found out that he had a feeling for all hunted animals, as if some sixth sense told him that a day would come when he himself would be hounded and driven to ground.

On the homeward stretch we managed to lose Tiernan O'Rourke who had stuck to me like a leech all day. Perhaps Dermot had given him some signal. O'Rourke went in awe of his king.

"Do you stay much longer, my lord?" I put the question I had been longing to ask. I remembered he was leaving soon and suddenly all the sparkle went out of the day.

He manoeuvred his horse nearer mine. "Dervogilla, pet, why so formal all of a sudden?"

My heart leapt at the endearment, but I controlled my voice. "My brother Donnchadh didn't dare ask your plans. If you intend to honour us with a few more days of your company I will need to consult the cook about a change of meals." Even as I said the words they sounded feeble. As if our kitchens were any concern of the King of Leinster. The only subject that had engaged his attention since he arrived was war. I swear he didn't know what food was put in front of him.

The snow started to fall, silently, thickly, flakes powdering my hair, touching my face. I drew up the hood of my scarlet cloak and gave Dermot a dazzling smile.

"You look like Red Riding Hood in the tale," he said easing his horse to a standstill. "Like the wolf I am ready to gobble you up."

He dismounted and lifted me down, taking me in his arms. My heart was singing and as he bent his head I parted my lips.

We celebrated the end of Christmas with a feast. Dermot had been generous with silver and gold and the kitchen had done him proud. I had ordered that the white wine be snow-chilled and the burgundy warmed. Jugs of mead and metheglin, a lethal mixture of hazelnut mead and wine, were set at intervals down the long table and there was a barrel of heather ale all the way from Dublin. My mind went back to that evening at the Thingmote and the brewer who had offered to trade the secret of the ale for a kiss. What would Dermot offer if I shared my bed?

As befitted the King of Leinster, Dermot was given the hero's portion which he insisted on sharing with me. I know we all drank too much. There are times when even the plainest of women can glow, and that night looking into Dermot's eyes I knew I was beautiful, in a low cut gown of green silk, with gold on my arms and neck. Diamonds powdered my dark curls which fell to my waist, and I had reddened my lips with the juice of berries. Tiernan O'Rourke sat watching me with the eyes of a sick dog.

That night Dermot came to my chamber. It had taken Rachel two hours to help me dress. It took Dermot two minutes to strip me of my finery. Yet he seemed in no hurry to have me, feasting on me with his eyes, wrapping my hair around his fingers, tasting my face, my hands, my body with his mouth and tongue. And when I thought I could stand it no more, he lay over me and began to make love. At first gently, then with a mounting rhythm, a passion that carried me with him to a country where I had never been. I had been married for most of a year but up to this night I had been as unaroused as a nun, a virgin.

"I have wanted you like this for years," I whispered.

His mouth dammed my words, as he sank into me again, and I held him fiercely, offering him everything I had, body, soul, my future, the damnation of my country if that was the price I must pay for his love. I tasted his sweat, and heard him whisper, "Nothing can take this night away." After a little time he eased himself out and we slept.

He stayed another six days and for most of the time the snow fell and we made love. While everyone in the castle was aware of what was happening – they would have had to be deaf and blind not to know – only Cinit had the courage to caution me.

"Dervogilla, be careful," he begged. "Dermot will never take you with him to Ferns. He dare not. The O'Tooles are too powerful. He cannot afford their enmity."

I didn't listen, I didn't believe him. I was too far gone, too besotted, too much in thrall.

On the last night we made love as if there was no tomorrow, and I prayed that the time would stand still while the stars burnt themselves out, that the night would never end. I slept for a little while and when I awoke it was morning and the sky was leaden. Yesterday's bright snows had vanished and rain was falling, sullenly, grime-laden. Dermot was dressing and in my heart I knew he was leaving for good.

I held out my arms. "Take me with you to wherever you are going."

He turned away, his voice muffled. "Dervogilla, what you ask is impossible."

My eyes swallowed him up: the straight back, the golden hair that no matter how he flattened it sprang back into curls, the proud stance.

"You must," I pleaded. "I have been in love with you since the first day I saw you ride up Cork Hill in Dublin."

He came over and sat on the side of the bed, taking me in his arms as he had done when Cormac died and I had been distraught.

"I didn't mean this to happen," he murmured against my hair. "God knows, I kept my hands off you as long as I could," He stroked my face. "Darling, you know I am married to Mor O'Toole."

I wrapped my arms around him. "What does she mean to you, what can she mean after our nights of love?"

He loosened my hold. "Don't, Dervogilla. I must go back to Ferns."

"Take me with you," I pleaded.

"I cannot. Mor is the mother of my sons Eanna and Conor, of my daughter Aoife."

Tears ran down my face. "I will give you sons, daughters." I pulled him closer, biting his lips. "Take me as your second wife. You can, it has been done before, it is allowed in the Brehon Laws."

His breathing was harsh. "I cannot."

"You don't love me," I sobbed.

He kissed away my tears. "I have wanted you since that evening in the Thingmote when you flirted with your brewer and made your funny little speech."

"*A ceiling of swans' feathers, and a company of fair men and women with a handsome king presiding over all.* It is what I have tried to arrange for your visit here."

He stroked my hair. "Oh, Dervogilla, I love you. I have asked Mor, reasoned with her, threatened her. But it is no good. If I bring you to Ferns she will take my children to Wicklow to the O'Toole clan and start a war. And this time the whole of Ireland will be caught up."

I pounded his chest. "And what if my brothers start a war? Do you forget I am a Princess of Meath?"

"Sweetheart, Donnchadh and Cinit and MacDara are my subjects, as are all the men of Leinster."

"Except the O'Tooles."

"They too, but it will be impossible to contain them if Mor goes back."

"Do I mean nothing to you?"

"You mean everything, but this is goodbye."

"What do you want?" I asked desperately.

"To be High King someday. Since Brian Boru there has been no king strong enough to rule all Ireland, not in a hundred years. If we do not unite as a country soon we are lost. What happened in Britain will happen here. We shall be overrun by a stronger force, our lands taken, our homesteads destroyed, our lands scorched."

"You are mad," I sobbed. "Ulster and Connaught divide the high kingship between them."

"And there is no peace," he finished sadly. He sighed and got up from the bed. He went to the table and poured wine into a goblet. "Drink this up, Dervogilla. It will steady you."

I gulped and swallowed. Resting in the bottom was a ring set with two enormous red stones.

"The dragon's ring," I whispered.

He fished it out and slipped it onto my finger. "It once belonged to Queen Maeve of Connacht. Ferdinand gave it to her. He told her that if ever she needed help she was to send it to him, and he would come, no matter what the cost."

"I will remember," I whispered.

He got to his feet and went heavily to the door.

"This can't be the end," I thought frantically. "Shall I see you again?" I called after him.

"It would be better not," he muttered and went out the door and down the stairs. Later as I watched from my window he mounted his horse and with his retinue rode away. And though I called after him, he didn't even look back.

Chapter 6

Soon after Christmas word was brought to the Maolseachlain stronghold in Meath that the black plague had broken out in Kildare, brought by a monk who had returned from a pilgrimage to Compostella. Within a day of his arrival in the monastery he had fallen ill. At first the infirmarian feared leprosy, but he knew it was even worse when the dreaded blue plague spots appeared on the monk's arms and neck.

Everyone had heard of the Black Death. Travellers who had witnessed the ravages caused by plague brought back stories of whole communities decimated in a matter of weeks. We in Ireland had never suffered the like. For centuries we had been complacent on this score. Didn't the old stories tell us that St Patrick had banished the plague from Ireland, when he banished the snakes? But now our beliefs in the old myths were shattered and men and women grew cold with fear and prayed that the plague would pass them by.

Immediately I heard the news I dispatched messengers to Kildare with orders to bring Grandmother and Bronwyn to Meath. I don't know if the wretches I employed ever arrived, or how far they went, or even if they ever took off. I suspect they stayed hidden at home with the money with which I had bribed them, waiting for the disease to die down.

I was worried sick and in the end decided there was nothing for it but to go to Kildare myself. Donnchadh and Cinit did their best to dissuade me, but I brushed them aside. I could afford to make my own arrangements. No one would tell me what to do.

On the morning I was due to set off Tiernan O'Rourke came to my room in the east wing of the castle. Below in the courtyard my horse was saddled and the guards who were to accompany me waited in sullen silence. Only Rachel was eager to come with me but I ordered her to remain at the castle and see that rooms were got ready for Grandmother and Bronwyn. I explained that they might need nursing and she could see to their needs.

I had been searching for a crucifix which contained a relic of the One True Cross to bring with me to Kildare. It had belonged to Grandmother, she would be glad to have it, perhaps it might contain a cure. I was on my hands and knees rooting under the bed after a fruitless search in trunks and presses, when I heard a cough and looked up to find the tall figure in black at the open door. Tiernan O'Rourke stood gazing at me for a long moment and then said in a flat voice, "You are not going to Kildare, Dervogilla. I forbid it."

Only that I was so upset I would have burst out laughing. "Grandmother and Bronwyn need my help," I said stiffly.

He took a step into the room, throwing out his

hands in appeal. "Mother of God, Dervogilla, do you know anything about the plague? Have you any idea how quickly it claims its victims, with what rapidity it spreads?"

I turned away and he shouted: "I have been in plague-ridden spots in the east, seen men beating their bloody heads against walls, seen babies suckling the breasts of their dead mothers. Can you conceive how plague victims look? Bloodshot eyes, coated tongues, bloody mucus and vomit spurting from mouths and nostrils and ears, maggots feasting on living flesh."

I fought back the nausea. "I don't care, I am going to Kildare." My voice was stubborn.

He said in a quieter voice, "From all I heard, the nuns and monks have enough on their hands without your storming in. No one is allowed go within five miles of the monastery. Orders from the Palace at Ferns."

"Dermot would let me go," I snapped.

"I doubt it," he said dryly.

"But what if Grandmother dies?"

"She very well may. She is old and frail. But your being there will not save her."

"I must know what is happening." It was like beating my head against a stone wall.

"I shall go to Kildare myself to see what help I can offer," he said evenly.

"What will Dermot say when he hears that you have disobeyed his orders?"

He went on, not listening to me. "You don't know what it's like. I nursed my best friend when the plague broke on the way to the Holy Land. His hair turned white overnight, his flesh was a mass of bleeding sores, swellings under his arms, in his groin. I held him in my arms and whispered the prayer for the dying in his ears. Do you know what it says, Dervogilla? Have you ever heard it repeated again and again while men and women died like flies?"

I put my hands over my ears, but he pulled them away roughly.

"Listen to what they recite: *Go forth O Christian soul out of this world, in the name of Jesus Christ the Son of the Living God who suffered for thee; in the name of the Holy Ghost, who sanctified thee.*"

I shivered. That prayer, the way he chanted the words seemed to fill the room with voices of ghosts. I was more scared by that prayer than by all the descriptions I had heard of the living dead. I collapsed on the side of the bed and he said gently: "Anyone who lives through a plague can never forget the horror."

I averted my eyes from his face. "What if you get the plague? Why should you escape?"

His mouth twisted in a smile. "I had the plague once when I went on crusade. There was an outbreak in Antioch. I was one of the lucky few. It seldom attacks a second time, there is a kind of immunity built up."

I put a hand to my mouth and rocked on the bed. "I can't bear to think of Grandmother and Bronwyn. What shall I do?"

"If they survive I shall bring them safely back to Meath. You must trust me. Will you give me your promise to remain here? You can get rooms ready, they may need nursing. And you can pray as you

91

have never prayed before that the plague will be contained. Otherwise it will spread like wild-fire. That is why I am going – not to please you, Dervogilla, though God knows I would do anything to win your favour – but this time it is for the sole reason of advising the community. They will need to keep the sick isolated, to wash them, shave their heads, burn their clothes, cremate the dead at once. A doctor who was on crusade with me will accompany me. He has medicines, herbs." He came over and sat beside me on the bed, taking my hands in his. "Will you be a good girl and trust me?"

I knew what he said made sense, but how I wanted to go to Kildare, run all the way if possible. It hurt to be beholden to a man I didn't even like. I would have covered Dermot with kisses, begged him to take care of himself, to come back safe. Then I was ashamed of myself. Tiernan O'Rourke was a good man, brave too; he was doing his best.

"I'll do as you say," I said shakily. "I would only be in the way."

He kissed me on the forehead. "Be good and storm heaven that this will pass." Then he was gone.

He returned a month later, gaunt and haggard and came to my room at once. He kissed me briefly on the cheek. "The plague is over, thank God. The danger is past."

"Grandmother, Bronwyn?" I could scarcely bring out their names.

He put an arm around me. "They were dead before I got to Kildare. They were amongst the first victims."

I was too stunned to say anything.

"Bronwyn fell ill of the plague almost at once. The Lady Deborah went to nurse her. Mercifully it was quick."

"Why did the Abbess allow it? Grandmother was too old to nurse anyone." I burst into a storm of wild weeping.

He wiped my eyes. "I asked the same question, but as you know the Lady Deborah was a strong-minded woman, used to command. The Abbess was scared to cross her, besides there was pandemonium, patients, visitors, nuns, even monks falling in their tracks. Take consolation in the knowledge that your grandmother went fast. Possibly she never knew what happened her. Likely her heart gave out before the disease could take a grip."

He was only speaking the truth. Grandmother had always insisted on nursing her servants when they fell ill, but knowing this didn't help the pain of losing the two who had been closest to me. Bronwyn, my nurse and confidante. I had drunk the milk at her breast and Grandmother – Grandmother who was all the family I had ever known. It was only now that she was gone I realised how much I had lost. I had never heard a word of complaint cross her lips in all the years of my childhood.

For months afterwards fancy mocked me. I would catch a glimpse of her dear face in a crowd only to realise it was a trick of the light. The hand of a stranger raised in greeting, the turn of the head, a voice would bring her back for the length of a heart-beat, then the jolting truth, the aching throat. It was hard to realise that she had passed into the shadows and that we would never again meet in this world.

Bronwyn's death brought back Cormac, the foster-brother beloved of my youth with his freckles, his spiky hair, his sense of fun, his loud voice. Once, I dreamt that Cormac and I were riding along the white dusty road on the way to the Tailteann Fair. The river rushed past and without warning a hare ran across the road, frightening my mare. I heard Cormac's laughing voice call out: "Don't you know a hare from a witch?" I was filled with dread, knowing our journey was doomed.

I was standing on the race course near the royal tent and the riderless horse was bearing down on me while I stood rooted to the spot. I saw Cormac lying on the ground, his brains spilling out. I shouted for Dermot to help me, but he was nowhere around. I awoke in a sweat, shaking, calling his name. It was dawn and Tiernan O'Rourke was holding me like a child. I pulled away angrily.

"What are you doing here in my room?"

His voice was gentle. "You were having a nightmare, Dervogilla. I have brought you a drink." He gave me hot milk and honey and I fell asleep almost at once. When I awoke the second time, it was morning and he was gone. It was only then I remembered that his room was at the other side of the castle. Had he been keeping watch on me, hoping I would call out, need him? I was too embarrassed to ask, yet in a strange way I was touched that he cared so much. In that grim stronghold where I now passed my days, my half-brothers were no closer to me than strangers. Indeed, remembering Bronwyn's hints I wondered at times if we were blood kin at all.

I took to walking the fields and woods around the castle, reliving my early years: Grandmother and I racing our horses across the strand; she always won. Grandmother and I sitting in that long bright room in her cottage beside the Boyne, while she told me so many stories of her young days that in the end I felt I knew her even better than I knew myself. I saw in my mind's eye the young girl in her fringed woollen skirt and blue linen bodice, red hair hanging loose, feet bare, walking along the edge of the sea at Anglesea on the day her beloved Ragnor had scooped her up in his arms and taken her in his dragon ship back to Dublin. She had known love and companionship. But she had also known heartbreak, the loss of a beloved husband and little sons. Her second marriage had been hard, but she never complained, had kept her part of the bargain.

There is another memory I have of her, sitting beside the fire on the night before she left for Kildare. She reached across and kissed me, cold hands, cold lips. *"Keep thy heart with all diligence, Dervogilla,"* she said, *"for out of it are the issues of life."* It was a passage she had memorised from the bible. In the years to come when my courage gave out and I felt near to despair, I often thought of those words.

Grandmother had left gold, houses, shops, even a trading ship which carried cargoes of pine marten skins, Irish wolfhounds, Irish silver and combs to Bristol and London and Normandy, bringing back silks and laces, sugar and spices which were rare luxuries, dried fruit, leather gloves and fine wines. Tiernan O'Rourke helped me settle my affairs, appointing an agent and steward, and making sure that the captain of the ship was trustworthy.

Captain Nils was to become my friend in the years to come, a beanpole of a man with a flowing white beard and the shrewd blue eyes of the sailor. He was Norse, and a man of few words, but as dependable as a rock. I nicknamed him Peter. I don't think he ever understood what I was getting at. After a time I reverted to calling him Nils.

I hadn't realised Grandmother was so wealthy. Apart from a couple of bequests, one to the nuns at Kildare, another to the Leper's Hospital outside Dublin, the bulk of her fortune came to me. She had always been charitable, supporting a string of beggars, and was good to her servants. They were loyal and faithful and remained in her service until they left to marry or died of old age. Even her maid, Greta – I blamed her Nordic blood for her taciturn ways – wept when Grandmother left Dublin to settle in the convent in Kildare. I have spoken little of Greta. I don't remember ever having had a proper conversation with her. I think she found children tiresome. Grandmother gave her a dowry before leaving Dublin and soon afterwards Greta married a baker with an infectious chuckle. It must have been the attraction of opposites: that jolly little man with the twinkling eyes and his fund of jokes and Greta who had never been known to smile in her life. I wrote to Greta after Grandmother's death, but she never replied. Perhaps she didn't know how to write.

Tiernan O'Rourke remained on in the castle, and because I was lonely – Donnchadh was always too busy and Cinit could talk of nothing except fine clothes and some handsome soldier who had caught his eye – I allowed the Breifne Prince to share my thoughts. He would listen with rapt attention and then pat me on the hand, telling me, "You have suffered a loss in the death of your grandmother, the Lady Deborah and Bronwyn your nurse, but you must put your losses behind you and go on with your life, like a good child."

I wished he wouldn't call me child, I was a grown woman; a widow, my own mistress. Sometimes I felt a hundred.

As the weeks went by in that dreary castle I withdrew more and more into myself. MacDara and his red-headed wife had returned to the south of Ireland. I wasn't sorry to see them go. They were company of a sort, but uneasy. You could hear them all over the castle. If I came on them suddenly, in the solar or in the Great Hall, or the stables, I felt I should apologise. It wasn't anything they said, just the way they looked as if I had interrupted something, as if they were about to make love. Yet I missed their high spirits in a place that was dead. Rachel tried to persuade me to go back to Dublin. I was answerable to no-one but it would take more courage than I possessed to walk again in streets where I had been so happy.

And as for the house on the strand, too many ghosts lurked in the shadows, too many voices could be heard in the wind whipping across the strand, echoed in the lone cry of bittern and curlew. It would have been too painful to visit the small sandy garden Grandmother had created with such loving care. We used sit there on dreamy summer evenings,

Grandmother singing, Cormac accompanying her on the harp. They were both very musical. She taught us all the songs she remembered from Wales, and Cormac sang the troubadour songs he had picked up from the students. Even when I was young and going through a difficult time, Grandmother never whipped me as most parents and guardians thought it their duty to do. Neither did she spoil me, except when I fell ill. Then she would come softly into my room with a gift, a honey sweetmeat, a toy, a ribbon. Once she brought me an orange she had got from a trader down by the Liffey. I had never tasted the fruit before. I can still get the bitter sweet taste, the pungent smell of the peel where the knife sliced through the skin, sharp juice running down my chin. No. I could not bear to go back to the places I had known as a child. Someday I would pluck up the courage, but not just yet.

Summer and autumn passed and in my memory they were sunless days. At the beginning of winter I married Tiernan O'Rourke in the small oratory attached to the castle. A priest performed the ceremony. Tiernan O'Rourke insisted that we have a Christian marriage. Donnchadh and Cinit invited a druid along. He was a stranger to me, a tall dark man with sallow skin and brooding eyes. I wondered had Crom Dorcha looked so forbidding on the night I was born, when he read my destiny in a falling star. After the Christian ceremony we were married according to the old druidic rites. The Brehon Laws decreed that if we divorced, any property, cattle or gold I had brought to the marriage would revert to me. My brothers thought this would make me feel secure, and

I agreed, knowing it was what Grandmother would have wished. Tiernan O'Rourke said he had no interest in my fortune, and I believed him. As hereditary Prince of Breifne he ruled over territory extending right across Ireland from the mouth of the Erne to the mouth of the Boyne.

On our wedding night when Tiernan O'Rourke took me in his arms I tried to put thoughts of Dermot McMurrough out of my mind and to concentrate on pleasing my husband. He was lusty enough, virile, mad for my body, but as he pounded away the thought struck me that I could have been any woman lying there, even a soft-buttocked boy. Did he care about me or was he only concerned with his own needs, pulling and tugging to make me fit his body? Maybe I wronged him, I do not know. It is hard for a woman who has found happiness in the arms of another to put up with second best. I kept telling myself that the Lady Deborah had kept faith with her second husband, Maolseachlain of Meath, had kept her part of the bargain, done her duty, borne him a son. I, her granddaughter, could do no less.

Then as if he could read my thoughts, Tiernan O'Rourke rolled over and got out of the bed. "Go to sleep, Dervogilla, and dream of Dermot McMurrough," he said bitterly and stalked out of the room. It was the only time he had mentioned the King by name and I wept into the pillow at my failure, tortured by memories of Dermot's love-making, how he had held me closely until the throbbing of our linked bodies slowly died away and we slept.

The next night my husband did not come to my

bed. Instead I went to his, begging him to allow me in, telling him I was cold. He took me in his arms gently, stroking me all over, then his passion took over and I shook under his hands. I closed my eyes to keep back the tears, knowing that this was my fate, had been foretold from the hour of my birth. What choice had I? After Grandmother's death, I had discussed my future with my brother Donnchadh. He had been blunt. For me there was either marriage or a nunnery. In my short stay at Kildare, I had seen what convent life did to a woman. I was privy to the stories, the jealousies, the back-biting, the bickering. Some of the nuns even came to blows over a stool, a cushion, a hank of thread, a seat in the solar where they took their recreation. And these were women of good class, used to every comfort. No, whatever the pains of marriage I could never endure convent life. It had been different for Grandmother and Bronwyn, they had lived their lives, had gone as honoured guests, ready to make their peace with God, sustained by faith.

We left Maolseachlain's stronghold before dawn, with a retinue of servants and soldiers. My husband was anxious to get back to his castle in Breifne in time to celebrate Christmas. He grumbled that he had spent too long in Meath and that there was a lot of unrest on the borders of his territory. He distrusted Torlach O'Connor of Connaught who called himself High King. O'Connor was hard and unscrupulous in an age when chivalry was becoming the fashion. I knew my half-brothers in Meath and Dermot in Ferns shared Tiernan's feelings about O'Connor.

I remember the day was crystal clear and cold, the

reeds on the lake beaded with icicles, glittering like diamonds. Misshapen snow-spangled bushes on the edge of the path had turned into faery trees. To our right a great lake fringed by a forest appeared to stretch out for miles. As I watched, four swans, necks arched, floated past. I pointed them out to my husband. "Look," I said, "don't they remind you of the Swan Children, Fionnuala and her three brothers?"

"Pagan beliefs," he said scathingly. "People should move with the times. No good Christian believes in such superstitious rubbish."

I kept my peace, but my heart was heavy. Dermot would have been delighted with my remark, would have told me more about the Swan Children. I knew in my bones that if we were to spend the next hundred years together Tiernan and I would never understand each other, never speak the language of lovers. It was a harrowing thought and a lonely one. And on that bright morning it was borne home to me what a mistake I had made in marrying Tiernan O'Rourke. I would spend the remainder of my life paying for my foolishness.

We were coming to wilder country where winter snows had piled up and hardened. Our horses were forced to pick their way along frozen paths. The Shannon had narrowed but there were boats on the river. I thought of how Dermot had sailed up the Shannon to Leitrim to help Tiernan O'Rourke fight Torlach O'Connor. The High King made merciless raids on everyone else's territory. Dermot told me O'Connor had a fleet of 190 vessels on Lough Derg and from there he had devastated Munster. I think everyone in Ireland except Dermot went in fear of Torlach O'Connor. I knew Dermot would make a better High King. At times I was afraid my husband could read my thoughts. I never mentioned Dermot's name. If I as much as breathed a word of how I had lived or what I had done before our marriage, Tiernan O'Rourke would retreat into a black silence, refusing to speak to me for days, until I coaxed him back to friendship.

Beyond the holly bushes crowding the river banks like spectres at a feast, I could see the tall walls of my husband's stronghold. The O'Rourkes had been Princes of Breifne for more than a thousand years. The great gates were flung open offering Gaelic hospitality in the traditional manner to any chance travellers. A line of servants were drawn up in the Great Hall waiting to welcome their lord and master and his new wife.

That was the first time I saw Tiernan O'Rourke's foster sister, Sunnivea. If her name gave the impression of light and brightness her appearance told otherwise. Her strange orange-coloured eyes burned in a pale face, and her black hair was pulled back in a bun. There wasn't a grey rib in her tresses, although her skin was wrinkled and weather-beaten. She greeted me stiffly, introducing me to the servants and turned a fawning look on my husband. From the first day I crossed the threshold I knew it to be an uncomfortable household. Before the maids and me, the Lady Sunnivea showed herself to be a belittling nag and bully, but to her foster brother she was meekness and docility. It made me squirm for all craven women to see her constantly make up to him, when he wanted nothing of her. There was something secretive in her face, something dark and unpleasant in her eyes. My husband treated me with all deference and I heard him remind her sharply on more than one occasion that I was now mistress of the castle.

Of course there was gossip within the walls and some of it came to my ears. Rumour said that she had once been a beautiful woman – I could well believe that – she had good bones in her face; that as children she and Tiernan had been close, they were reared together. When she had come to womanhood it was said she had fallen violently in love with him. Or maybe indeed she had loved him all along. It was even whispered that a child had been born, one of God's innocents, who had been put out to nurse. Once, I came on a shambling figure of a young man with a vacant face and drooling mouth down by the lake. He muttered something unintelligible about the Lady Sunnivea, calling her Mother.

I puzzled why Tiernan O'Rourke allowed his foster sister to remain when he so obviously despised her, until the day my eyes were opened. Whether by accident or design I do not know, the sleeve of her gown fell back, revealing a brand that ran from elbow to wrist. She saw me wince, pulled down her sleeve and smiled, a smile both cruel and pleased. No words passed between us but I knew in that moment that I had the answer to the enigma. It was because of that weal, and whoever had inflicted it – my mind shied away from the truth – that she ruled the castle and all in it with a rod of iron.

Part V

Breifne, 1142

Chapter 7

A year later I gave birth to a son, a fat, complacent baby who seldom cried. Tiernan O'Rourke was beside himself with joy. He heaped me with jewels and silks, and had a goldsmith fashion a loving cup in which we toasted each other. The baby was christened Tiernan Óg. Rachel adored him. He would lie in her arms gurgling and smiling and playing with her ribbons and tassels.

Rachel had become my firm friend. When she first came to our home from the London slave market, she understood only a few words of what was said. But she was clever and had a good ear and soon learned to speak not only fluent Norman French but the polyglot mixture of Norse and Irish used by the Ostmen of Dublin. At first she was shy, but little by little she opened up.

Her story was sad and strange. She came from a village near Edessa on the far side of the Euphrates where nothing much had ever happened until trouble broke out between the Saracens and the Christians, resulting in the Second Crusade. Her tribe were Jewish, peace-loving people, and they had no defence against Turkish raiders, who made swift forays, shooting their bows from the saddle before closing in with short sabres. In one of those raids her home had been destroyed and her family killed. She escaped to the hills, hiding for weeks in wild places, living on berries and nuts until captured by bandits. They sold her to a slave trader and she was taken to London where young boys and girls fetched a handsome price. She said it was like arriving in the "promised land" when I took her to live in our mansion overlooking Westminster Palace. I paid little attention to her in the beginning. She was just another pair of willing hands amongst a houseful of servants, a young girl, not more than fifteen years old with a smile that lit up her face so that one forgot the swarthy skin, the nose too big for the face and the slave's brand on the forehead. After Grandmother and Bronwyn died, she tried in her own way to comfort me and I realised there was great kindness in her nature.

Since the birth of our son I had seen little of my husband. Tiernan O'Rourke spent much of his time patrolling the borders of Breifne fending off Torlach O'Connor, perhaps the bloodiest and most ruthless man ever to reign. When one of the annalists complained that Ireland had been reduced to a trembling sod by the High King, even his heir, Rory, turned against him. In a fit of revenge O'Connor imprisoned the son in a castle on Lough Mask and swore to put out his eyes.

It is laid down in the Brehon Laws that a man with a blemish can never be king. If O'Connor carried out his threat to blind his son, it would mean he could not be elected king. Before long the whole of Connaught was divided into two warring camps. Castles, churches and homesteads were destroyed, families driving their cattle before them fled into Leinster and Munster. When the Abbot of Cong was killed and his monastery fired, the Church thought it time to intervene. Gilla Mac Liag, Coarb of St Patrick and Archbishop of Armagh, summoned a great hosting and convention of all the kings and princes of Ireland to Armagh. After weeks of charges and counter-charges interspersed with prayers, hymns and the High King's threat of immediate and terrible war over all Ireland, a peace pact was signed. Torlach O'Connor was ordered to make an offering of a thousand pieces of silver to Cong and to free his son unharmed. There was general rejoicing, fifty white doves were let loose and the Archbishop preached a stirring sermon in which he promised peace. The peace lasted one year.

On his way back to Ferns from Armagh, Dermot McMurrough stopped off in Breifne. My husband, who accompanied him, was none too pleased at this, but Dermot was his Overlord. Besides, he must honour the laws of hospitality.

"You will comport yourself with dignity," my husband stated as I dressed for dinner in the Great Hall. I could see he was angry. Behind his back Rachel's eyes implored silence. She went in fear of Breifne's prince.

"I have never done otherwise," I said coldly, turning my back.

"You are my wife and you will obey my orders." The veins stood out on his forehead. Jealousy was eating him up. He would have locked me up in my chamber had he dared.

I had determined to treat Dermot with a cool politeness. There would be no tender passages, no resurrection of our love affair. I had a baby son to consider and no wish to create trouble for myself.

"I know my duties as an hostess," I said coolly. "I am a princess of Meath."

"You will speak to the Leinster King only when necessary. And you will retire to your chamber as soon as dinner has ended. Do I make myself clear?"

"As clear as mud," I muttered under my breath and watched as he strode out of the room, banging the door so hard that the tapestries trembled on the wall before falling in a heap on the floor. It was as well the doors were made of solid oak. Banging doors was a sign of my husband's displeasure. It was one of his habits I most disliked.

Humming tunelessly under my breath I inspected my gowns hanging like sentinels from poles: silks, brocades, fine linens, wools, cut lace, embroidered and dyed rainbow colours. Rachel was a superb seamstress and I loved clothes. Through sheer cussedness I determined to dazzle every man in the Great Hall, and to hell with the consequences. I picked out a jewel of a gown in apple green, finely pleated, with long flowing sleeves and a sweetheart neckline.

I bathed in scented water and perfumed my skin with attar of roses. Under the gown I wore neither shift nor tunic, smoothing down the thin linen which clung to the line of breast and hips, and fell in elegant folds to the ground. Rachel wound a girdle of soft gold leather twice around my waist, fastening the broad decorative band in front at hip level. I brushed my hair loose, though it was the custom for married women to wear plaits. Finally, I fastened a gold torc around my neck, arranged a couple of bracelets on each arm and slipped the dragon ring onto the index finger of my right hand. In the firelight, the dragon's eyes came alive, gleaming ruby red. My husband wasn't to know that the ring was Dermot's gift. He thought I had inherited my jewels from Grandmother. With a final glance at myself in the long polished bronze mirror I swept out the door and down the curving staircase to where the company were gathered.

Dermot was seated in the place of honour at the top of the high table and I sat at his right side, with the Lady Sunnivea at the foot of the table beside my husband. Down either side sat the most important members of Dermot's retinue, and next to them local chieftains with their ladies, a couple of wealthy cattle barons and our local bishop with his mistress. She came of a poor family but had taught herself housewifely arts. She was very popular with bards, Brehons and visiting clergy who considered that an establishment without a chatelaine was scarcely worth visiting. Who else would see to the dairy, oversee the kitchens, keep tally, spin and sew and warm a man's bed on a winter night? Besides which the laity approved.

Never by as much as a flicker of the eyebrow did Tiernan O'Rourke show the annoyance he felt when I swept into the Great Hall in a gown that left little to the imagination. He was the perfect host, pressing the hero's portion on Dermot, seeing to it that goblets were constantly filled with finest wines. The Lady Sunnivea and I had buried our differences for the time being and worked hard to decorate the Great Hall which looked truly enchanting, hung with tapestries and carpets, silver and gold plate and appointments gleaming in the wax candlelight, the ceiling hung with baskets of flowers, and greenery everywhere. In the minstrels' gallery, harpers played soft seductive music and the sparkling conversation was broken with laughter. Once I thought I felt something brush my thigh but when I looked around Dermot was chatting amiably across the table using his hands to describe improvements he had made in his stone castle in Ferns, shouting an invitation to my husband to come back with him on a visit. He had employed the architect sent over from France by Abbot Bernard to design the new Abbey at Mellifont where a foundation stone had been recently laid, and was anxious to get Tiernan O'Rourke's opinion.

When the meats had been eaten the servants set out dishes of fruit and cheeses, and my husband called for the loving cup fashioned for our son, filling it to the brim with metheglin. Dermot toasted our son and passed the cup around the table so that all might drink. When it reached the Lady Sunnivea's place she appeared to reach out awkwardly, knocking over the loving cup so that the drink spread over my husband's damask coat, staining the fabric. He passed it off though I noticed his face mottled with anger. That coat was his pride and joy. He had brought it back with him from a crusade to the Holy Land. Sunnivea, wiping the stains with a linen, made matters worse by spilling a jug of water over coat and trews. With a muttered exclamation of annoyance he got up from the table. She followed him out of the Hall and as she passed she threw me a triumphant glance. I knew it was no accident. Whatever her motive I no longer cared. My head was spinning and I longed only to be alone with the fair-haired man at my side.

As if he could read my thoughts, Dermot put a hand under my elbow. "Will you take me out into the garden, Dervogilla, and show me the god with three faces? Your husband was telling me about the marvel. I understand the time to see it is when the moon is high."

"It will be my pleasure, my lord." I smiled and took his hand as we left the table and went out into the courtyard and through an orchard. A narrow winding path led to a grove in the middle of a hazel wood where a great stone pillar decorated with swirling scrolls and swelling curves formed the base for the three-faced god. In the drifting shadows the high foreheads, blunt noses and tight-lipped mouths looked stern. Only the eyes seemed alive, large and luminous gazing at some distant scene hidden to mortal man. The glade was littered with coins, ribbons, shells, feathers, corn dollies, sheaves of straw and strands of gaily-dyed wools.

"People come in secret to worship and leave offerings," I whispered. Someone had crowned the head with a wreath of wild flowers. Under the moonlight the dead flowers looked obscene. With a grunt of annoyance Dermot lifted the crown and threw it into the wood where it fell with a soft plop. Something rustled in the undergrowth, there was an unearthly scream, a patter of hooves, and then silence. I wondered was it the god Pan himself. All around us the scent of night stock was overpowering. Dermot put an arm around my shoulder. "This idol was fashioned in pagan times, in the days of Balor and Aengus, Lugh and the Dagda. For centuries pagan priests spilled wine in libation to the Unknown God."

I could feel the cold of the stone gather around my heart.

"And make sacrifice," I said. "They still do. I have seen dead birds and a lamb pierced through the heart. They spill the blood as they do around the lintels of the door and the windows at Martinmas. They say if you make a wish when the moon is full it will be granted."

"There is an old saying," Dermot said. "I first heard it from a travelling man from the east. It goes, 'Take what you want, say the Gods, take it and pay for it.'"

Someone was walking over my grave. I shivered. Overhead the clouds rolled back and the moon sailed across the sky. Dermot said: "Now is the time to make our wish."

At that moment, so much in love was I, that all I wanted was to be with Dermot. My husband, my baby son, my position in life, all that I held dear were no more to me than shadows. "Please, stone god," I prayed silently, "make Dermot mine."

In the bright moonlight I could read Dermot's lips. He was asking for power to unite Ireland, to put an end to strife and madness.

"Let my name echo and re-echo down the

centuries, when others are forgotten," he prayed. "Let the annalists write my obituary when I am gone," he said. He hadn't even mentioned my name. I meant nothing to him. I protested but my words were drowned out by a sudden crash of thunder. Was the god with three faces angry or was he granting our wish? Jagged flashes of lightning tore across the sky, fireworks of the heavens. Dermot caught me by the hand and raced me back to the castle, just in time. As we reached the door a cloudburst exploded like the cataract of a waterfall. In the darkness of the outer hall he pulled me into his arms and I held up my face for his kiss.

"I love you, Dervogilla," he whispered into my hair. "I shall always love you." For a long moment he held me, then put me away. "Not now, Dervogilla, not now. I dare not risk Tiernan O'Rourke's jealousy, he would tear apart the peace we have put together and with such difficulty. Did you know I journeyed to Breifne specially to see you?"

I stroked his face. "I know, my love."

His hand closed over mine, pressing the dragon's head into my flesh. "If ever you have need of me, send the ring and I will come."

"I promise," I breathed and slipped away just in time. I met my husband coming down the stone staircase. "You are going to bed?" His eyes raked the damp spots on my gown.

"I was caught in a cloudburst," I said in a composed voice. "I fear I may have taken a chill. Dermot expressed a wish to see the god with three faces. We went to the grove."

He frowned, but said nothing.

115

Rachel was waiting to help me undress. My husband did not come to my bed that night. I heard afterwards from the servants that he had sat up half the night carousing with his guests. When I arose the following morning he and Dermot had left for Ferns.

There is nothing dramatic about the landscape of Breifne, but the eye never tires of the scene. I love the sea, but the vista of countless lakes made up for the ever-changing tides lapping the strand where I was brought up and which I missed so much. Hedgerows of whitethorn, ash, green oak, holly, wild cherry, sloe, sycamore, divide the rushy fields. And everywhere is the rustle, the movement, the busyness of life: mice and insects and small birds, darting and mating and feeding and quarrelling. I had many walks but my favourite was along the shore of Lough Erne.

Rachel would accompany me, carrying my baby son in a sling on her back and he would gurgle with delight and put out small starfish hands attempting to catch the sparrows and hawks hunting for food. Later when he learnt to walk I made a rein of soft leather and this allowed him stumble along at his own pace, which he loved. He would plop down when tired, stuffing his mouth with the sticky blue marly clay that adheres to the shallows, chuckling with joy at the sight of the mother otter feeding her young.

He was a very good baby and seldom cried. We came to an understanding. In return for a honey sweetmeat, he would allow Rachel scoop the clay out of his mouth. I would point out a snipe or pheasant or a grey heron standing on one leg in the mud and he would scream with excitement. Once he saw a fox loping by and he went mad to give chase. These were our happiest hours. I planned that when he was old enough to ride I would buy a small pony and take him with me on a visit to Dublin. We would stay in the house on the strand. I saw him paddling in pools, searching for crabs, making sand castles with Rachel's help and galloping his pony across the beach while I rode my black mare, even as Grandmother and I had once done.

At the beginning of summer as the Lady of Breifne I accompanied the villagers on their annual excursion to the Iron Mountains for the Booley. The custom of Booleying is very old. There is good reason why people drive their cattle to summer pastures; fresh grazing is provided for the herds, fields of clover and good grass abound on the heights. Then too the home fields where the cattle had wintered can be used for tillage or meadowing.

As we set off in single file on that May morning, our path to the peaks took us past hedges of whitethorn, foaming into streams of pink and white glory. There was sally too, the first to green and the first to die. Donkeys, panniers slung across their backs, carried pots and pans, crockery and churns. A group of the young girls would spend the summer tending the cattle, the rest of us would bid them goodbye and make our way down the mountains and home at nightfall.

My year-old son was perched on a pannier, Rachel keeping a steadying hand on the animal's back. The young man with the foolish face whom I had met on my first morning had decided to accompany the villagers. The locals said he was an omadaun, but they were kind and saw that he came to no harm.

The journey took three hours, the cattle herded along the mountain track by excited young boys and barking dogs, while each girl carried her own spinning wheel, comb and needles. My young son squealed with excitement at the lowing of cattle and smiled up at the omadaun who patted his head. The gesture was curiously tender, and when we stopped for breakfast half-way up the mountain, I called the young man over and shared our bread and bacon and milk. I tried to draw him out, but either he couldn't or wouldn't speak. Afterwards when I enquired about his family the villagers fell silent. It was better to ask no questions.

When we reached the heights everyone went to work with a will. Men and older boys set about building small dwellings of clay and wattles to house the girls who would remain herding the cattle for the length of the summer. Rachel helped the women gather armfuls of black sedges and when my son yawned made him a bed. I could hear her telling him the old legend of how on Christmas night St Joseph had made a bed of black sedges for the newly-born infant in the cave at Bethlehem, and that anyone sleeping on such a bed never knew pains or aches. Some of the girls listening vouched for the truth of the story. During the summer months they would make their beds of bracken and rushes and sedges and wake each morning fresh as a lark. I thought it a beautiful story and was moved when the poor young man with the foolish face lay down on the sedges putting a protective arm around my sleeping son.

Later when the small houses were built, the cattle let out to graze and holes dug in the bogs to hold the newly churned butter, a bonfire was lit, to roast the meats for our supper. We would be leaving the mountains soon, we would not see the young dairymaids until Hallowe'en when the harvest was in and the cattle driven down to their winter quarters.

It was a beautiful evening, with scarcely a breeze. Though I was not to know it, I was experiencing the last moments of my carefree youth. Oh, I would have many more years before me, my life would be long. I would know days of happiness, moments of ecstasy with Dermot in the wildness of Wicklow; in my house on the strand; looking down over the ramparts of that enchanting palace at Poitiers, but never again would I know heart's ease. It is one of the gifts of the gods that we cannot see into the future. On that spring evening, I was conscious only of the buzz of voices around me, a voice singing an old lament and the smell of sizzling pork that made my mouth water.

After we had eaten our fill I lay with my eyes closed and was awakened from a half-dream by a cry. I started up and saw a grey wolf making its way down the face of the rocks, drawn by the smell of the food. My son slept on his bed of sedges away from the bonfire. To reach the scattered bones the wolf would walk over my baby, snatch him up. In a second that lasted an eternity I could hear in my head teeth scrunching, my child screaming with fear. I was on my feet, but the omadaun had moved fast, a knife in his hand. As I watched paralysed with fear, he plunged his hand into the grey furry chest. Man and beast seemed to go into a slow motion dance. When we got to them both were dead, the man mauled, the wolf's back arched in its final agony. And my son still slept.

They carried the body of the foolish young man down to the village and waked him in the castle as befitted a hero, with stories and tears and funeral meats. Of all those present only the Lady Sunnivea was dry-eyed. On the morning her son was buried she came up to me in the solar. "My son saved your changeling child," she said with a dreadful smile. It was the first time she had acknowledged his birth.

"I'm sorry," I said. I wanted to tell her I was heartbroken, that her son had been noble, a prince, that she should not grieve but glory in the manner of his death. The look in her eyes stopped my words. "My little boy loved him," I stammered. "He died saving Tiernan Óg's life."

She grimaced. "I am without a son. Soon you will know my pain."

"What do you mean?" I thought she was half-mad with grief and maybe she was. She turned away, shrugging me off and went to her room.

A week later Tiernan O'Rourke broke the news. "I have decided," he said one night as we prepared for bed, "to foster our son. It is all for the best."

I collapsed on a chair. I had been dreading something like this. "Did the Lady Sunnivea advise you?"

He patted my head, as he would his hound. "Sunnivea was sensible, she said the younger he goes the better he will settle down."

I opened my mouth. At first no words came, then I managed to bring out the question, "Where will you send him?"

"To Connaught. The High King has agreed to receive him into his household, to rear him as his son."

To Torlach O'Connor! Was my husband mad? I found myself shouting, "And what if you displease him and he puts our son's eyes out as he threatened to do to one of his own?"

"Dervogilla, be sensible." O'Rourke attempted to hold me but I fought him off.

"Leave me alone!" I screamed.

He said wearily, "You know well that fosterage is the custom. Our son would have had to go sooner or later. This will cement peace between Breifne and Connaught." His face twitched. "Dermot McMurrough is not the only man who loves peace."

I lost control. "If you give my son away to that man, I shall never speak to you again, never lie in your bed, I swear."

"Dervogilla, there will be other children, other sons, daughters."

I slapped his face. There was a mist in front of my eyes. "Never, never, never," I sobbed, biting the hand that was holding me down.

With an oath he let go of me and I wrenched open the door, ready to throw myself down the stairs, to run to the nursery, to snatch up and hold my son safe. O'Rourke was rapping out orders, servants were dragging me back into my room, tying me to the bed, locking the door behind them as they went out.

They didn't even let me kiss my baby goodbye. For weeks I lay ill. The surgeon who tended me bled me to lessen the fever. Rachel brought me honey drinks, potions made from poppy seeds which sometimes made me sleep. But when I did I was caught up in a dreadful nightmare. I could see my small son drowned, his eyes open, a water lily clenched in his small hands.

When I awoke I determined to recover, to live, to regain my senses. A day would come when my son would need me. I must be there. But my marriage was over. I would never trust Tiernan O'Rourke for as long as I lived.

Chapter 8

*B*efore the year was out, Torlach O'Connor had invaded Munster with his Connaught army and the peace that was to last for all times was broken. Leinster was caught up in the wars and my husband set off with his soldiers for Cork. There were a couple of skirmishes, culminating in the Battle of the Great Bog which took place in a spot called Gougane Barra where the river Lee rises and where St Finbarr founded his monastery. It had long been considered a holy place, a place of sanctuary, but in the bitter wars that were consuming Ireland nothing was sacred.

Back in Breifne we waited for news. It was brought to us by my husband's dwarf, nicknamed Beg. He had set off with O'Rourke's army, perched high on a wicked black horse. How he managed to control the animal I never could fathom, but manage he did. I was in the solar working on my tapestry frame when he returned. I sent for the servants; their husbands and brothers and sweethearts had gone off to war in my husband's train, and they were as anxious as I to learn what happened.

"The Lord Tiernan O'Rourke with King Dermot McMurrough was in the forefront of battle," Beg began, settling himself down on a stool at my feet. "Begod, one eye and all as he has, the Lord Tiernan did us proud. He killed seven Munster warriors with a blow of his axe. I saw their heads dance like footballs across the field. 'Twas a pity I hadn't a hurley stick."

I shuddered. "You are a bloodthirsty rascal. Get on with your story." Beg held out his beaker and I filled it with beer. For so small a man he had a thirst that would sink a ship.

"Tell me, your Ladyship, were you ever on the field of battle?" he asked slyly and some of the servants tittered.

"I was reared amongst the Ostmen of Dublin," I said coldly. "Civilised people, merchants and craftsmen, more interested in trade and commerce and building a city than in tearing each other apart."

Beg took a long swallow, and nodded. "Sure Brian Boru beat the spirit out of that lot at the battle of Clontarf. Ach, we're a quarrelsome people but what matter. We only fight when the time is right."

"When the time is right? And when might that be?"

He arranged the hem of his purple shirt, smoothed down his green trews and inspected his shoes. They were very fashionable and had turned up toes. I wondered from what dead warrior he had filched his finery. He reminded me of Cinit. By the flirtatious look he was throwing the blacksmith, a burly fellow with arms of steel, he had similar tastes. "You see 'tis like this," he explained. "In the spring, there's the land to be tilled and the seeds planted, then in autumn the harvest. Winter is horrid. 'Tis only in summer, when nature can be left to get on with her own devices that you'll find men ready and willing to shoulder their axe and take to the field of battle. It stands to reason."

He smacked his lips. "Begod, that is a good drop of beer. Nearly as strong as the stuff brewed by the Norsemen of Dublin. Tell me, Lady Dervogilla, did you ever hear tell of the heather ale?"

The heather ale. It brought a smile to my lips as memory went helter skelter back down the years: shadows dancing on walls, fires blazing, the light of wax candles in chandeliers and lamps in alcoves throwing the great dais into relief and the young Dublin brewer with eager eyes flirting with me promising to trade the secret his people had brought with them when they swept around the coast of Ireland. All for a kiss.

There was a story about how a Viking ancestor of his had been taken prisoner after the battle of Clontarf. In return for the secret of the heather ale, the Irish chieftain promised to spare the brewer's life, whereupon the Norseman wrapped his arms around his captor's neck, whispering in his ear and then jumped over the cliffs, taking both secret and captor with him to death on the rocks below.

But that evening in the Thingmote I had no time for my young admirer, had eyes only for Dublin's new Overlord, Dermot McMurrough. I had fallen hopelessly in love with him earlier, riding up Cork Hill, looking every inch a king. That evening when I was just fifteen years and wore golden balls at the end of my curls.

"Get on with your story, Beg," I said stiffly. "Otherwise we'll be still listening to you at cock crow."

Beg smirked. "I can't be rushed." One of the kitchen maids giggled delightedly, and the blacksmith cleared his throat in a growl of admiration. "A storyteller spins his words the same way a spider spins his web, there's a pattern in his story," Beg continued imperturbably.

"Tell us what happened," I said wearily, knowing he had every intention of giving a blow by blow account of the battle and all that had gone before. My only interest lay in learning who had survived.

He held out his beaker for more. "'Tis like this," he explained. "The field of battle resembles a play with the actors coming in on cue. Oh, 'tis a sight to behold. The two sides marching in with their pipers leading the way and arranging themselves on opposite ends of the field. As each clan appears, a herald with the voice of a bull calls out, 'The Hy Kinsellas of Kinsealy; The O'Tooles of Wicklow; The O'Maolseachlains of Meath; The O'Rourkes of Breifne.' Before they enter the field, every man throws a stone on a mound as he passes by," Beg ran a hand across his mouth and I poured him a drink. "When the battle is over, the survivors pick up their stones on the way out of the field, so they can tell how many died on either side. The stones that are left are built into cairns to honour the dead."

"Did the Leinstermen fight in their pelt? Did they swing hatchets, gouge out their enemies' eyes?" a dairy maid with long red hair and mad eyes shouted out. "God, I wish I'd been there."

Solemnly Beg upturned his beaker on the floor. "Some fought naked and some wore shields; they fought with axes and spears and stones and hand to hand. Our soldiers drove the Munstermen back into the bogs where they belong. Their king, Conor O'Brien of Thomond, escaped on a horse, in a fairy mist. They say his mother came out of a fairy mound."

I could contain myself no longer. Beg's rigmarole could go on all night. "What happened to Dermot McMurrough?"

Behind me someone gave a cold mocking laugh. Sunnivea had slipped into the hall unnoticed. Beg turned around, his small apple face puckered with concern. "King Dermot, praise be, is safe. He fought as brave as a lion, side by side with the Lord Tiernan O'Rourke. My master has gone into Connaught to visit his son who is hostage there."

Sunnivea frowned. "The child is fostered."

"Fostered, hostage, 'tis one and the same if there's trouble, and eyes to be put out," Beg muttered and held out his beaker for ale. I emptied the jug. "Until the sands of the sea and the stars of the heavens are numbered, no one will ever reckon all the sons and kings and chiefs and lords of Munster who were killed in the Great Battle of the Bogs," he chanted and got a round of applause.

I gave the dwarf a silver penny. He had been a match for Sunnivea. Leinster was safe for the moment and if Tiernan O'Rourke had gone to Connaught on a visit it would be weeks if not months before he returned.

To distract my mind I decided to visit Dublin, taking Rachel with me for company. We opened up the house on the strand and Rachel employed a couple of serfs to wash away the cobwebs and dirt of years. Soon it was as if I had never been away. I walked the narrow streets of the city, up High Street, past the Thingmote, down by the Shambles and into Hogg's Green. On an impulse I stopped at a stall that sold children's toys. I bought a wooden ship, a hurley, a wooden spade and a bucket. I would send them to a small boy in Connaught. A small boy who had once laughed and put out baby hands to catch the sparrows and hawks hunting for food on the shores of Lough Erne and who loved to eat blue marly clay. Would he remember his Mamma? Or had he already forgotten my face?

I was filled with pain and rage at the princes who ruled us, their lust for power, their greed for land and cattle and gold. Their subjects only wanted to get on with their simple lives, to marry, bear children, see their sons and daughters grow up handsome and comely, to do the hundred and one small tasks that gave them pleasure, to tell stories and make music. Instead of which they were pawns in a deadly game of war. Dermot McMurrough alone wanted peace. He dreamt of a time when Ireland would be united. He had promised to endow foundations, build schools of learning, make roads. Craftsmen would flourish. He had promised a return to Ireland's Golden Age. Was it all a dream? Could it ever happen? I would make an offering of silver to the Cistercian monastery they were building at Mellifont that this vision of a peaceful united Ireland would one day become a reality. And I would pray too that my small son would be returned to me safely before long. If the price I must pay was never again to see Dermot McMurrough, well I would keep my part of the bargain and with a good grace.

That evening when the tide was far out I rode my black horse to the edge of sea and sky and as I cantered along the ghost of a small boy rode beside me, brown hair blown in the wind, starfish hands holding the reins, baby cheeks dimpling. And in that deepening twilight I knew that whatever there had been of goodwill or kindness between Tiernan O'Rourke and myself was dead. I would have divorced him without a second's thought except I knew that if I did so I would almost certainly never set eyes on my small son again.

I had gone down to Wood Quay where ships plying between Dublin and Bristol tied up. Rachel was with me. Beg had joined us in Dublin, there was nothing for him to do in Breifne when the Lord Tiernan was away. He was entertaining a group of sailors with a hornpipe and I sent him off in search of Captain Nils.

"What do you intend to do?" Rachel asked nervously. She didn't like the sea and was suspicious of strangers. She never thought of herself as a foreigner, she had adopted the Irish.

"I think I'll make a voyage to England," I said recklessly. "The sea air will do me good, blow away the cobwebs." The truth was I couldn't bear to go back to Breifne, not yet and Dublin still held too many memories of the past.

Rachel saw Nils before I did. Beg was hanging out of his coat tails, gazing up at the big Norwegian with something akin to adoration. "Oh, isn't he big, isn't he handsome!" he squealed.

Nils lifted the little man up in the air and dropped

him in the river.

"Why did you do that?" I shouted indignantly. "He'll drown."

"It is time he cooled off," the Norwegian said calmly.

Beg was being pulled to safety by the sailors he had been entertaining. Nils tossed them a handful of silver, and, blowing kisses all around, Beg went squelching along in his tattered finery to the nearest inn, accompanied by a band of hangers-on.

The next morning I sailed with Nils for England. Beg and Rachel refused to come with me. Nils had made friends with a Norman merchant, Robert FitzHarding, chief magistrate of the town of Bristol where we dropped anchor. We went to his house, a fine stone building and he received us in his study, the walls of which were lined with maps and manuscripts.

When they were finished their discussion, Robert FitzHarding clapped his hands and a servant brought in wine and cakes. At first he spoke to me in halting Gaelic and seemed both surprised and delighted when I answered him in fluent Norman French.

"You are wife to Tiernan O'Rourke, Prince of Breifne?" he began. He smiled showing strong white teeth. "I have heard tell of the Princess Dervogilla and that she has a fine son."

My heart skipped a beat. "My son is fostered with Torlach O'Connor of Connaught."

FitzHarding pursed his lips. "An unruly man. I trust your husband is wise."

"If ever the Lady Dervogilla requires help in recovering her son she can count on me," the big

Norwegian growled. He patted my hand with his large brown capable one, his kindness all but unnerving me. I had to bite back the tears. I would not let the Norman magistrate see my weakness.

"We have a splendid king in Dermot McMurrough," I blurted out. "He holds the peace in Leinster between his hands."

Robert FitzHarding drank his wine and smiled. "Dermot McMurrough encourages trade between our two countries. He sent me a gift of heather ale."

I smiled. "His favourite drink. He once tried to coax the Dublin brewer to come to his castle in Ferns."

Nils gave a great belly laugh. "We Vikings will never part with the secret, but we are prepared to export our best brew. It travels well."

Soon after, Nils and FitzHarding concluded their business and the Norman magistrate escorted us to the courtyard.

"We Normans believe in law and order. Peace is much to be desired," he said in his deep voice. "We are soon to have a new ruler in King Henry, son of the Empress Matilda. He recently married the Duchess Eleanor of Aquitaine. She is a great heiress. Pope Adrian sent Henry an emerald ring with permission to invade Ireland."

My heart sank at the news. Was there never to be an end to wars?

"By what right does the Pope give this permission?" I demanded.

Robert FitzHarding gave a dry smile. "The Church is all powerful. The Pope claims jurisdiction over all these islands. He says the Irish church is in much need of reform."

I began to protest but he held up his hand. "Do not bother your pretty head, Lady Dervogilla, it may never come to pass. King Henry will have much to do to control both Aquitaine and England." He laughed. "And to control his new wife. Like all beautiful women she is mettlesome."

"Have you met her?"

"I saw her once in Paris. I was there on business. The streets were crowded. A high silver trumpet blast alerted us to her coming. A herald called, 'The Queen rides out.' Forerunners pushed back the crowds but I stayed in front. I lifted a child high on my shoulder so he could see the outriders jogging by in parti-coloured cloaks and hoods, followed by a gilded coach. The windows were covered by red velvet curtains. As the coach passed us the curtains were pulled back and we saw an oval face and widely-spaced eyes. Then she was gone. People around us could be heard remarking that Louis of France had taken another and plainer wife, that she would be faithful but that Henry got the better bargain."

Robert FitzHarding pointed to his library. "Homer wishes his guests godspeed with the words: *May the god grant you all the things which your heart desires and may they give you a husband, a home and gracious concord.*"

At that moment I could have wept for the wish that never could come to pass. Once I had prayed to the stone god with three faces and had been given my answer in a peal of thunder, a flash of lightning. Maybe what Dermot held was true. Happiness was not for those of noble blood. On an impulse I kissed

Robert FitzHarding on the cheek. "Goodbye, my friend, and thank you for your kindness."

He held my hand in his. "If ever you are in need of a friend I am here." I did not expect to see him again. I little knew how wrong I was.

Nils took me shopping in Bristol where I bought leather purses and belts and stuffs to make a gown for Rachel and a brightly-coloured waistcoat that would gladden Beg's heart. The sea trip had done me good, lifted my spirits, given me courage. I promised myself that when I got back to Ireland I would return to Breifne and give my marriage a second chance.

I still nourished the hope that my son Tiernan Óg would be returned to me. I would never rest easy while he remained in the care of that bloodthirsty king. The man of whom the annalist had written that he had made a battleground of his country.

Chapter 9

I was back in Breifne by the autumn. On the eve of
Samhain, November night, the cattle were driven
down from the top of the Iron Mountains and the
local people prepared to celebrate the harvest which
had been gathered and stored. From this night
onwards no more field work would be done, not even
blackberries or apples picked. It was believed that the
puca spat on the fruit the night after Samhain and no
one would eat them for fear they were poisoned. My
husband who had recently returned from Connaught
was in high good spirits and promised to give a
hosting to his tenants, their wives and families. Even
the serfs and kitchen scullions were welcomed.

On my return from Dublin he had come to my
bed and I had not refused him. He was tender and
passionate by turns and aroused in me feelings for
him which I thought I had not possessed, or perhaps
it was that I had slept alone for most of a year. So
much had happened since I had last set eyes on
Dermot McMurrough that his image was fading. That
night for the first time I found comfort in my
husband's arms and when he said, "Let us make a new
start," I stroked his face and coaxed him with small

134

kisses and tender touches to bring back our small son.

"It would complete my happiness," I whispered.

"He is well and content," my husband said, but when I pressed him again he promised he would.

I lay awake in the darkness a long time after he had fallen asleep thinking about Breifne, of my first sight of the bushes, ablaze with red winter berries, the river banks jewelled with icicles, the snow-capped mountains. Spring and summer had brought their own promise. I had known happy hours gathering foxgloves, orchids and the thousand other wild flowers that grew at the lake's edge, and deep in the quiet woods. I rowed out to the crannógs, the small artificial lakeside dwellings which generations of farmers had used when they moved their cattle to different pastures.

The people had an old world courtesy. They said it was an honour to have the Lady Dervogilla under their humble roofs. They had a fund of stories relating to the kingdom of Breifne. Magh Slech had the most dramatic history of all. In ancient times it was known as the plain of prostration and it was the custom for druids to make human sacrifices to Crom Cruaich, the King Idol of Ireland and his sub gods twelve.

How were they chosen, I wondered? A young prince offered to the gods for his bravery, a young maiden for her beauty? Or perhaps the sacrificial victims had been slaves. A great bonfire lighted, osiers and wicker lashed together to make a cage. The victims given a drink of herbs crushed in wine to deaden their senses. It was an eerie thought. Were the ghosts of the long dead still weeping, the spirits of the druids asking Crom Cruaich to grant them a good harvest, victory over their enemies?

On that same visit I came on an old woman sweeping up fallen twigs in the sacred grove. It was considered a holy spot. She pointed out a circle of upright stones. A bishop known for his cruel austerities had come on a crowd of dancers one Midsummer's Eve, and struck them with his crosier, turning them to stone. One standing apart from the rest looked older and worn yet had a jaunty air. The old woman said it was the piper who had supplied the music on that fatal Midsummer's evening when six young girls, their sweethearts and the musician were frozen in stone forever.

But there was no heartless cleric to curse the revels on the night we had our celebrations in the stronghold. I will say this much for my husband, his family had long been noted for their hospitality and he spared no pains to entertain his guests. Crowds of people, old and young, had been gathering in the forecourts since dusk, and as soon as the doors were thrown open they surged into the Great Hall where a banquet had been laid. Trestles heaped with food had been set up; apples and hazel nuts, dishes of smoked bacon, piping hot sausages and blood puddings, roast pork and beef and fowl, oaten and wheaten bread, honey cakes and hot apple pies, hard and soft cheeses, tankards of ale and beer, wine and metheglin and foaming jugs of creamy milk. The young girls who had spent the spring and summer months Booleying on the Iron Mountains were surrounded by young men eager to catch their fancy, to hear their stories.

"There was never the equal of the butter yield," the girls boasted. They likened the cattle to the mythical Glas Cow which had once crossed the mountain leaving a gap so huge it could still be seen. The Glas Cow belonged to the Tuatha de Danann, the faery people who had come out of the clouds and when their day was done had vanished into the hills and hollow places. The Glas Cow could not be milked dry. In the end, the people were forced to milk her into a sieve until she had died from exhaustion.

Looking back down the years I see that night in the castle through a golden haze, the music, the dancing, the storytelling. I reminded myself how kind my husband had been after Grandmother and Bronwyn had died of the plague in Kildare. I watched him sitting in his high carved chair, legs stretched out to the blazing fire, at his ease, pleased with the company. He was wearing a fine linen shirt which I had embroidered in the early days of our marriage, a golden torc and the bracelet circling his wrist glinted in the firelight. His one good eye danced with delight as Beg took the floor. Servants ran around replenishing goblets and horns, and people sated with food and drink settled deeper into their seats on benches or sprawled on cushions, called on Beg to tell them a story.

"You all know the Valley of the Black Pig," Beg began in his treble, and people nodded, for the Black Pig's Dyke was a great ditch that ran through Breifne, skirting lakes and rivers until it entered the sea in the far north.

"We have the picture, tell us more," someone

called out to give Beg the encouragement that every storyteller needs.

A servant handed him a horn of metheglin.

"The origin of the Black Pig's Dyke was a race," he continued, "and here's how it happened. A certain schoolmaster who lived beside the Boyne had the horrid habit of turning his pupils into hares and hounds and setting them on each other. But he met his match when he enchanted the two sons of a red-haired widow, turning one into a hare and the other into a hound. The hound killed his brother, and the widow was so enraged that she turned the schoolmaster into a black pig. The herds of swine drove the enchanted pig out and the animal raced across the country leaving a huge track behind him."

"And what was the end of the rascal?" the blacksmith called out in his deep-throated growl.

Beg gave a little dance of delight. "A washerwoman hanging out her linen on bushes to dry near Rooskey put a stop to the pig's gallop. He had trampled on her clothes and she caught him up in her great strong arms and tossed him into the middle of the river Shannon where he drowned."

When Beg finished there was a roar of delight. Next the floor was cleared and sprinkled with sawdust and Tiernan O'Rourke stood up and led me out for the first dance of the night.

These were the last happy hours I spent in the castle. Soon afterwards, word was brought that our son had fallen into a river. He was rescued but too late. They tried to pump out the water, but he was dead.

I was distraught and when my husband tried to

comfort me he only made things much worse. "It happens all the time," he said. "My mother had fifteen sons and reared only two to manhood."

"I don't care," I sobbed. "Had he remained at home I would have watched over him. You gave him in fosterage to Connaught to further your own ends. I never trusted Torlach O'Connor."

At this my husband lost patience. "Torlach O'Connor was not to blame. Our son was treated with every kindness, the drowning was an accident. The High King has promised to foster any more sons you may bear."

Hearing this I think I went mad, tearing out my hair, tearing my clothes to ribbons, screaming that I would give him no more children. "Do you think I am a brood mare to produce sons to be given away as bribes?" I wept.

Rachel gave me a potion that put me to sleep for hours. When I awoke I felt drained. I have written it before: there was always the hope that while my son lived we could make something of our marriage. But no more, I would not suffer such a loss again.

I saw little of my husband in the months that followed. All around the castle the land slept in the silence of winter. The flocks were gathered in their quarters and the fields were rain-sodden and deserted. I found it hard to sleep and walked the ramparts of the castle in the damp heavy dawns. Tiernan O'Rourke was constantly on the move, sometimes conferring in Connaught with Torlach O'Connor, again patrolling the borders that divided us from Ulster. It was well known that O'Connor fomented trouble. Divide and rule had always been his slogan and he followed this through while Dermot McMurrough strove hard to keep the peace of Leinster and Ulster. The North held the Pass of Ulster. They had sworn an oath that the next High King of Ireland would come from the powerful McLaughlins.

The Cistercian Abbey of Mellifont which Archbishop Malachy of Armagh and that saintly monk, Bernard of Clairvaux, had planned and executed was nearing completion. My husband and I, together with the High King and other noble families, were invited to the consecration. I had promised to give gold and silver for the safe return of my little son but now he would never come. As I rode stony-hearted and dry-eyed along the miles to Mellifont, it occurred to me that numbness has its advantages. Nothing moved me – not the beauty of an April day; not the gusts of wind sweeping the sky so that the blue of the heavens showed through and sunbeams lit up our road; not the air scented with young growing things. I was blind to the herd of young deer raising startled faces at our approach, deaf to the woodland song. Not even the magnificence of Mellifont, a miracle of stone set among living foliage, decorated with delicate tracery and pointed soaring arches that glinted gold in the bright morning, could lighten my mood.

The Father Abbot took us on a tour of the cloisters, the pilgrims' hospice, the flower gardens, broad lawns, the stable and granaries. Only the scriptorium, where the monks were putting the finishing touches to a copy of the gospels for the High King, gave me solace of a sort. It was probably the air of quiet purpose. A youngster not more than eight years old was rubbing sheets with pumice stone to smooth the parchment which the monks would illuminate with strange and wonderful beasts in delicate colours. Next to each scribe stood a lectern on which the codex to be copied was placed. There were rows of pots containing inks of gold and various colours. In its way it reminded me of the workshops in Dublin where craftsmen made horns and combs and painted the hulls of the long ships in vivid purples and blues and reds which would flash and glitter at sea. I was wrenched with sudden longing for a return to my carefree girlhood when my only worry was whether or not I would be allowed wear golden balls in my hair. And I realised with pain and for the first time that one thing is certain: we can never go back.

When the High King arrived, the ceremonies got under way. Gorgeously mitred and coped priests filed onto the altar and the monks took their places in the choir. During the Mass that followed I tried to keep my thoughts on the majesty of God and the glory of his heavens but tumbling through my mind was the picture of my son. Would my little boy be lonely in these celestial mansions? He was too young to spend an eternity singing and praising God. He needed laughter, joy, the company of other young people. Tír na nÓg, the afterlife of my pagan ancestors had always sounded more appealing: that land of youth, its rivers teeming with silver salmon and speckled trout, trees bearing marvellous fruit, music and storytelling to delight a young boy's heart.

When the Mass was ended, one by one the kings

and princes stood up to make their pledges for the upkeep of Mellifont. My husband promised one hundred pieces of silver, which set the pattern for those princes and chieftains that followed him. Dermot McMurrough pledged five hundred silver pieces and Torlach O'Connor, High King of Ireland, one thousand silver pieces. There was a pause while the Archbishop murmured a benediction and then I stood up and said in a loud ringing voice:

"I pledge fifteen hundred silver pieces, a herd of cattle and gold for altar vestments." There was an audible intake of breath around the church. Dermot McMurrough looked around at me in amazement, while my husband hissed, "Have you taken leave of your senses, woman?"

I shook off his hand and continued. "I give the offering in memory of my son Tiernan Óg O'Rourke who died while in the care of Torlach O'Connor of Connaught. And I make an appeal that the Brehon Laws be changed and that no child under the age of seven be sent away in fosterage."

Had I slapped the High King in the face I could not have created a greater stir. But my gift was too handsome to be refused. The clergy cleared their throats and the Abbot murmured something about God giving me grace to accept His will.

The Mass was followed by a banquet in which I took no part. Instead I retired to a small house they had placed at my disposal outside the gates of the monastery. Women were not allowed sleep in the sacred cloisters. When the festivities were over my husband would take his rest in the lavishly arranged guest chamber with the other kings, princes and chieftains. In later years when I was old and widowed and could do as I pleased, I built a nunnery outside the walls, so that women who wished to spend a week or a lifetime beside the Church, could do so in some comfort and feel free to walk the gardens and take part in the holy offices without asking permission of any man, be he Abbot or simple monk.

As I sat alone toying with a supper for which I had no appetite the small novice I had last seen in the scriptorium arrived with a letter bearing the King of Leinster's seal. The message was brief. Dermot was waiting in the chapter house. Could I come to him? Wrapping a warm cloak around me, for the night had grown chilly, I followed my guide, through the Abbey gates, under the arch, down the cloister. The child left me at a richly decorated doorway. Here the monks assembled during the day to hear readings from holy scripture but now it was empty and dark as a tomb. I closed the door behind me, gazing down the dim vaulted space.

He was standing in the embrasure of a window, his eyes fixed on a further door. So intent was he and so silently had I entered that his ear had caught no sound.

"I said to the Abbot that I must talk with you for a little while, that you were distraught after the death of your son," he said as I came up. "I told him that I am an old friend. I think he understood."

I threw back the hood of my cloak and looked at him. "Then no-one knows we are here except the Abbot and the messenger."

"And he is dumb, or had you not noticed?"

"No, I questioned him but he walked on. I

143

thought he was too much in awe of me to talk. Are they all asleep?"

"The banquet went on for hours. Nine courses and wine with each course. The monks have retired to their dormitories, the others to the guest houses, most of them sodden with drink."

I shivered. "Was there no other place we could talk?"

He shook his head. "Darling, we have such a little while. I knew I must see you, be near to you. You looked so forlorn."

I sighed. "I had hoped we could make something of our marriage, but my husband insisted on sending our son into Connaught. I shall never forgive him."

"Hush," he murmured. "Children are fragile plants; a frost, a wind, a wetting can have fatal effects."

I thumped his chest with my fists. "And yet there is this fosterage, this law which sends them away when they are little more than infants."

He stroked my hair. "If ever I have the power I promise you I shall have the laws changed. No boy shall leave his home until he reaches the age of seven years."

"Indeed," said a mocking voice in my ear. My husband was standing at my shoulder. "Quite a touching scene," he said bitterly. "The King of Leinster wiping away a woman's tears. Tell me, Dermot, what other things will you change when you are High King? God's commandments? Will adultery no longer be a sin? Will coveting your neighbour's wife become a virtue?" He swayed on his feet. He was very drunk.

Dermot took him by the arm. "It is time you were

in your bed, Tiernan O'Rourke. I am sorry you think ill of me. I had thought to comfort Dervogilla in her loss."

"Aye, comfort your whore," my husband shouted, and swinging away aimed a punch at Dermot. He missed and fell heavily to the floor.

There was a commotion and a couple of monks burst in through the door, carrying torches. At the sight of the Leinster King they drew back.

"There are no bones broken," Dermot said wearily. "A small accident, over-indulgence in wine and mead. Carry the Lord of Breifne to his bed."

Between them the monks got my husband out of the door. He was snoring loudly. Whether it was the fall or the drink I neither knew nor cared. Lurking in the background, a scared look in his brown eyes, was the messenger who had fetched me. Dermot touched him on the head and told him in a gentle voice to escort the Lady Dervogilla back to her lodgings. He took my hand in his and pressed the dragon's ring. "Remember, if you need my help, send this token."

I nodded speechlessly. I was suddenly overcome with fatigue. I longed at that moment to be away in some quiet place, by myself, with no man to bother me. I wanted no quarrels, no passion, no comfort, nothing but to be on my own.

"I am like the Glas Cow," I told myself as I stumbled along the path behind my guide, back down the cloisters, through the arch, out the gates to the thatched cottage where I would spend what remained of the night. "Milked dry of any emotions. I shall never feel anything again."

Chapter 10

Rumours about the marriage of Eleanor of Aquitaine and Henry, Duke of Normandy, son of the Empress Matilda who had fought so long and bitter a war with King Stephen of England, reverberated through Europe, even reaching us in the backwater that was Breifne.

Beg was the first with the description of the wedding that was destined to change not only England and France but Ireland too.

"The Duchess of Aquitaine is the most beautiful woman in Christendom," Beg said eyeing me slyly, "saving only the Lady Dervogilla."

"Get on with your story," I said crossly. I had no illusions about my looks. I was hollow-eyed and gaunt from worry and abuse. My husband came to my bed repeatedly, insisting on his conjugal rights in what was tantamount to rape. When he left me in the early hours I was bruised and battered. But for Rachel's kindness and her skill with brewing sleeping draughts I might have been tempted to put an end to myself. She constantly counselled patience. She was the sister I never had.

"You all know of Eleanor's wanton reputation,"

Beg was saying.

Rachel hid her face in her hands, and a couple of my waiting women tittered behind their hands.

"There is no need to go into details," I interrupted. "Tell us what the wedding was like."

He screwed up his tiny face in concentration. "Louis agreed to an annulment in the end. They had been married fifteen years and she hadn't managed to give him a son."

I thought of how nightly my husband tried to get a son on me and how I prayed that I would not conceive. Listening to Beg meander I had a certain sympathy with the Duchess Eleanor. I envied her her freedom to do as she pleased, marry or divorce as she chose.

"There was gossip because her bridegroom was younger," Beg continued, biting his thumb. "Eleanor is twenty-nine years old and Henry is eighteen. Not that it matters, he is said to be as besotted with her as was Louis of France. Troubadours in Aquitaine sing of her beauty," Beg went on in his fluting voice.

Nils, my ship's Captain, had told me many stories of Aquitaine. Eleanor's lands stretched from the Loire as far south as the Pyrenees and from the Bay of Biscay to Auvergne. It was a country of many landscapes, heaths and sandy wastes, mountains, flat lush plains and impenetrable woodlands. I wondered how Eleanor would settle in the damp and gloom that was England, she who had known yellow-walled and red-roofed towns with their Romanesque cathedrals and rich abbeys, she who had enjoyed slow sleepy days in the sunlight when troubadours sang. It was said of the troubadours that their poetry demanded no other inspiration than a May morning, the dawn chorus, a hawthorn tree in blossom, and a group of knights templar, with bright banners fluttering, on their way to crusade.

Beg finally took himself off to the kitchens where his stories would be better appreciated, and I applied myself to my tapestry frame. I was hoping for a couple of weeks of peace. Murtough McLaughlin of Ulster, after a couple of skirmishes, had made peace of a kind with Torlach O'Connor of Connaught and now they were busy dividing up Meath. It was rumoured that one day they would divide up Ireland. They were even nibbling on the southern half of Breifne. My husband had taken a force of men and word was coming through that he had been driven back. I stifled a wish that they would take him prisoner and hastily prayed for forgiveness. Torlach O'Connor was in the habit of blinding those who got in his way. Since her foster brother's departure, the Lady Sunnivea had taken to her sick bed. I sent her gifts of flowers and fruit. She threw them out the window and once when I called she ordered me out of the room.

I heard my husband's return even before I laid eyes on him, there was such bustle, tramp of feet, horses' hooves, clash of arms and the hoarse voice that I had come to dread. I gathered my courage around me, determined to have a "show down." I was a princess of Meath, an heiress. If Eleanor of Aquitaine could have her marriage to Louis of France set aside, why should not I? I was sick of cowering like a kitchen scullion when he came to my bed at nights. We ate supper in silence and when he attempted to follow me to my room I stood outside the door with my arms stretched out. "Enough is enough," I said. "We were, as you will recall, married according to the Brehon laws and I am entitled to demand a divorce."

He pushed me before him into the room. When I attempted to escape he dragged me back by the hair. "I have lost men and part of my lands thanks to your brother's stupidity," he panted. "Your family has been a millstone around my neck for years."

"What you or my half-brothers do is no concern of mine," I said, struggling with him. "I want to know nothing of tussles for power between kings and princes."

"Only in so far as it affects your paramour, Dermot McMurrough," he sneered.

I tried to break away but he twisted back my arms. "I have not slept with Dermot McMurrough since our marriage. I have not slept with any other man," I shouted. "But I no longer intend to be raped by you."

He slapped me across one side of the face, and then the other, dragging me across the room, beating my head against the wall.

"I would crush your head in my two hands, I would reduce it to pulp if it would put thoughts of your paramour out of your mind," he snarled.

Blood was pouring down my face and Rachel who had come into the room threw herself between us. "Strike me if you must strike anyone," she cried.

"So you want to take your mistress's place?" He kicked me in the ribs and then lifted Rachel onto the bed, tearing off her clothes, raping her before my eyes while she wept and pleaded with him to stop.

He had dropped his dagger and slowly, painfully, I pulled myself along the floor to the bed. Holding on to the bed posts, I lunged at his arm, drawing blood. He turned and cursed me. It was then I saw the Lady Sunnivea standing in the doorway. In her long grey draperies, a lighted brand in her hand, she was like a figure from some inferno. "You used it on me once, Tiernan O'Rourke," she said with a laugh that froze the very marrow of my bones. "Now tame the bitch you call wife."

O'Rourke crossed the room in one leap, snatched the brand and lashed out at me. There was a sickening smell of flesh burning and a searing pain down one side of my face. I think what he had done shocked him into sanity but the Lady Sunnivea appeared to have gone berserk.

"Ireland's Deirdre of the Sorrows," she cackled. "Now, Dervogilla, you have sorrows and to spare."

My husband was shouting orders. Servants were dragging Sunnivea from the room. My women were tending to me. Rachel, bloody and bruised, was crawling down the bed, telling me she had ointment which would heal, that everything would be alright. I collapsed on the floor and remembered no more.

I lay in a darkened room, one side of my face covered with a veil. Days passed when I allowed no one near me except Rachel. Then O'Rourke came, pushing aside the guards I had set at the door. He stood at the bedside, gazing at me. I thought he had aged.

"I shall do all in my power to make up to you," he said hoarsely. "I never meant to injure you. I am going to the holy island of Lough Derg to do penance."

"You may go to hell for all I care," I muttered. "Just as soon as I am well enough I intend to leave this place for good, taking with me the mark of your favour." I put my hand to the side of my face where the skin had shrunk. The pain was still intolerable. "It is bad enough that you have destroyed me but that you should abuse Rachel is more than I can bear."

He bent his head and I forced myself to meet his gaze. I would not show fear. He patted my hand. "Don't, darling. It would be useless. I have left word with the servants that you are not to be allowed out of your room while I am away. There are guards everywhere. You must be a good girl, get better soon. You will be a more amenable wife and make me sons, now that your beauty is marred, and Dermot McMurrough will no longer covet you . . ."

I closed my eyes. "He is mad," I told myself. "I am in hell, out of which there is no redemption."

Beg put his head around the door. O'Rourke had left the castle, gone on his pilgrimage to Patrick's Purgatory in Lough Derg. He might drown in the lake for all I cared.

"They have tied the Lady Sunnivea to the bed. I fear she has quite lost her wits," the little man said, edging into the room. Somehow the sight of his apple face and childlike eyes undid me and the tears I had been holding back for days burst like a dam in full flood.

Beg perched himself on the end of the bed. "Don't cry, Lady Dervogilla. Rachel will be cross with me. She says she will heal your face, that you will be as beautiful as ever."

"I don't care about my looks," I wept. "If only I could get away."

Beg put his little head to one side. "If King Dermot knew what happened he would help." I wasn't surprised at Beg's words. Little that went on in the castle was secret from him.

I turned the dragon's ring on my finger. "Would you help me? Can I trust you?"

"My friend the blacksmith says I am the most trustworthy person he knows." Beg said boastfully.

I thought, dear God, am I reduced to this, begging help of a little man who is my husband's creature? What if he has been sent to tempt me? What if he fails me? But there was no-one else.

"Would you take this ring to King Dermot McMurrough? All you need say is that the Lady Dervogilla sent it."

I had barely time to take the ring off my finger before it had vanished. "How will you make the journey to Ferns?" I fretted. "It is so far, it will take so long."

Beg climbed off the bed and did his little dance on the floor. "King Dermot is at the borders of Breifne, a day's hard ride away. The blacksmith will find me a horse. Never fear, Lady Dervogilla, but he will get your message, and come like a knight in shining armour to your rescue."

He paused at the door and then ran back to whisper, "You must promise to take me with you when you leave. If you do not, the Lord Tiernan O'Rourke will brand me and then hang my head on the flagpole of the castle as an example to traitors." He giggled. "I'm not a traitor, I just love a bit of diversion." He ran out the door and I lay there wondering was I as crazy as the Lady Sunnivea, taking such a chance. Beg had always prided himself that he was my friend. I had been kind to him, but how did I know what went on in his little head?

When Rachel came to my room to anoint my face and bring me something soothing to drink I told her what had happened.

"Beg will do what he can to help," she said cheerfully. She was brave and had done her best to recover her spirits. "He is the only one who can slip past the guards. No-one knows or cares when he comes or goes. They are used to his ways."

A couple of days later Dermot McMurrough came. I heard the commotion outside before I saw him, heard the shouts, the cries as the soldiers guarding the castle fell back before the ferocity of the Leinster King and his men. He swept into the room, gathered me up in his arms, and carefully lifted back the veil that covered one half of my face. Only that morning I had asked Rachel to bring me a polished bronze mirror to inspect the damage. The skin was wrinkled and brown where the brand had seared flesh and bone leaving a jagged scar from brow to chin. Dermot kissed me tenderly. "Don't worry, Dervogilla," he said, touching my face with gentle fingers. "Everything will heal in time."

I sighed. "Will you take me to Dublin, to the stone house by the sea? I think I might recover there. Rachel will come with me. O'Rourke raped her. Here in this room, before my eyes."

Dermot rubbed his tousled hair which was matted with blood from a blow. "O'Rourke is mad," he said flatly. "I have thought so for a very long time and feared for your safety."

"What of Beg?" I asked.

Dermot laughed. "By now he is halfway to Dublin. He has appointed himself my jester."

It was a soft autumn day when we reached the house on the strand, the air scented with seaweed and the tang of the sea. Slaves were being off-loaded from a boat carrying a Saracen's flag and hauled across the mudflats to where a group of traders waited to take them to the slave markets behind Smock Alley. Rachel put a hand to her mouth to smother a cry and I hugged her. "You are safe, my dear, whatever happens me in the future," I promised her. "I intend to give you your freedom. You have suffered because of me and it is only right I should try to pay my debt."

"It was of no account. Not like you," she whispered, distressed. "I was raped before by the slave master. There was no harm done, I have had my flux."

I kissed her. "Put the past behind you. You will always have a home with me." I thought I read disappointment in her face, but when I looked again she was smiling.

Beg was turning somersaults on the sand in his excitement, squealing, "Nils is coming. I sent him word we were on our way."

I looked around and saw the Norwegian thundering across the strand. He paused only long enough to pay his respects to King Dermot and to me, and then swung Rachel up in his arms. And I thought, what will he say when he hears she has been raped by Tiernan O'Rourke? But Nils was smiling broadly and I knew that Beg had told him everything.

Later that evening as I sat at my front door, watching the sun set over the mountains, he came again and this time asked me for Rachel's hand in marriage. I knew by the look in her eyes that she was in love with her Norse giant and for his sake was prepared to brave the sea which she hated. But there would be no need of this, he said, he had rented a house on the estuary. I think I completed her happiness by giving her a dowry. It wasn't the money that mattered but she had her pride. She promised to stay with me for as long as I would need her. I was glad she would have Nils to take care of her. We were living in dangerous times and if even a princess of Meath was not safe from ravening beasts such as O'Rourke, what hope was there for a girl who had been branded a slave?

In the clear salt-laden air my skin healed and my spirits lifted. I would always be marked but a veil would hide most of the damage.

Dermot was staying with the new Ostman King, Hasculf, but came to me each evening for supper. I would meet him on the strand and we would ride far out to where sea and sky met. He was very gentle, making no demands. He said our time would come and, truth to tell, I was relieved that he was prepared to wait.

Then one evening he came to give me the news I dreaded to hear. Tiernan O'Rourke was back in Breifne, swearing vengeance on Leinster for what he called my abduction. "He says you were carried screaming from his stronghold," Dermot said. "He has appealed to Torlach O'Connor for help to get you back. They say he is quite unhinged."

The tide was lapping around the stone wall that enclosed the garden and I looked towards Howth rising out of the sea. "I would rather walk out until the water covers my head, it would be easier to drown than go back," I said, meaning every word. "There would be peace in the blue green waters, and I would take my chance in the hereafter. Tiernan O'Rourke branded his half-sister, the Lady Sunnivea, on the arm. She showed me once."

Dermot put his arms around me. There was comfort in his embrace, strength in the lines of his face, love in his hazel eyes, his deep voice. This was a man who held the peace of Leinster in his hands, a man who had fought many battles, a man who had been scarred, yet he was gentle as Rachel. "You must come with me to Ferns, Dervogilla," he said. "You will be safe in my stronghold. I must return soon, I cannot leave you behind me in Dublin. Tiernan O'Rourke would find you and drag you back with him. Will you trust yourself to me, will you come with me?"

I pondered. I loved Dermot, but all I wanted at that moment was to be by myself, to have a little peace. "What about Mor? What will she say?"

He got up abruptly and took a turn around the room. "She must welcome you. There is no other way."

There was always England. Nils would take me across the Irish Sea. I could go to live with cousin Gwyneth, but I was bone weary; her incessant chatter would drive me mad. It was easier to let Dermot make the decisions. I thought about Rachel. "When would we need to leave?"

"As soon as possible. O'Rourke has not yet left Breifne. He is not sure where I have taken you. But no doubt he has spies."

"Nils means to marry Rachel. I would like to be at her wedding."

Dermot frowned. "Then she must be married tomorrow. There is no time to lose. She is no longer of interest to Tiernan O'Rourke, but he will kill her if he gets the chance. It would be revenge of a sort."

"The Ostmen will take care of one of their own. Grandmother taught me that. We must take Beg and his friend the blacksmith with us."

Dermot threw back his head and laughed. "I can always do with a jester and storyteller at Ferns and show me the blacksmith who is not needed. If I could just coax the brewer of the heather ale to come with us my court would be complete."

Nils married Rachel the next day in the Thingmote. The ceremony was performed by one of the City Fathers. Nils was urged to take his bride away on a sea voyage for the good of her health and Rachel said she would be happy to go. The Ostmen didn't want any trouble when Tiernan O'Rourke came storming into Dublin. They were wise, the Norwegian giant would have taken Breifne apart, stone by stone, if one of O'Rourke's men dared lay a hand on his beloved wife.

Dermot sent Beg and the blacksmith ahead with his men-at-arms, and he and I rode our horses along the south-east coast on our way to the Black

Country. It was the first time we had ever been alone together and I could feel contentment creeping over me, and began to sleep again at night.

Summer was still with us, breathing its warmth on our skins. We took the mountain road out of Dublin and into Wicklow. Far below us the white-tipped waves soared over the heather-strewn cliffs. Kittiwakes, petrels, guillemots and puffins rode the sparkling seas and a golden eagle soared high in the blue skies only to be lost to sight. That night and for many nights after we made our bed in the heather and when I told Dermot about the Iron Mountains and how I remembered my little son asleep in a bed of sedge so soft that it felt like swans' feathers he kissed away my tears and covered my body with his. And the thought came to me, how strange love is, how unpredictable. Who can tell when it will happen and why? But how comforting and how complete. The fact that we were both married to other people and were out of God's grace seemed to matter so little in the night, in the silence and under the vast canopy of stars.

Part VI

Ferns, 1152

Chapter 11

The days and nights of that Indian summer when Dermot and I journeyed to Ferns were magical. We left the sea behind us and took the narrow winding path to the Sallygap, down into Glencree and over Kilakee. We dismounted and let the horses loose to feed while I prepared supper. Dermot caught a couple of trout and I cleaned and wrapped the fish in cabbage leaves, baking them over the hot coals. A farmer's wife had given us bread, milk, cheese, apples – she mistook us for beggars which was not surprising for we wore old clothes and our faces were streaked with dust. No supper ever tasted as good as that meal eaten in the shelter of a rock, washed down with clear spring water, more intoxicating than heather ale.

We gathered wood and built up a fire so that it blazed high in the night sky. Dermot leaned back and began a story of far-off days. He had cut his teeth on the legends and history of Ireland, had been schooled by the monks at Clonmacnois. Watching his face, I thought: he is a man of vision and would change the face of Ireland, yet he loves the old ways best. In that moment I was sick with bitterness for my lost beauty.

161

What was Dermot feeling for me now? Sympathy, a protective tenderness, and, harder to bear, pity. As if he could read my thought he pulled me to him and kised me passionately, then pushed me away and laughed.

"Not now. Later, Dervogilla. First I must finish the story of Oisín's return from the Land of the Ever Young.

"Through Glenasmole, the valley of Thrushes, Oisín rode, stopping only to watch a crowd of men trying in vain to roll a boulder out of a field they were clearing.

"In pity the last of the Fianna leaned down, picked up the rock with one hand and flung it far down the valley. As he did so, the girth broke and he fell. Between the saddle and the ground he changed from a giant of a hero to a withered old man too feeble to move."

Dermot paused and flung the butt of his apple in a wide arc, just as he had described Oisín hurling the rock.

"One of the men, braver than his companions, lifted Oisín up and asked him who he was.

"'I am Oisín, son of Finn,' the old man replied.

"'The Fianna are gone from Ireland these hundreds of years,' the rest said, gathering courage and drawing near. 'Their names and deeds are now but a bedtime story mothers tell their children.'

"And Oisín told them how he had gone riding over the sea with Niamh of the Golden Hair and how what had seemed but three days in Tír na nÓg, was in our time three hundred years."

No one could tell a story like Dermot. He was

happy, at ease, yet I sighed with foreboding. What had happened to Oisín might all too easily happen to Dermot. Puny men unable to lift their own burdens could drag him down into the dust. "Don't frown, Dervogilla. One day, I shall bring peace and prosperity to Ireland," he said and there was bright hope in his voice. "Already Connaught and Ulster are quarrelling. When the time is right I shall call a hosting of the men of Ireland at the Hill of Tara and they will elect me High King, God willing."

Later, as the sun went down behind the mountains, he laid his cloak on the ground and we made love. He fell asleep suddenly, but I lay awake a long time watching the flames send golden sparks higher and higher until it seemed they must reach to where stars wheeled and turned. And I thought how wonderful it will be to awaken in the fresh dawn, his arms around me, and the song of the birds filling my head.

The early September days continued hot, but in time all journeys must come to an end. Reluctantly we took the narrow track down into Glendalough, sombre in the midday heat and rode into the black country, fording a river, skirting the base of Carraig Rua. We had taken two weeks to make a journey that could be covered in three days, bathing naked in clear streams, making love at noon and under the stars and in the ardour of his desire I forgot I was marked. I could almost convince myself that the past had never happened. Together we were invincible, making space and time our own.

"I love you, Dervogilla," he told me in a hundred different ways and it struck me with chilling force that my husband Tiernan O'Rourke had claimed my body, had tried to control my mind, but in the years of our courtship and marriage, he had never once spoken of love. And in a curious way I was glad.

Ferns was a surprise to me. It was at once bigger and more prosperous than anything I had been led to expect. Dermot's stone castle dominated the valley and the market square was surrounded by houses and workshops. In the blacksmith's forge I saw Beg perched on a high wooden bench. An Augustinian monastery stood on a hill outside the town, surrounded by cloisters, refectories and a hospice. Night and day prayers were offered in the church, and candles burnt on altars and shrines for the intentions of its benefactor, King Dermot McMurrough.

The villagers had turned out to greet us, and in a charming welcome had spread green rushes under our feet along the path to the castle. The castle was designed on the Norman style, perched on the side of a hill, its foundations stretching down into granite rocks. It was well defended with an inner and an outer bailey and a keep overlooked by battlements, commanding a view of the countryside for miles around.

For the two years I was to spend in Ferns, I saw a steady stream of workmen on the move, busy with plummets, windlass and pulleys; masons and carpenters, painters and roofers. The noise of their labours was a constant background to the other sounds of castle life.

My quarters were comfortable, furnished with oaken furniture, the walls hung with tapestries and carpets covering the floors. In the bedroom presses and alcoves lined the walls, and under a diamond-shaped window was a comfortable low-slung bed covered with a fine wool quilt of scarlet and gold and dotted with cushions. I wondered would Dermot lie with me now that he was home, or would his duties, and more to the point, Mor and his family, make this impossible.

He kissed me quickly on the forehead when we arrived and said I should rest.

"Will Mor welcome me, will she be displeased I have come?" I asked in a small voice. I had lost much of my confidence and longed to be back in the safety of my own house on the strand. But I knew it was an impossible wish. Tiernan O'Rourke was even at this moment tearing Dublin asunder in his search for me. I would rather be dead than go back with him to the living hell that was Breifne.

"Mor will do as I ask her," Dermot said and went out the door.

A servant brought a pitcher of hot water and helped me bathe and wash my long black hair. I saw her startled eyes when my scarred face was revealed and worried that before morning the castle and all in it would know my story. Then I chided myself for my foolishness. Knowing Beg, not only the inhabitants of the castle but the whole town of Ferns would have been titillated already with his stories of Tiernan O'Rourke, the Lady Sunnivea, and the madness that had gone on in the castle. The young maid was nervous, spilling water, snarling my hair into knots. I longed for Rachel's capable hands and thought, "I am wealthy and well-born and once was beautiful and here I am at the mercy of strangers."

Later, another servant brought me supper; chicken breast and watercress, fresh bread and imported figs and wine. Beg and the blacksmith had carried my travelling boxes with them and these were set down in a corner of the room. I wrapped myself in a red silk gown, let my hair down, half covering my face and waited for a visit from Mor. But it was Dermot who came after supper in the Great Hall.

"I thought you would prefer to be alone on your first night here," he said, kissing me on the forehead. "Whenever you feel the need for company you must join us."

Who did he mean by "us"? His wife, his children, his entourage, guests? Once I would have had the courage to meet anyone, now I preferred the security of my own room.

Dermot had the servants set up a chessboard in front of the fireplace. He said he had a couple of hours free and then must return to his quarters, where a mountain of work awaited him. There were many decisions he had to make. When I joked him about the stakes he said the winner could name the prize.

I am a skilled chess player. Grandmother taught me well, but Dermot far outstripped me. I played fiercely. My prize would be that he would spend my first night in Ferns in my bed. He had his own clever strategy involving the queen and knights. Each time I thought I saw an opening he closed it, twice I checked only to have him break free and force a bishop and rook. Then too late I saw the danger. "Checkmate," he said triumphantly and I stared at the board through a mist of tears.

"I won," he said, "and now I claim as my prize that you will come riding with me tomorrow morning."

I nodded speechlessly.

He must have seen the disappointment in my face. "Kiss me good night, Dervogilla," he said softly and I wrapped my arms around him, holding him as if I would never let him go. I could feel the rising surge of his passion and strained myself to him so that he would feel the pounding of my heart and my breasts and thighs melting into his body. With a little sigh he swept me up and carried me to my bed. "You are like Helen in the old story," he said in my ear. "For you, men would risk all," and as he took me I thought: my beauty is gone and I am alone and friendless and yet he likens me to the legendary Queen of Troy. It was cock-crow before he left my side.

"You are the Princess Dervogilla," the child said insolently, standing at the door of my room. She could have been no more than seven years old, gangly, with pale freckled skin, intelligent eyes, and a head of flaming hair. "What are you doing with that quill and parchment?"

I looked her up and down. "Writing a letter to Rachel who was my maid and is now married to a ship's captain, if you must know."

She moved nearer. "What is his name?"

I hid a smile. "Nils is Norwegian and has had many encounters with pirates. He brought back with him from such an encounter a chest of gold and a parrot that can talk. Who are you?"

She paused as if wondering would she divulge her

name, and then tossed her red hair. "I am Aoife, King Dermot's daughter. Is it true you are marked for life? Beg told a story."

"I am," I said severely. "But at least the scars grow fainter each day, or so I am told."

"What happened?" she said, sliding even nearer.

"As if you didn't know! No doubt Beg gave you graphic descriptions of how my husband, Tiernan O'Rourke, threw a lighted brand at my face. Do you want to see the marks?" I threw back the veil that covered one side of my face and she winced. She hadn't expected this. I hoped the truth would flummox her and I could handle her better. "Is there anything else you want to know?" I demanded. "I have this letter to write to Rachel."

She grinned. "Tiernan O'Rourke is my father's enemy. My mother says you are my father's whore."

"We are old friends," I said evenly. "I prefer the term mistress."

She circled the room. "What have you got in your trunks?"

I threw back the lid and allowed her rummage amongst the silks and laces. She opened my jewel case and let handfuls of diamonds, amethysts, river pearls, stones of red jasper slip through her fingers. She admired a necklace of shells. I told her that my foster brother Cormac had bought the necklace for me at the Fair of Tailteann before he was killed by a run-away horse.

"Misfortune follows you," she said, eyes round as saucers. "Were you ever cursed by a witch?" She didn't wait for an answer, she had discovered the gold balls I had worn in my hair on the evening Dermot came to take Dublin. I knew she was dying to try them on but hadn't the courage to ask. Instead she swung her thick red plaits in an arc around her face. "I tie stones in the end of my plaits," she boasted. "It frightens my brothers and scares off enemies who bother me."

"The golden balls would serve better," I remarked.

She rubbed her freckled nose with her fist. "Would you lend them to me?"

"If your mother agrees, you may have them," I said carelessly. "Perhaps I might discuss the matter with her, as well as other things."

She ran out of the room, banging the door behind her. I knew that before long I would have a visit from Mor whom I hadn't seen since my arrival in Ferns.

Mor was tall and broad, plain of face, with a deep voice and a commanding presence. She was wearing a quilted gown when she came to my rooms that evening. The first thing she said was, "Why did you promise Aoife golden balls? Are you trying to seduce her as you did my husband?"

"I thought hollow balls would do less damage than the stones she boasted she ties in her plaits," I said calmly. I indicated a chair and Mor sat down.

"You're right," she said. "I'm afraid she'll put out someone's eye one of these days. Is it true what she told me – did Tiernan O'Rourke mark you?"

I was tempted to tell her to go to hell, but what was the use. Beg had seen my face, the maids had seen my face, Aoife had seen my face, Dermot had kissed the scars. She was entitled to know. She hadn't invited me to Ferns. I had come at her husband's behest. She had been presented with a fait accompli, difficult for any woman to take. I pulled back my hair which I had allowed hang over one side of my face.

"My husband Tiernan O'Rourke used a lighted torch."

She sucked in her breath. "Why?"

"Because I refused to sleep with him. I was tired of being raped."

"Why did you refuse?"

"He sent my baby son to Connaught to be fostered by Torlach O'Connor." I bit back a sob. "They let him fall into a lake and he drowned. I would never have allowed it happen."

"Aren't men sods?" she said mildly. She leaned her elbows on the chess table that separated us, pushing the pieces to one side and studied me. "You aren't at all like what I was led to believe. Tell me, when did you set your cap at my husband?"

She was like her daughter, she would demand the truth. "I first saw him on the day he rode into Dublin, on my fifteenth birthday. I fell in love with him and have been in love with him ever since. But," I said bleakly, "he married you."

She got up abruptly and went over to the fire, poking it hard so that a cloud of smoke drifted up to the rafters and hung there. "It was a made match. I am the daughter of the chieftain of the O'Tooles. The marriage cemented peace between my people and the Hy Kinsellas. They had been warring for years. I never expected Dermot McMurrough to be faithful. He told me before our marriage that he loved another, I presume he meant you, but I have no intention of divorcing him."

"Or even allowing him to take a second wife?"

"I want to make sure that my children inherit when the time comes. I want no competition from by-blows."

"You know the laws," I said levelly. "The tribes will decide who is the next King of Leinster."

"High King of Ireland," she corrected me. "My own people, the O'Tooles and the Hy Kinsellas will decide."

"You hope he will be next High King?" I said.

"I know he will be High King, that is the reason I married him."

Her words depressed me. Heaven knows I wanted the High Kingship for Dermot but it was the first time I had faced up to the fact that he shared his hopes and dreams with another woman and it didn't help one bit.

"What will you do?" she asked suddenly.

The idea had been forming in my mind. "I think I shall go to England. I have a friend in Bristol, a Norman baron, Robert FitzHarding. He might befriend me."

"Make you his wife?"

I shrank back in misery. "No, nothing like that. I am still married to Tiernan O'Rourke, he will never let me divorce him. At times I think I might enter a nunnery."

She laughed and rang a hand-bell furiously. When the maid dashed in she abruptly ordered wine which was brought at once.

"Drink up a goblet, Dervogilla, it will put heart in you. You would never make a nun, there is too much life in you and you have the quality that appeals to men."

"With my scarred face?"

She swallowed her wine and smacked her lips. "A good vintage, we get it from a merchant in Wexford, he imports from France. You can cover your scar with a veil, in time it will fade though some marks will always remain. Not that it matters. Did it never occur to you that people seldom, if ever, really look at a person? Especially lovers. They are captivated at the first meeting and never really see what is before their eyes after that. You have a beautiful body and know how to charm. You have bewitched my husband, my daughter Aoife and she is difficult, as I know to my cost."

"I spoke to her as woman to woman," I said. "It is how my grandmother treated me." I drank some wine, it was rich and mellow and heart-warming. "What would you advise me to do, Mor?"

"Remain at Ferns until you are stronger and have charted your course, or until Tiernan O'Rourke is killed. Many would wish him dead."

I drank another glass of wine to give me courage. "And what if your husband continues to visit me in my tower?"

She finished the flagon. "It will not worry me. One does not expect fidelity from a king, one hopes for loyalty. He has kept his word and has not sent our children out to fosterage. For that I am grateful. He has promised me that when he is High King I shall stand beside him as his queen. He is a man of his word." She stood up, shaking her skirts. "You will not see that much of him. He spends most of his time travelling Leinster, when he is not battling in Connaught and Munster. No, I think it is best you stay."

I held out my hand to seal the bargain and she shook it firmly, like a man. I judged her as practical and fair in her dealings, her head ruled her heart. At that moment I wished we could be friends.

On the journey with Dermot through Wicklow and down into the Black Country of Kinsealy, I had laughed, made love. At times I had experienced pleasure such as few can know. In the still reaches of the night when we came together I had longed for that ecstatic moment to stretch into eternity, but these were delights out of time and place, perhaps never to be repeated. I always knew my story would end badly. Yet, all things considered, I was content to be in Ferns, as day followed uneventful day. I had my routine, spent a certain number of hours spinning, weaving, doing tapestry work. I had even taken up pottery. If the day was fine I might walk the dogs with the red-haired Aoife or we might pick fruit in season. At times Beg diverted me. I had the occasional heart-warming laugh as he told some joke. No, I was not complaining, I was thankful for the lull after the storms of Breifne.

Mor had been right when she said I would not see much of Dermot. He spent most of the year travelling the kingdom of Leinster, settling disputes, strengthening borders, visiting the Norse cities of Dublin, Wexford and Waterford. The country was still in a state of turmoil, with Connaught fighting Munster, Ulster raiding deep into Connaught and always the rivalry over who would be next High King of Ireland.

I knew I could not spend the remainder of my life in Ferns, where I would always be a stranger. I would have liked another child, Dermot's child, but after my second miscarriage, the midwife said I would not conceive again. She said that she read it in the lines of my hand. I think it more likely that she had heard from Beg of what happened me in O'Rourke's stronghold and, wise woman that she was, had based her prognostication on my ordeal there. Whatever the reason she was to be proved right.

When Mor heard what the midwife said, she offered to allow Dermot take me as a second wife. She confided that she no longer shared Dermot's bed. She had developed a fondness for her cousin, the Captain of the Guards, one of the O'Tooles of Wicklow. I thanked her for the offer but reminded her that Tiernan O'Rourke had sworn he would never divorce me. He had the support of the Church. It occurred to me that Grandmother would turn in her grave if she heard I even considered becoming Dermot's second wife while his first was there to take precedence over me. And she would haunt Tiernan O'Rourke if she knew the mess he had made of my life. Maybe she did, for all I know. People who saw him described him as having a haunted look.

On the few occasions that Dermot was in Ferns and came to my bed our love-making was sweet. It was comforting to explore each other's bodies and fall asleep in each other's arms, but the wild headiness of our earlier days had gone.

When I think of Ferns I shall always remember my first summer there. Once Dermot took me with him on a visit to Wexford city. We dallied on the journey. They were halcyon days of blue skies, painted here and there with gossamer clouds. When the rain fell it was soft and warm, and gave back the smell of good earth; bird song seemed to go on all day, and there were splashes of silver everywhere; in the sky, in the bark of birch, in the flash of trout and salmon rising to the fly. But more than anything else I remember the kindness of the people we met, and how Dermot was loved and trusted by them. I little knew how brutal and sudden the end would be, when I would be forced to leave Ferns and seek sanctuary elsewhere.

Chapter 12

Nils and Rachel came to Ferns on a soft spring day. It was now almost two years since I laid eyes on the girl who had once been my maid and best friend.

Nils had been in London and Rachel had gone with him to buy silks and threads, polished bronze mirrors and cheap jewellery in the markets at Charing Cross. To occupy herself while Nils was away at sea she had opened a shop in the High Street in Dublin, and did a brisk business selling bits and pieces to the Ostmen wives and daughters.

On their return journey, Nils put into the Norse city of Wexford and came directly to see me. He had some business matters to discuss with me. I should buy another ship, I should go into the wine business, he was extending trade to the east. To all this I agreed without argument or even much discussion. I had confidence in Nils, he had a good business head as well as being an expert seaman. The fortune Grandmother left me had increased substantially during the years Nils had been in my service. When we finished our talk, Rachel kissed me and said that my face had improved. She had brought me a paste from London which she said would cover the scars.

"Are you happy in Ferns?" she asked. "Do you miss Dublin?"

They both seemed to be preoccupied with my happiness. As if happiness was a possession, not a state of mind.

Aoife sidled into my room. I had been expecting her. She constantly questioned me about Nils: stories of his life fascinated her. Now that he was here in person, she couldn't take her eyes off him and when he produced a silk scarf from his sleeve and conjured a singing bird out of thin air, she almost died with excitement. She watched with shining eyes as he coaxed the bird into a golden cage, covering it with the scarf and presenting the treasure to her. She never lost her admiration for Nils, even when she married Strongbow and became the most important woman in Leinster, if not in Ireland.

We were joined by Mor who had come to hear of Henry's crowning at Westminster Abbey which had taken place on the eve of Christmas. She had brought her two sons with her, Conor and Eanna. They were older than Aoife and very different in manner. One loved books and gardening and the other hawking or hunting. Yet they both sat drinking in every word but saying nothing.

"It was the most glorious sight," Nils began. "A single horseman leading the procession rode down the strand, followed by the knights, the barons on their chargers and the bishops and abbots. Henry was last. He rode alone, stright backed, regal, dressed in gold and purple, his legs melting into the sides of the stallion, a wicked black horse, nostrils flaring."

"Did the king notice you?" Aoife demanded. She had a great interest in royalty and never forgot she was a princess of Leinster. She said that when she was of an age, she would marry a knight.

Nils chuckled. "Henry's eyes missed little, darting here and there, noting the size of the crowd lining the wide surburban road that led into the city. After him came the Duchess in a painted litter."

"As the Duchess rode by, she pulled back the curtains," Rachel put in, smiling down at the three intent little faces. It must have seemed like a faery tale to the children. "She wore a gown of gold and her bracelets and rings flashed in the light."

"We followed the crowds under the city gates and into the narrow strets," Nils continued. "As the royal party reached Westminster, a roar went up from those gathered around the Abbey Church. Some gave the old Saxon cry: 'Waes Hael.' Others called out 'Vivat FitzEmpress.' The bells of one hundred churches rang out over the city and there was free ale for all."

Soon afterwards Nils and Rachel took their leave and set off for Dublin. Mor, with unusual expansiveness, had the cook prepare a delicious basket of food: smoked salmon, smoked ham, cold chicken, apples from the loft, imported figs and a flagon of best French wine. The weather was sunny but frosty. I urged them to be sure to light fires at night and to wrap up well in the mountains. I envied them the journey, remembering the magical week Dermot and I had spent travelling from Dublin to Ferns.

Aoife took me by the hand to see the preparations for

the very important Norman visitors arrived from Bristol. We stood at the door of the buttery and watched Conor the steward checking plate and cutlery as it was carried into the Great Hall for the feast that would take place that night. We saw gilded platters, plates of silver and gold, mottled green glass which the Bishop of Ferns had brought back with him from a crusade and presented to Dermot, drinking horns of silver and gold and polished wood.

"I think the chief guest is to be the Magistrate of Bristol," Aoife confided. "I listened at the door of my father's library. My father knows hardly any French though he is fluent in Latin. I think you are to help him make sense of the Normans. Will you teach me to speak French, Dervogilla?"

"Yes, of course," I said absently. So Robert FitzHarding had come to Dermot. I wondered why.

Mor sent her women to help me dress. I bathed and perfumed my skin with attar of roses, then stood naked while the women helped me into a linen underskirt, an inner robe of saffron-coloured linen as fine as silk and an outer robe of apple green with wide sleeves and a heart-shaped neckline. I slipped on my rings, set my bracelets spinning and sat down opposite a long polished mirror to attend to my face. I used the paste Rachel had brought with her to cover the scars, reddened my lips with berry juice and had my maid brush my hair till it shone. I let it fall like a curtain over one side of my face.

Dermot was seated in his accustomed place at the top of the high table when I made my entrance into the Great Hall. I was placed at his right hand with Robert FitzHarding on my left. I was glad that my scars were on Dermot's side, he was used to them. Mor smiled in an absent-minded manner at me, her attention focused on the handsome Captain of the Guards who was beside her. An attendant struck a great bronze gong for silence, and the Bishop of Ferns intoned grace. There was a scraping of chairs and benches as we all sat down again and Conor the steward clapped his hands. Immediately a succession of servants came through the door, platters containing venison, sides of roast beef, mutton in pastry held high. The cook himself, wearing a tall hat, bore in a dressed swan and was followed by a bevy of boys carrying golden pheasants and geese and ducks, fish freshly caught from the river, honey cakes, apples stewed in honey and pitchers of thick cream. Throughout the meal, wine, mead and heather ale flowed until all the men except Dermot and Robert FitzHarding were well into their cups.

Dermot leaned towards his guest, face serious, eyes sharp. "Tell me, what are King Henry's plans?" His French was atrocious, heavily accented and almost unintelligible, but Robert FitzHarding appeared to understand and said in a low voice, "The King promised at his coronation to restore law and order to England after the nineteen year winter of his predecessor."

I began to translate, but Dermot shook his head impatiently. "I understand that much. What does Henry now intend?"

Robert FitzHarding stroked his beard. In the candlelight his eyes were heavily pouched and lines criss-crossed his face, yet he was still a handsome man, and imposing. "The greatest danger has been the robber barons who infested England during Stephen's reign," he said. "They built castles without hindrance, robbed the rich and took the poor as captives and slaves, so that one could travel a score of miles without seeing a lighted hearth or a field of corn, or hearing the lowing of cattle in a field. Since his arrival in England Henry has pulled down over one thousand robber strongholds."

I repeated all this in Irish for Dermot's benefit and he nodded. "Ask FitzHarding what he wants of me."

"Help in Wales," the Norman said, running his finger down the blade of his knife. "Henry has already ridden into Wales, covering in a day five times the distance a normal man might ride. His energy is boundless. Some of the robber barons have joined the Welsh outlaw Owain Gwynedd."

Dermot raised his head. "And who is this Owain?"

"A princeling who commands the loyalty of many Welsh chieftains. Henry has chased the Welsh back into their mountain fastnesses. What he needs are ships from Ireland to block the escape routes from Welsh seaports."

I ventured to intervene, to express a certain sympathy for the Welsh prince and his followers, but neither Dermot nor Robert FitzHarding would hear me out. They both had a passion for law and order and respected King Henry for what he was attempting to do in his new kingdom.

"We have robber barons here in Ireland," Dermot said bitterly, "and there is no peace. Would that I had Henry's power. Tell Robert FitzHarding that I shall arrange for ships and Ostmen from Wexford and Dublin to go to Henry's aid in Wales. Tell him they are young men, descendants of the Viking pirates, who love adventure and are prepared to serve any master for gold. They are invincible at sea."

Dinner ended and Dermot and Robert FitzHarding went off together to drink in peace in Dermot's room, and speak in bastard French and Latin. They were happy now that they had struck a deal.

"I have heard of your misfortunes since coming to Ireland," Robert FitzHarding said as we were parting. "Once before I promised you help if you should ever need it, Lady Dervogilla. That offer still holds." I thanked him warmly, little realising that a day would come when I would hold him to his word.

The summer passed and Dermot was busy in Dublin and Wexford. Later, when fair-haired young men with Viking names and sea-blue eyes set off for Wales to harry Owain Gwynedd and earn King Henry's gold, Dermot returned to Ferns.

I was traversing the castle wall on the leeward side when I saw the watch beacon give the alarm of approaching danger: great pillars of smoke rising in the translucent air. Behind me Beg played softly upon his silver pipe, sweet as lark song. Aoife, red pigtails swinging, tugged at my arm. She had eyes sharp as an eagle's. "See away in the distance, Dervogilla, an army is approaching." I craned my neck and saw foot soldiers running fast, bowsmen with their arrows notched coming at a steady pace.

Then all was confusion. Dermot was going out to meet the Connaught army and the High King was arriving surrounded by his mounted guard.

Mor had come panting to the castle wall. "A

messenger has brought word that Tiernan O'Rourke has arrived with Torlach O'Connor," she called up. "They mean trouble for Ferns."

Aoife wanted to stay but was ordered inside by her mother and reluctantly I followed her, with Beg now playing a lament.

Mor locked me in my rooms in the tower for safety, while Dermot parleyed with the High King and Tiernan O'Rourke, who had come swearing vengeance, demanding my return. I leaned out the window and saw them in the courtyard below, and in a frenzy of rage and fear shouted: "I swear I will throw myself from this window to the flags below, rather than go back to Breifne." I tugged at my hair. "Look well, Torlach O'Connor, see what your friend and ally did to me. Scarred me with a flaming torch." I knew I sounded like a fish wife but I didn't care.

The High King was too far away to hear what I said but he could see my face, recognise my distress. He must have thought that Tiernan O'Rourke was crazy to demand the return of such an unwilling wife. Little he knew the dark obsession that had destroyed my husband's mind. Then I heard a voice raised, screaming something about "wife price." I closed the window, sat on the floor and put down my head and wept.

Later, Beg came to my room and told me that a settlement had been reached. "King Dermot does not want trouble," he piped. "He has offered Tiernan O'Rourke one thousand silver pieces. The Lord Tiernan O'Rourke called you a name I will not repeat and said the compensation was not enough. But the High King ordered him to take it and go."

I wept and Beg patted me with his little hand. "Do not fret, Lady Dervogilla, the High King and King Dermot and Prince Tiernan O'Rourke are fighting their own battles, they hate and distrust each other. Unfortunately you are caught up in a spider's web of intrigue."

"I am not a possession, a thing to be bandied about, bought and sold. I am my own person, a princess of Meath," I said passionately.

"Do not be angry with King Dermot. He is doing his best for you and Leinster," Beg said in his small wise voice. "The Lady Mor will bring you a hot drink of wine and honey which will make you sleep."

He went away and when Mor came I was composed, like a child, doing her bidding, taking the drink, lying down on the bed and eventually falling asleep.

Whatever potion Mor used, I slept for twelve hours. When I awoke it was morning and Dermot was sitting beside my bed. He looked tired and heavy-eyed, but he bent and kissed me gently on the lips. "They are gone, Dervogilla. you will not be bothered again."

"You paid Tiernan O'Rourke a wife price?" I choked on the words.

"Under the law he was entitled to compensation. I took you away. He has promised never to approach you again. There is no question of your going back to Breifne."

"But I am to leave Ferns?"

Dermot rubbed his eyes with the back of his hand. "I had to think of the peace of Leinster. I do not want a war, nor, I think, do you, Dervogilla."

I gave him a wan smile. "I am no Helen of Troy. Where am I to be sent? To Kildare, to a nunnery, or maybe to a hermit's cell?"

He took me in his arms. I could feel his heart pounding. "You are free to go wherever you wish – to Meath, or Dublin, or anywhere else in Leinster."

"I would be happy to go back to my house on the strand in Dublin. You have all been kind to me in Ferns, but it is not my home."

"Aoife will miss you," he said into my hair.

"She can come and spend some time with me," I promised. "Maybe you will visit me if you can spare the time."

"As if I could keep away," he groaned. He laid me back on the bed, hands busy with my gown, and then he was touching me, taking me and I was whispering wildly how much I loved him – and after that there was peace.

Chapter 13

It was autumn and I stood at the door looking out across the wide expanse of sand and sea. In the distance the city walls glowed rosy pink in the evening sun and beyond the turrets and towers smoke spiralled into the sky from houses and workshops. Tallest of all the buildings was the Thingmote on Cork Hill.

The sun's red disc was low in the heavens, and I shaded my eyes. The tide was coming in fast. He would likely take the main road running south-east that skirted farms, a church, a mill, a cluster of fishing cottages, a forge and a pond before veering off at the small dusty lane that led down to the sea. Or he might chance beating the tide, following the river, then cutting across the sea shore. Already the narrow channels were rapidly filling with water, leaving on either side of sandy ridges a brown frothy scum that resembled the top of a beaker of ale. Bubbles formed, expanded and burst and the waves carried a mass of dark green seaweed, birds' feathers, twigs, all the debris of some autumnal gale that had happened far out at sea. Overhead, flocks of screaming gulls followed the tide to make their way to the city ramparts where they would settle down for the night. These in turn were followed by waders and small sea birds skimming the waves.

Already the strand was darkening over, though patches of blue still showed in the crimson streaked sky. Then I saw him, cloak billowing out behind him, fair hair shining in a sudden last burst of sunshine, riding over the waves, like Oisín in the old story coming back from Tír na nÓg. Why was it, I asked myself, that the first sight of him always made my heart turn over so that I was again a love-stricken girl standing with my nurse watching him lead his army into the city all those years before? He leaped a pool and I heard small churning sounds, the suck of the sea and the horse's hooves striking off rocks and pebbles.

I had been afraid he would not find time to come and with delight ran out to meet him, kicking off my shoes, wading into the sea, at first catching up the hem of my gown, then allowing the waves to carry me until the water was up to my waist. He saw me and let out a shout, spurred his horse onwards and, bending, swung me up on the animal's back. We clung together wetly, laughing, and I rubbed his cheek. "I thought you would never come, Dermot, I have been waiting for hours."

He kissed me briefly on the mouth. "King Hasculf and the leading Ostmen received me with a list of complaints. They need money for roads, drains; they say fifty people died of a summer fever, and that the shipping trade is bad. They think my purse is endless. But enough of all that. What I need now is a hot bath and something to eat. The last food I remember

187

was a handful of oats mixed with butter, good iron rations for marching men, but it leaves a gap. I quartered the men with farmers north of the city, promising recompense."

We clattered over the paving stones of the courtyard where an ostler stood patiently waiting at the stable door. With a grunt Dermot lifted me down and tossed the reins in the direction of the boy.

Inside the house a bright fire burned in the entrance hall; servants were lighting candles, setting the table with silver and cutlery and carrying plates and beakers into the dining parlour. From the kitchens came the clatter of pots and pans and the delicious aroma of roasting meats.

Dermot threw himself down in a chair in the hall and a boy ran forward to pull off his boots. "God, it's good to be back." He rubbed his face dry of rivulets of sweat and sea water. "Get out of that gown, Dervogilla," he laughed. "You look like a sea nymph. You'll catch your death of cold."

I perched on the side of his chair, conscious of the fact that my wet gown clung to my body in curves. My face might be marked but my body was still considered seductive by Dermot.

"Is it true that Torlach O'Connor is dead?" I demanded. The question had been hovering on my lips all day.

Dermot nodded briefly and took me by the hand. "What we both need is a hot bath, warm clothes and mulled wine. Later I'll tell you all you need to know."

He led me briskly out to the bath house. Steam rose from red hot bricks and piles of warm towels and pitchers of cold and scalding water were everywhere.

Dermot sent the servants away and we soaped and sluiced each other. When we were rosy and squeaky clean we went back to the bedroom where my silken bedgown, his night-shirt, dressing robes of fine wool and slippers were laid out.

We sat contentedly sipping the hot spiced wine talking about the demise of Torlach O'Connor. "Is it true he was poisoned? Rumours have been sweeping the city for days. No one seems to know the truth. When I heard you had arrived in Dublin and were closeted with Hasculf, I guessed it was serious."

Dermot turned my hands over and kissed the palms. "The High King died of old age, in his bed, in his stronghold in Connaught, with his priest in attendance. On his deathbed he named his son Rory as the next High King of Ireland."

I drew in a deep breath. "How long did he reign?"

"Fifty years. Even before the funeral games are over, the scribes are writing his obituary."

"And what do they say?"

"They are calling him the Augustus Caesar of the west of Europe. They say he lived and died in a flood of glory and princeliness. They praise him as a king with veneration for church and clerics, one who never lost a battle."

I said furiously, "The monkish scribes have short memories. A few years back they were cursing him as the man who had destroyed Ireland."

"He endowed monasteries." Dermot was always moderate.

"Aye, and laid waste Desmond, church and lands. How many churches were burnt? Seventy, I believe. Then there was the fleet he assembled on Lough

Derg. You told me about it yourself once; one hundred and ninety ships and soldiers sent out plundering as far north as Tory Island and Tirconnell and as far south as Valentia and Cork."

Dermot stroked my hair. "Don't upset yourself, Dervogilla. He is dead and gone beyond our judgement."

"For as long as I have breath in my body," I said passionately, "I will condemn the man who demanded my baby son as hostage."

"The boy was fostered, and with his father's approval."

"Fostered, hostage, it's one and the same to Torlach O'Connor who would have blinded his son Rory but for the intervention of the Archbishop of Armagh. You were at the peace conference, Dermot, you know what happened, a peace that was to last our time. What a joke! It didn't endure twelve months. Can you honestly catalogue for me any good he did, any one thing that will be a memorial to a name that stinks?"

Dermot sipped his wine, and for a while was silent. His voice had a note of nostalgia when he spoke. "Torlach O'Connor leaves behind him a treasure, of which any king would be proud, the Cross of Cong. When I was a boy in Clonmacnois an old monk, Maelisa was his name, told me about the young High King for whom the Cross was made. The year was 1123. They say O'Connor rode like a young god. He started off well, with great plans for his country."

I put a finger to his lips. "Enough of our late High King. Tell me more about the Cross of Cong."

"Torlach O'Connor had a relic, a splinter of wood from the One True Cross, brought back from the First Crusade by a Connaught man. Maelisa described the excitement in Clonmacnois the day of the High King's visit. High Mass was celebrated, afterwards there was a feast . . . Skilled craftsmen and artists were brought to Conmacnois. It took ten years to complete the Processional Cross. Once I had the honour of holding it between my hands. It is a marvel of gold, set with rock crystals and embossed with strange animals and dragons' heads. Inscribed on the back are the words: '*Remember Maelisa, son of Bratan O Echan who made this Cross.*'"

Dermot's voice shook. "I tell you, Dervogilla, it is worthy to take its place beside the Ardagh Chalice or the Book of Kells. Maelisa's name will be remembered, aye, and Torlach O'Connor too, when you and I are dust and forgotten, remembered and honoured whenever men see and revere the Cross of Cong."

This was the Dermot I loved. Passionate about Ireland, her heritage, her treasures, her ancient lore. He, more than any other, had patronised artists, craftsmen, given them gold, and an honoured place at his table.

No one had been more generous to the church, founding the Cistercian Abbey at Baltinglass, endowing the Priory of All Hallows with the lands of Baldoyle, building the Convent of St Mary de Hogge and his own Augustinian monastery at Ferns. But I kept these thoughts to myself.

We sat down to supper and Dermot ate ravenously of his favourite dishes, roast pork from a pig that had fattened on the mast of the oak and which gave so delicious a flavour that the gods themselves might die for a bite; salads, garlic bread hot from the oven, nuts and dates from the Saracens' ship.

He sat back replete and in an expanse of good will sent a gold piece to the kitchen. He confided that he had asked Hasculf for support in the bid he would make for the High Kingship of Ireland, and the King had given his promise. His eyes were bright in the firelight. "It is my one chance. Ulster, as you know, has the support of the princely O'Neill clan. McLaughlin intends to march on Connaught soon. There Rory O'Connor considers himself the uncrowned king, now that his father is dead. They will battle it out and meanwhile I shall rally the men of Leinster and Munster. Pray as you have never prayed before, Dervogilla, that I may be successful."

I had little faith in my prayers but surely all over Ireland women and children and men too must have been down on their knees begging God to grant them peace after more than a century of war and strife.

The hosting was held on Tara's hill. It is my firm belief that if Dermot had been successful in his bid to become High King, he would have built a palace worthy of the name of Royal Tara on the spot.

It was Beg who brought me word of what happened. He had gone to Tara with Dermot and his army and had perched and squinted and listened to all that had been said and done and stored the words and actions in his capacious memory.

"It was a glorious sight," he said, wagging his head sagely. "King Dermot stood on a platform, surrounded by the chief men of Leinster. Down below, far as the eye could see, the men of Ireland were massed, ready and willing to have him crowned High King of Ireland. The princes and chieftains dared not go against their followers. King Dermot spoke of the past, calling up the glorious deeds of the heroes of old. Once again Finn and the Fianna walked the land, once again Cuchulainn held the Pass of Ulster and the Red Branch Knights awoke from their enchanted sleep. King Dermot told us of the Ireland he would build, and there was not a man present but saw a future of peace and plenty, another Golden Age."

"And what happened then?" I asked.

"Well, it was your husband, Tiernan O'Rourke who upset the apple cart," Beg said, sulky at the interruption. "The men of Breifne were laughing and cheering with the rest, when their lord and master climbed up the hill and jumping up on the platform pushed King Dermot aside. The guards wanted to intervene but King Dermot said to give the Lord Tiernan leave to speak." Beg sniffed. "Anyone could have told him that was a mistake."

"What happened?" I repeated with what patience I could muster.

"The Lord Tiernan O'Rourke as you must know has a voice life a fishwife, and it carries. 'Is this the man you would appoint High King of Ireland?' he shouted, pointing at Dermot. 'The man who carried off by force another man's wife and keeps her as his mistress in his castle in Ferns for all of two years. Will your wives and daughters know safety if this whore-master and his followers gain power, or must they be locked away for safety? And what of the Church? Shall our nuns and priests be debased?"

I was shocked. "And they listened to this? Did no man raise his voice in protest?"

"Lady, the men were uneasy, they like to think their families are safe, especially the women. They don't relish the idea that King Dermot carried you off to his castle in Ferns."

"But I sent for him. You know that better than anyone else, Beg. My husband was doing his utmost to destroy me."

"Even so," Beg said in a stubborn voice. "They asked each other, why not your brothers? King Dermot tried to intervene, to explain, but the Lord Tiernan O'Rourke shouted him down. 'No woman is safe from Dermot McMurrough,' he screamed. 'Remember the rape of the Abbess of Kildare, and the shame he brought on Leinster. Rory O'Connor is the rightful High King of Ireland.'"

"And that was the end," I said miserably.

"King Dermot might have salvaged something except a young fool from Kildare rushed forward bent on avenging the rape of the Abbess."

"But it wasn't a rape," I said almost in tears. "Everyone knows she chose marriage."

"Maybe you're right," Beg said, though he sounded unconvinced. "Whatever the truth, the guards ran the young madman through, and before we knew it the whole of Tara was in an uproar. Kildare men attacking the Hy Kinsella clan from Ferns, and men from Breifne and Ossory and Wicklow and Meath dividing themselves into factions, clawing and fighting each other like cats and dogs. Not content with fists and sticks and feet, they drew knives. Fifty were killed," Beg said with a kind of gloomy satisfaction. "The army intervened but King Dermot ordered his men to sheath their swords and he left the platform. I never saw a man so cast down," Beg sighed. "He had been so sure of success, it was all the fault of the Lord Tiernan O'Rourke, though as my friend the blacksmith said, you must take your share of the blame, your Ladyship. Not that I mean any disrespect," he added hastily.

"I know that, Beg," I said, "go away and leave me alone. The servants are waiting to hear your story in the kitchens below, cook has kept you a meal. Be careful how you criticise me, they are loyal to their mistress."

"It's not that I blame your ladyship," Beg said, complacency written all over his tiny face. And as he minced away I thought, did I ever think I would live to see the day when an undersized, itinerant storyteller and jester would insult a princess of Meath to her face, and not even realise the harm he had done.

Later I heard that the forces of Connaught and Breifne battled it out with Ulster, but Ulster had the superior force and while Leinster and Munster looked helplessly on Murtough McLaughlin was crowned High King of Ireland by the Archbishop of Armagh. Afterwards, he went on a circuit of Ireland and Dermot bent the knee, as did Rory O'Connor and Tiernan O'Rourke and the rest. It must have gone hard with Dermot, but with McLaughlin lay the best hope of peace and to give him his due, the Ulster King worked hard. Oh, he was arrogant and scornful of little men, but he confirmed Dermot as King of Leinster, lent his support to my half-brother as Lord of Meath and even acknowledged Tiernan O'Rourke as Lord of Breifne, though he knew the man was a born troublemaker, constantly urging Rory O'Connor to rebellion. But for the moment Ireland enjoyed a fragile peace.

During the years of McLaughlin's reign I saw Dermot from time to time. He never reproached me but the wonder was gone from our love-making. We were like any old couple, friendly, used to each other, gentle, considerate. But I yearned for the days of our youth, when lightning flashed and we were caught up in the storm of our passion; the times when we could argue and laugh and shout each other down. Even our fights had been sweet, followed by nights in each other's arms when we experienced ecstasy such as the gods themselves might have envied. And I knew with a heartbreaking certainty that our youth had gone and with it all the high ambitions and hopes that Dermot had once nourished and that I had been privileged to share.

Chapter 14

Clonmacnois was an oasis in a turbulent world on that morning in spring when I made a pilgrimage there. Murtough McLaughlin had been High King of Ireland for almost a decade, and though there was peace of a sort, they were uneasy years. At least Dermot seemed secure in his kingdom in Ferns, high in favour with the northern powers, both king and clergy. Under him Leinster flourished.

He usually managed to visit Dublin three or four times a year, to confer with King Hasculf and receive tribute as King of Leinster and Overlord of the Ostmen, tribute most unwillingly given, I may add.

He would steal time to visit me in the house on the strand and our hours together were very dear. We would ride for miles over the wide expanse of golden sand, right out to the water's edge, to where the Hill of Howth rose out of the sea, and play a game of charting the flight of the legendary lovers, Diarmuid and Gráinne. Later we would return to the grianán where we liked to eat supper, play chess or just sit looking out of the east window at the sun going down on the sea in a blaze of glory.

Aoife sometimes visited me. Now a handsome

girl, she still wore the golden balls I had given her at the ends of her thick red plaits. I had not laid eyes on Mor since the day I left Ferns. I heard she paid frequent visits to her clan, and Beg, who had all the gossip, said that when she was in residence in the castle she spend her nights in her captain's bed. Dermot didn't appear to object and indeed why should he? All his hopes and ambitions were centred on his two sons. Eanna, a quiet pale boy, with his father's golden hair and hazel eyes, was approaching his eighteenth year. He desired nothing more than to enter the monastery at Clonmacnois. Conor, a year younger, had inherited Mor's red hair, strong features and iron will and his father's vision of how Ireland should be ruled.

"Conor should have been my heir," Dermot said on more than one occasion. "Eanna has no interest in power. All he loves are his books, but the Hy Kinsellas and the O'Tooles will not change the law. It is written down that the eldest son inherits his father's mantle."

I wondered had Conor inherited his father's ambition to be High King of Ireland and what would happen Eanna in the years to come.

Murtough McLaughlin had managed to hold the peace but Ulster was in a state of turmoil, with the septs of Down and Antrim turning against their High King. They had expected help and support from one of their own, instead of which McLaughlin had harried their lands and killed their people, and they had sworn to depose him. Meanwhile, Rory O'Connor in the fastness of Connaught and Tiernan O'Rourke in Breifne bided their time.

"I think I shall pay a visit to Clonmacnois," I said to Dermot one evening as we sat finishing our meal. It was high summer and I had a sudden yearning to spend some time on my own, to be in a quiet place where my days would be ordered and where I could hear the voices of the monks intone the holy office and inhale the sweet pungent smell of incense. Maybe it was that I had a premonition of the storm clouds that would shortly gather and wished to hide away. I felt I had endured all the heartache and disappointment I could take in one lifetime. Dermot seemed unusually happy. It was the last time I was to see him in such high spirits.

"You will love Clonmacnois," he encouraged me. "It is where I spent my happiest years as a boy."

And so, partly on impulse, I went to the foundation which is really a city set in the heart of Ireland beside the deep blue waters of the Shannon. Clonmacnois had been founded some five hundred years before by St Ciarán, owner of the famous Dun Cow. In the centuries that followed the monastery had been plundered eighteen times: by Vikings, by Munstermen and by roving bands of robbers.

"But each time the monks rebuilt the damage done," the Abbot told me tranquilly gazing out on the Shannon. "Only the Nuns' Chapel is in ruins, and the Vikings were not responsible for that. Their chapel was destroyed, accidentally, by fire many years ago. It is the fervent prayer of the sisters that some day a benefactress will restore the chapel to its former glory." He smiled. "You will be the guest of the nuns while you are with us, Lady Dervogilla?"

"Perhaps some day I may join them."

He shook his head. He was tall and broad and with finely chiselled features and a spiritual look, yet withal he had a sense of humour. "I do not think King Dermot would like to part with you," he chuckled.

"Then you forgive me my sins?"

"Child," he said, "who am I to condemn or forgive? I think all the good God asks of us is that we love our fellow men, and do good."

The Abbess met me in her garden and took me on a tour of the small convent which had an aura of peace. The community numbered no more than a score of nuns. We walked in the ruins set in a spot so beautiful that I decided to rebuild the Nuns' Chapel.

It was to engage the skill of many craftsmen and stone masons and took five years to complete, but the result was a gem of Romanesque architecture with the most beautiful west doorway and exquisitely executed chancel arch. I was not present at the consecration. At that time I was far away in Aquitaine but I heard that the nuns sang a *Te Deum* of thanks.

Lulled by the serenity of convent life, savouring the slow passing days, I might have spent the remainder of my life at Clonmacnois but for a twist of fate. Murtough McLaughlin was killed by his fellow Ulstermen in a small but fierce battle in Tyrone and, to use Beg's own words, "After that, Ireland and the High Kingship were up for grabs."

I returned to Dublin in time to hear that Rory O'Connor had claimed the High Kingship and was hastening to Armagh with his ally Tiernan O'Rourke, to be crowned. It was said he put the crown on his own head. Dermot, no longer able to count on the fidelity of the Leinster tribes, could only stand by while one after another of the petty kings, always jealous of his power, submitted to the new High King, on his circuit of Ireland. In a place called Coill Dorcha, the dark woods, in the fastness of Carlow, Dermot came face to face with his enemies. The woods held the gate to the Kinsealy stronghold of Ferns and Rory O'Connor forced the pass. He took Dermot's son Eanna hostage and killed him, then went back to Connaught. Dermot retreated to Kinsealy, but Tiernan O'Rourke, gathering the men of Breifne and Meath, marched on Ferns.

"King Dermot was caught like a rat in a trap," Beg said, his small face wrinkled in concentration. He had come in some haste to give me the latest chapter of the drama.

"But surely he had the support of the Hy Kinsellas and the O'Tooles of Wicklow?"

Beg shook his head. "King Dermot's support has fallen away. When the Lord of Breifne marched on Ferns there was only a handful to stop him. He cut them to pieces and set fire to the town, then he demolished King Dermot's castle, stone by stone. I was there, I saw it all. A horrid sight, black smoke rising, people screaming, men butchered, women raped, even the children were not spared."

"And was there no one to raise a hand?"

"Lady, what could the townsfolk do? The Lord Tiernan O'Rourke blinded King Dermot's son Conor when the lad spat in his face. He said he was avenged at last for the abduction of the Lady Dervogilla."

I put my head in my hands. I did not want Beg to see me weep. This, I thought, is the worse moment of my life. Dermot destroyed, Conor blinded, Eanna dead. What must Dermot be thinking and what of their mother, Mor?

"And Aoife," I said in a choked voice. "Did they molest her, rape her?"

Beg allowed a smile. It was his morsel of good news. "They got her away. She is safe with her uncle, somewhere in the Black Country. O'Rourke is gone back to Breifne. He can do no more harm."

"And where is King Dermot?"

"Hiding in a woodsman's cottage. Will you go to him, Lady? He is friendless and alone. He would like to see you." Beg cocked his knowing face and I caught him by the sleeves of his gaudy jacket.

"Do you know what you're saying? Are you making this up? Did he ask for me?"

Beg drew himself up to his full three feet. "King Dermot wished me to take a message to the Lady Dervogilla."

"And it was?"

"That it would be a comfort to see her, but it is too dangerous. I think," Beg added slyly, "King Dermot means to leave Ireland if there is anyone to help him get away."

Nils took me by boat to Wexford. Beg came with us. He insisted, I could not refuse. Besides, he knew where Dermot was in hiding. But when we reached the woodsman's hut it was to be told that King Dermot had taken refuge in the Augustinian monastery.

I met Mor in the guest house parlour. Her eyes

were swollen with weeping and she had aged ten years. When she saw me, she made the sign of the cross. "You are evil," she said. "You and your husband Tiernan O'Rourke have brought ruin on my family."

Her hate scorched me, yet I could not find it in my heart to blame her.

"I am sorry," I said. It sounded inadequate, was inadequate. How can one comfort a woman whose husband is deposed, whose home is destroyed, one son put to death, the other one blinded?

I put out a hand. "I would never have left Breifne had I known it would end like this."

She swept past me, out of the room. Afterwards I heard she had gone back to her own people in Wicklow. I never saw her again.

At first the Abbot refused me permission to meet Dermot. But I insisted with all the arrogance I could command as a princess of Meath. He relented and left us alone in the Chapter House. Dermot wore a monk's robe, tied with a cord. He was unshaven, old and ill, yet when he saw me he managed a smile. I thought of the first time I had met him and his dancing eyes, his confident voice, his merry ways. I fought back the treacherous tears. I would not let him see my cry.

He said: "You came all this way to me. It is dangerous. I am like a fox or a stag at bay."

I gathered my courage. "A boat is lying in a secluded cove in Wexford. Nils will set sail to wherever I say. Come with me to London. I have gold, jewels."

He caught my hands, his grip was a vice, like a drowning man. "We could go to Bristol, to the

Norman baron, Robert FitzHarding. He owes me a favour."

"There is no need to go begging. I have cousins in London. We could rent a house, you could rest."

He wasn't listening to me. "I could ask Robert FitzHarding to find me mercenaries."

"For what, in God's name?"

"King Henry might help me. The Pope gave him permission to invade Ireland."

I twisted out of his grip. "What you are saying is madness."

His eyes were feverish. "My own people will rally when they see I am strong."

"And what if Henry decides to invade?"

Dermot looked at me as if seeing me for the first time. "Don't worry, Dervogilla. Henry has trouble enough with his Archbishop Thomas à Beckett and the English church. You know nothing of such matters, leave them to me."

I was sure madness lay his way, but the die was cast. I must help him, whatever the cost. I owed him and his family that much. I would instruct Nils. We would leave Ferns at once and take boat to Bristol. I prayed we would never come back.

Part VII

Aquitaine, 1166

Chapter 15

We left Ferns on a day in August, drinking in the good smell of new mown hay and peat smoke. Woodbine scented the hedges and the trees were heavy with fruit. Wild flowers raised velvet faces to the sun, children playing around a pond waved as we passed. Ducks squawked and women with graceful carriage, bearing pitchers of water on their heads, glanced at us from under dark lashes. We were nearing the sea, we could smell the salt marshes and hear the raucous cries of the gulls. Fishermen mending nets called out "God speed on your journey." Did they recognise the broken man wearing a monk's habit as their once proud king, or know that the woman riding beside him was Dervogilla, the Meath princess whom he had kept as his paramour in the stone castle in Ferns for two years? Did they know or did they care?

Tiernan O'Rourke had done his worst. Ferns lay in ruins and now the people of the surrounding districts were re-thatching their roofs, re-stocking their farms, carting seaweed in panniers to fertilise their scorched earth and getting on with their lives as best they could. Meanwhile, their king was taking leave of his kingdom and making his way to the harbour where Nils was waiting to sail with the tide.

Ireland had never looked more beautiful than she did on that autumn morning and I wondered as our ship slowly slid into deep waters would I ever see my country again. Beside me on deck Dermot stood rapt in silence, hazel eyes dark with pain. My heart twisted as I saw the first streak of grey in his hair, the lines on his face, the monkish habit soiled and torn. Had I brought him to this: a hunted man in his own land, a refugee seeking help from Norman upstarts and adventurers across the sea? In that moment I all but despaired. Rushing in on me were voices and figures from the dead past, Bronwyn reliving the story of that storm-tossed night when I was born; my mother sobbing with birth pains; the banshee wailing and shrieking around the castle; the doom-laden voice of the druid Crom Dorcha prophesying my ruin; Maolseachlain's bitter curse; the bright star born in the heavens which for a moment had lit up the sky before plunging into the darkness. Then I remembered Grandmother in the grianán of our house on the strand, her soft warm voice as she read her favourite passage from the Bible: *Keep thy heart with all diligence for out of it are the issues of life*.

God knows I had done my best to keep my heart when they wrenched my little son out of my arms and took him to Torlach O'Connor's dark castle in Connaught, when they brought me word my darling was dead, on that terrible night when Tiernan O'Rourke branded my face and raped my maid. I think my courage failed me when I heard that Tiernan O'Rourke had marched on Ferns for the final act of revenge. But for Dermot's need, I might have left the world, run back to the convent in Clonmacnois where I had known such peace, but I was glad that Dermot did need me, glad I was going into exile with him, that I would be there when the final act of the drama was played out.

With fair weather, a good wind behind us and Nils's skilful navigation I enjoyed the sea voyage to Bristol rather more than I would have thought possible. When we put into port we took lodgings in a sleazy inn down by the docks. The people looked with curiosity at our party: Nils blonde and handsome; Beg, who had insisted on coming with us, garish as ever in bright blues and yellows and wearing a totally unsuitable cloak, much too large for his small frame, and lined with fox fur. I had travelled sensibly in a dark travelling cloak, bodice and skirt, but Dermot's monkish habit was stained with sea water and food and had a rent in the skirt. We requested a private room which we got with difficulty and the payment of a handful of silver. Here we changed into clothes more befitting a visit to the most important man in Bristol. I dressed in a fashionable mantle of soft wool the colour of hyacinths, over a gown of fine linen pleated into folds and a girdle studded with gems, slung around my hips.

Beg stood on a chair holding up a mirror while I spread the white square of lawn that was my wimple on my finger and floated it over my head so that one corner hung down over the left sleeve of my gown, hiding the side of my face that was marked. I made little tucks in the linen on each side of my forehead, and placed a small gold band on my brow. Beg sighed with pleasure and even Dermot was forced to smile. He had brought with him a suit of clothes salvaged from the ravages of Ferns: a fine wool tunic of green, leggings of worked doeskin and soft leather knee-boots, his cloak of scarlet was caught with a gold pin.

According to the innkeeper, Robert FitzHarding had recently purchased land in the immediate neighbourhood of the town and had built himself a fine mansion north of the Abbey of St Augustine. Thither we sent Nils with word of our arrival. He was back before long with a litter, shut in by curtains, which four sturdy servants would carry.

I would have preferred to walk or go by horseback, but evidently the Lord of Bristol thought it more fitting for me to ride. An ostler had a wicked-eyed stallion for Dermot. It kicked and frothed at the mouth when mounted, but Dermot could handle anything on four legs and the animal, recognising authority, trotted sweetly along beside the litter.

Very skilfully Dermot guided the beast through the crowded streets, pivoting around pedestrians. Watching him from behind the curtains I was reminded of the young Dermot, leading his army up Cork Hill on his way to the Thingmote.

To reach the northern gates which led to Robert FitzHarding's mansion, we were forced to traverse the length of the city. Bristol is an important port and commercial centre and on this fine September morning it had a prosperous air, with men from all arts and parts jostling for space in the narrow streets. Norman knights were there with their squires, lords with their retinues, their accents proclaiming them newly arrived from Maine and Anjou, Aquitaine and

Paris. Small dark Welshmen, some carrying bows, rode their ponies bare-backed and were none too careful of the strolling merchants and barons easily recognisable by their self-confident strut.

We heard Irish accents too: fishermen from around the coast of Ireland who had put into Bristol to sell their catch and traders from the Norse cities who nudged each other and stood to stare at Dermot riding by in green and scarlet, wearing his royal collar of gold. A couple of young Dubliners even managed a cheer.

New buildings were going up everywhere. We passed a market where busy housewives were shopping for fish, fowl, fruit and flowers. I averted my eyes as we went through the shambles. I can never bear the sight of bloody carcasses hanging from hooks and on this hot morning the haunches of beef and mutton were black with flies while men with stained aprons wielding cleavers drove maddened animals into slaughter houses.

It was a relief to move into the industrial centre, alive with workshops, tanners, weavers, silversmiths, goldsmiths, a moneyer where silver and copper were coined. It was even more agreeable to move into the suburbs with fine houses, and well-kept lawns and orchards and fruit gardens running down to the river. Such was the air of wealth and self-confidence all about that I began to change my views on the visit. If the small fishing port that once was Bristol had grown to this great port under Henry's rule, perhaps Dermot was right to seek Norman aid.

Robert FitzHarding had grown old since we last met in Ferns. His hair had silvered and thinned, and his shoulders were stooped but his eyes were still sharp and clear as a boy's, though I guessed he was nearing seventy years. He greeted us courteously, kissed my hand, and when we had eaten the meats his servants brought in, and drunk a goblet of very good wine, he took us to his room at the top of the mansion which had a clear view of the surrounding land that had been cleared of trees. Away in the distance a silver ribbon of water snaked to the sea. The mullioned windows were thrown open and a tame blackbird and finch flew around the room, alighting on the Norman's arm, chirruping happily as he fed them crumbs from his pocket. They perched on his fingers and he stroked their feathers and held them out the window, urging them to fly off. I thought this little play said much for his kindness.

He beckoned Dermot and me to be seated and settled himself at an oak table piled high with parchments and pens. Dermot attempted some remark but, weighed down with his troubles, he appeared to have forgotten the little French he once knew and I was gratified when Robert FitzHarding asked me to act as interpreter. He opened the conversation by remarking that he had heard of the situation in Ireland and was sorry that Dermot had been deposed as King of Leinster. He smiled grimly. "Such are the fortunes of war."

Dermot frowned. "I have come to Bristol in the hope of raising a small army of mercenaries. My clan, the Hy Kinsellas, remain loyal, they will rise up and fight if I but give them the word."

I translated this dutifully. I thought Dermot too abrupt, he should have paid his Norman host the courtesy of asking his help and advice. Robert FitzHarding waved a hand in the direction of the open window where the turrets and spires of the town gleamed golden. "You will have noticed as you rode through the city that the place is growing apace, out there are opportunities for men willing to work. Few would be prepared to leave their families and homes for the uncertainty of war in a misty island away to the west of which they know nothing."

"There are always land-hungry barons and knights," Dermot insisted.

FitzHarding shrugged. "The marcher lords build their castles and are kept busy in border warfare with the rebellious Welsh."

"And what of King Henry?" Dermot demanded. "I understand he received Pope Adrian's Bull."

I drew in a deep breath. Forgetting my role as interpreter, I burst out, "By what right does Pope Adrian dispose of our country?"

Robert FitzHarding gave a dry smile. "His Holiness claims jurisdiction over all the islands. It has been brought to his notice that Irish morals are a scandal. I understand bishops are frequently succeeded by their sons and the Brehon Laws recognise six sorts of marriage, most of them concubinage, as well as divorce."

"I am only concerned with gathering an army to take back with me to Ireland to recover my kingdom," Dermot said sullenly.

I said in exasperation, "You are talking about invasion, Dermot. Our country overrun by ambitious men."

Robert FitzHarding patted my hand. "Do not

distress yourself, Lady Dervogilla. Pope Adrian's gift of Ireland to King Henry did not recommend itself to his mother, the Empress Matilda. She told her son as much. Moreover, the King's time is taken up with Thomas à Beckett, who was once his chancellor and friend. It has turned into a battle between Church and state. They are both in France, hurling invective at each other." He sighed. "I fear it will end badly. My loyalty is to the King."

I had heard from the monks of Clonmacnois that Thomas à Beckett owed his rise to high office to Henry. Once he had been a worldly cleric, but he was now a fanatical champion of the Church's rights. He had changed since his consecration as Archbishop. Now he fasted and abstained and gave all his goods to the poor. It must have been hard to oppose Henry, but Thomas à Beckett was said to have the courage of a lion. Yet it seemed to me that there was much to commend the King's stand. More than a hundred priests had committed manslaughter in the years since Henry had come to the throne of England. The turning point came when a priest in Worcester raped a girl and murdered her father. Henry wanted the wrongdoer answerable to the laws of the land. Thomas à Beckett said it was up to Rome to try his case and name his penance.

Of course I did not discuss this with our host. Instead I enquired if he was well acquainted with the King. He shuffled his papers, then decided to answer my rather gauche question.

"The Prince spent part of his youth in Bristol Castle with his uncle, Earl Robert of Gloucester. I was the Earl's friend. I supported the Empress

Matilda, in her struggle with her cousin Stephen for the throne of England. When Henry was crowned King of England he remembered his friends and rewarded them with honours and lands."

Dermot had been listening impatiently while I translated what had been said. Now he burst out: "Remind our friend that he came to my castle in Ferns seeking help and that I sent Ostmen from Dublin and Wexford to fight Henry's battles in Wales."

FitzHarding's voice was suave. "I have not forgotten, but who knows when Henry will return to England? He is a man who likes to be constantly on the move."

Dermot chewed on his thumb for inspiration. It made me smile. The legendary Finn MacCool had the gift of wisdom and chewed his thumb when in a quandary. The same magic must have worked for Dermot, for his face cleared and he said confidently, "I will go to France and seek out King Henry. If you are not prepared to help me, FitzHarding, say so and I will make other plans."

I put this rather more tactfully and the Norman magistrate smiled. "I shall give you what help I can, Dermot McMurrough, if not for your sake, then for the sake of the Lady Dervogilla who has been caught in a spider's web of intrigue and who reminds me of my dead wife, the Welsh princess Ermina."

I thought of Grandmother and the day she had walked over the sunlit strand of Anglesea and seen the dragon boats, a cluster of scarlet shields draped alongside and how Ragnor had scooped her up and carried her off to Dublin. For her sake, I loved the

Welsh race. I kissed FitzHarding's withered cheek. I was touched by his words. Someone else had likened me to a fly caught in a web. I think it was Beg. "I have blamed myself for all the misfortune that has happened to Dermot and to my country," I confessed.

Robert FitzHarding put an arm around my waist, and led me to the window. He appeared to have forgotten Dermot. "Down there, Lady Dervogilla, people are going about their business: craftsmen, farmers, soldiers, barons and knights. They are each responsible for what they do, the decisions they make. The Church teaches us we are given free will. Do not fall into the error of taking the sins of others on your shoulders. You are no more to blame for the bloody rule of your Irish High King, Torlach O'Connor of Connaught, than am I, a Norman lord who never served under him. Remember, we are not answerable for the mistakes of others. It is hard enough to suffer our own."

I knew he was right. Grandmother would have told me the same. But since her death there had been no-one close enough to me or maybe brave enough to tell me the truth. And for the first time since the destruction of Ferns and Dermot's flight, I felt a weight lift from my heart.

A week later we made the channel crossing to the fishing port of Barfleur in Normandy, accompanied by Beg and Nils and a strong armed escort provided by Robert FitzHarding. In his satchel Dermot carried the all-important introduction from Bristol's Chief Magistrate, addressed to Henry, King of England, Duke of Normandy and Aquitaine and Count of

Maine, Touraine and Brittany. Beg told us a lengthy story of how Henry and Eleanor had set out from Barfleur, to claim the throne of England all those years before.

"We were luckier than they were in our journey," he piped complacently. "They crossed from France to England in a storm so bad that it took the fleet half a week, and they all but sank. We made the journey over the same stretch of water in a matter of hours and the channel was like a milk pond." He preened himself. "But then, as I always say, I bring luck to people."

Nils threatened to dump him in the "milk pond" if he didn't cease his boasting, but I was glad of Beg. Dermot was riddled with impatience and the only one who could bring a smile to his lips was his small jester.

Robert FitzHarding had done us well. Each day his messenger went ahead to prepare our lodgings in the next resting place, and to ensure we had comfortable beds, a change of linen, and food and wine. Yet though our path was smoothed by Norman gold and Norman power, Dermot continued uneasy and when I thought of his lost kingdom and his sons, one blinded, one dead, I could forgive him his silence and his dark moods.

We went down through Normandy and into Brittany, passing Maine and Anjou on our way to Poitiers where Henry planned to spend Christmas. If our journey had not been so important, or if the outcome had not been so doubtful, I might have been tempted to dally. I loved the red-roofed and yellow-walled towns. We saw orange trees, over-ripe plums and apricots, fields of golden grain. We were invited to join harvest and wine festivals where men and women danced, crushing the vine with bare feet, and afterwards got drunk and made love. Once we ran into a hawking party and another time we came on a hunt, the men sweating in heavy leather coats, red-faced, important. Riders shouted and cursed, hounds circled whimpering, and servants scurried around dragging the wooden sledges on which they stacked the game. Venison would grace the tables of their Norman masters that night. And I recalled a winter's day in Meath and the eyes of a stag at bay. Now Dermot was the hunted one, and all I could do was to reach out in pity.

We reached the town of Poitiers at the end of September, and were overawed by the majesty and beauty of the palace, which was perched high on a cliff and defended by massive ramparts. Word of our coming had preceded us. We were warmly received by courtiers and lodged in the Maubergeon Tower, in a lofty keep that rose above the fortress. The ducal palace had been built by Eleanor's grandsire, William of Aquitaine.

King Henry was absent on a hunting expedition. Queen Eleanor had gone on a visit to the Convent of Fontevrault of which she was patron. Beg, who had all the gossip of the court before we were rightly settled in, regaled me with a scandal, concerning the Duke, that had rocked Aquitaine some sixty years before. Seemingly he had fallen in love with a lady aptly named Dangerosa and had carried her off from under her husband's nose, to lodge her in the very apartment we were occupying. Duke William was ordered by the Pope to return the sultry Dangerosa to her husband, but he only laughed when threatened with bell, book and candle. When he was eventually excommunicated he cocked his snout at Rome by buying his mistress the priceless black pearls that had once belonged to the Caliph of Baghdad's favourite wife. According to Beg, Duke William was shriven on his death bed and buried with pomp and ceremony and Dangerosa had taken the veil at the Convent of Fontevrault. She had ended her days as an Abbess renowned for her piety and good works.

Later, when the moon came up, Dermot and I went through the painted door that led to the ramparts overlooking city and sea. I told him the love story of Duke William and Dangerosa.

"You should have been born in one of the fascinating cities of southern France where the troubadours sing of courtly love," he said. "You were made for happiness, Dervogilla. You should have fallen in love with a king who would have risked damnation for your sake, and not a failure like me."

I laid my head on his shoulder. "I would not be happy in Eden itself without you, Dermot. We have known the two days."

Without warning he swept me into his arms, raining down kisses. Was it my imagination or did I hear a ghostly peal of laughter, followed by a deep-throated chuckle? Were the shades of William and Dangerosa looking on? That night we took cushions, a swansdown quilt, soft pillows and flagons of wine, mellow and potent, onto the balcony and there made our bed. It was the first time we had made love in more than a year, but it was as sweet as the nights we had spent together in the Wicklow mountains when we had bathed together in clear pools and watched the flames from our bonfire light up the sky, those nights when Dermot had sworn undying love.

For a week we were feasted, and entertained by poets and troubadours. Eleanor had returned from Fontevrault and there was a round of tournaments and plays and a romantic song contest over which she presided. I had not yet been presented to her, but I watched her from a distance.

I had never seen a more beautiful woman. She had a heavy sheaf of golden hair, a perfect nose, eyes like irises in twilight, purple and clear, and an oval face. She wore an air of fragility though it was whispered she had the constitution of an ox. She must have been all of forty years but she was like a young bride with her swelling belly that gave her the appearance of a golden pear. I thought it must have been hard for her to hold the attention of a restless king like Henry who was twelve years her junior. Beg whispered in my ear that the king had a new and exciting mistress in England, Rosamund Clifford, daughter of one of his Welsh knights. But Eleanor seemed unperturbed or perhaps she did not know. Henry was an uxorious husband and in the twelve years of their marriage she had borne him seven children and was about to give birth to an eighth.

Eleanor sent for me soon afterwards greeting me warmly, slipping her arm through mine, leading me through suites of rooms, decorated with wall paintings depicting the exotic fruit and birds she had come to know on crusade. Floors were covered with carpets, walls hung with exotic tapestries and fountains played in the gardens around which the palace was built. Smelling deliciously of some strange and exotic perfume and trailing clouds of silk and lace behind her, she led me through a wrought iron door into a secret garden, where she said we could exchange confidences away from prying eyes and ears.

"Henry is a man who likes to surround himself with scholars and travellers and kings from foreign parts," she said, settling herself on a marble bench. "He shares his thoughts as he does his bed, with me, but I like to form my own judgement. I understand that this Dermot McMurrough who was King of Leinster, bears a letter from Robert FitzHarding seeking help to recover his lands. I wondered why you thought it necessary to make the journey with him, Lady Dervogilla?"

I was on the horns of a dilemma: if gossip about Rosamund Clifford were true, Eleanor would scarcely look with kindness on an Irish princess who had stolen a queen's husband.

As if she could read my thoughts, Eleanor smiled. "I know all about your affair with Dermot McMurrough. There are no secrets at Poitiers, the place is like a seraglio. But that you thought it necessary to leave Ireland for his sake?" She spread out her hands in pretty bewilderment.

"Dermot McMurrough saved my life," I said flatly. "I owed him that much. And there is more." She should have the truth. I pulled back the wimple to reveal the scars running from forehead to chin. "My husband, Tiernan O'Rourke, branded me through jealousy, though he had no cause."

Eleanor did not draw away, nor did her voice alter. "And your children, did they not support you?"

I poured out the whole of our sad and bloody tale to the Queen.

Eleanor's eyes hardened. Then she repeated something Mor had once said: "Men can be such sods, even the best of them." She touched her stomach. "A soothsayer told me that this child I am carrying will be known as John Lackland because his father will deny the boy his heritage." She smiled grimly. "If ever a day comes when King Henry dispossesses his eaglets, they will tear out his eyes."

If this sounded strange coming from a woman who in her own right was the greatest heiress in Christendom, it must be remembered that she was also Duke William's granddaughter. And it was said of Duke William that he never forgot or forgave an injury. Something told me Henry would regret it, great king though he was, if he played Eleanor false.

"Robert FitzHarding has thought fit to befriend you," Eleanor went on, drawing her veils about her. "He is a man whose opinion my husband values." She patted her stomach. "I also have some influence while I carry his son."

"All Dermot asks is the King's permission to recruit an army to help him recover Leinster, Ma'am. He will pay King Henry tribute."

"And Henry will see that he gets his pound of flesh in time. You will have heard that at the moment his time is taken up with Canterbury. I warned him against raising up a merchant's son. Beckett was once Chancellor of England, and lived in greater style than did his king, but be assured that ere long Henry will make the proud Archbishop bite the dust."

I shivered involuntarily, though the day was balmy. I smelt blood in the air.

Eleanor gave me a radiant smile. "I have quite enjoyed our chat."

I helped her rise. She raised her rounded arms to the midday sun, and her bracelets made tinkling sounds harmonising with the playing fountains and birdsong. "Poitiers is my favourite place in all the world," she said as we slowly paced back to the palace. "Henry will tire of me when he can no longer fill my belly with sons and daughters. When that day comes I shall make this palace my home. If ever you grow weary of your misty isle, Dervogilla, and the men who use and abuse you, come to Aquitaine."

It would have been so easy to remain in Poitiers and to forget the heartbreak and sorrow I had known, but I felt the pull of my own land, and I knew I belonged there, that I was still needed. Or was I? Maybe it was Eleanor's words, almost a warning, about the fickleness of men, or maybe it was the fact that Dermot was obsessed with recovering his kingdom, beside which anything I had ever meant to him paled into nothingness. I wondered, not for the first time, would I have any part to play in his life in the years to come.

Chapter 16

I found Dermot in the Maubergeon Tower surrounded by sheets of parchment, his hair dishevelled, his brow furrowed, broken quills on the floor and his fingers and shirt spattered with ink. The moment he saw me he broke into a tirade: "Henry is back in Poitiers more than a week and he hasn't yet sent for me, though I have given Robert FitzHarding's letter to his secretary, and requested an audience." He glared at me as if I were responsible for the delay. "Have I come all this journey to hang around like a beggar at a monastery gate?" he shouted.

I sat beside him and counselled patience. "Queen Eleanor has spoken with me. She knows why we have come, but wished to form her own opinion. She has promised she will speak with Henry."

Dermot said with barely suppressed fury, "Why should Eleanor discuss my affairs with you?"

"I think she was curious about me. She could be a good friend."

He grunted. "Maybe so. At least when the King grants me an audience I will have no need of your services as translator."

Only the knowledge of what he had been through over the past months saved me from sweeping out of the room. He had never spoken to me before in such a manner. I was tempted to remind him that I was no serving wench to tremble at his moods but a princess, his equal in birth.

"What do you mean by that last remark, Dermot?" I was cold as ice.

He had the grace to look ashamed. "It was badly put. One of the courtiers mentioned that Henry speaks fluent Latin and moreover likes to converse in that tongue."

"And you are a Latin scholar as you have so often boasted. Well it is no pleasure to me to act as interpreter though I am always willing to help."

"I know that," he muttered. He pushed a sheet of parchment across the desk. "Henry must see me soon. I have been making a draft of what I shall say. Tell me what you think."

He had written in Latin: *To King Henry of England, Duke of Aquitaine and Lord of Poitiers: May God who dwells on high reward and save you, King Henry, and likewise give you heart and courage and inclination to avenge my shame and my misfortune brought on by my own people. Hear, noble Henry, how I was born of noble blood in Ireland and acknowledged King of Leinster, but my own people have wrongfully cast me out.*

He continued in this vein for a further page, listing the injustices and insults heaped upon him by everyone from the High King to his stable boy who had jumped on a horse and fled when Tiernan O'Rourke had fired Ferns. But worse was to come. He had finished his letter to the most powerful king in the western world with what was tantamount to an insult. *I shall become your liege man all the days of my life on condition that you help me, so that I do not lose everything*, he had written.

I could just picture Henry's face if presented with this, from a petty prince from the barbarous country which sophisticated Normans thought Ireland to be. Everyone knew Henry had a short temper. It was said he was unable to sit still but prowled about, ate standing up, refused to scan more than one page of a document, and did not suffer fools at all. Yet one would not know except by hearsay that those mild grey eyes were capable of bloodshot rage; that if annoyed he would roll and kick on the floor like a recalcitrant infant. I doubted if Dermot would have the time to say more than a couple of words before being thrown out the door. I began to fear that troubles had turned Dermot's brain.

"Well, how do you think of my efforts?" Dermot was looking for my approval.

"I think," I said carefully, "it would be better to say as little as possible about the injustices done to you. Robert FitzHarding has explained all that is necessary. Henry is a man with tremendous responsibilities, his kingdom is vast."

Dermot scowled. "And what do you advise that I do: stand there dumb, like some half-witted villein called to his master's hall?"

I decided on flattery and laid it on with a trowel. "This is not your style, Dermot, you are a reasonable man. It is your gift to hear the other person out and then perhaps make a suggestion. Queen Eleanor will

226

doubtless smooth your path."

In a temper he tore up the parchment. "I am going for a walk along the ramparts to clear my thoughts," he barked. "If you care to accompany me you are welcome to do so."

I had the beginning of a megrim, all I wanted was to lie down in a darkened room with a damp cloth over my eyes, but Dermot, in his present mood, was capable of insulting anyone who had the misfortune to cross his path, from Beg to King Henry himself. I took my cloak and followed him out the door.

We walked the ramparts in silence, then, descending flights of stone steps, found ourselves in the royal stables and mews where the King kept his birds. Here Dermot paused. He loved hawking and was fascinated by birds. Forgetting his grievances he began to instruct me in the ways of the wild. Out of the corner of my eye I noticed Henry standing a little distance away. Though the figure was carelessly dressed in shabby huntsman's garb, one could not mistake that close-cropped reddish hair and beard, the barrel chest, the freckled face, the grey eyes that took in all there was to be seen. Dermot noticed nothing, he was busy explaining how to trap and tame hawks. I kept my counsel. I thought it better that Dermot did not come face to face with Henry in his present mood. Besides, the King obviously wished to remain unseen.

I stole another glance. Henry still stood in shadows. Was he listening? I put my hand on Dermot's arm. "Let us speak in French. We should practice all we can. It is no bother to you, you have become quite proficient." If Henry was playing eavesdropper, better he understood, especially as Dermot was praising the King's birds.

Dermot was only too glad to oblige. "When you have caught a hawk," he began. His accent was still poor but he was fluent enough, "You've got to realise that she is lonely for her freedom and wants to fly away."

"And how do you prevent that from happening?" I asked, though long ago my foster brother Cormac had taught me all there was to know about birds and their ways.

"You have to keep her in the dark so she won't fly away, then when she's quiet you must coax her to take food. This takes patience for though she is hungry she won't eat."

"And how do you go about persuading her?"

"Give her a piece of meat and rub a feather on her leg. When she eats the food let out a low whistle. After a bit she will recognise your call, and associate it with meat. When she's out hunting, whistle and she will fly back. A hawk's a living thing, wild, beautiful and swift. I once had a falconer who taught me a jingle."

I could have recited the jingle backwards. Cormac had taught it to me when I was no more than five years old, but I waited patiently while Dermot said, "*An eagle for an Emperor, a grey falcon for a king, a peregrine for a lord, a merlin for a lady and for priests and boys a sparrow hawk.*" Behind us someone gave a deep chuckle. Dermot swung around but the mews was empty.

That evening word was brought to the Maubergeon Tower that King Henry would receive

Prince Dermot after Mass on the following morning. The courtier who brought the message said rather loftily that Prince Dermot would have ten minutes of the King's time.

As Bronwyn used say, Dermot was "like a hen on a hot griddle." He kept making notes for himself, asking my advice, then sulking. Eventually I coaxed him into bed, kissing him so tenderly and skilfully that I aroused his passion. After we had made love Dermot fell into an untroubled sleep. I lay awake for hours, asking the intercession of all the saints that the meeting with the great king would go well, and that Queen Eleanor would remember her promise.

Dermot awoke at cock-crow, much refreshed, gave me a hasty kiss, jumped out of bed to wash and dress in such high spirits that he could be heard from one end of the tower to the other, bellowing out the latest ditty, that had more of bawdy humour than wit. I covered my ears and tried to catch up on my sleep.

I was sitting on the balcony overlooking the ramparts when Dermot returned. I knew by the look on his face that things had gone well. Had Queen Eleanor rubbed her eagle's leg with a feather, and was this the result? Dermot caught me up in a bear hug and whirled me around. "I spent the best part of an hour with Henry. When we met he opened the conversation by telling me that he had enjoyed the jingle about hawks that the falconer taught me. He made me repeat it. He was in the mews and overheard our conversation."

I kept a straight face. "What an extraordinary

coincidence, Dermot. What else did the King tell you?"

Dermot threw himself down on the wooden bench. "He spoke of the thrill of waiting for the quarry to break cover and the chase, be it stag or bird. He showed me his favourite gauntlet, which his eagle knows. It has been repaired many times. He is marvellously well-informed about the wild, and described how best to remove the falcon's hood and cast her off. I swear I could almost hear the bells tinkling on the hawk's legs and see her climb wild and free only to plummet on her prey."

I let out a sigh of relief. Dermot had evidently got off to a good start. "Did King Henry promise you help?"

Dermot said importantly, "The King cannot spare the time at present to organise an expedition into Ireland on my behalf. His contest with that scoundrel Beckett is now in full swing. The Archbishop has repaid his kindness by stirring up many enemies against him. He says his whole attention is devoted to counteracting their machinations."

"And what does he suggest?"

"He accepted my homage and oath of fealty, and had his scribe prepare this document." He untied a sheet of parchment which he took from an inside pocket and there was pride and triumph in his voice as he read aloud:

"From Henry, King of England, Duke of Normandy and Aquitaine and Count of Anjou, to all his liegemen, English, Norman, Welsh and Scots, greetings. Whensoever this letter shall come to you, know that we

have received Dermot, Prince of Leinster, into our own grace and favour; wherefore whosoever within the bounds of our territories shall be willing to give him aid as our vassal and liegeman in recovering his dominion, let him be assured of our favour and licence in that behalf."

Dermot folded the Letter Patent reverently and put it in his satchel. "I am to be given sufficient gold to recruit an army, and a gift of two Arab steeds for my own use."

I kissed him on the cheek. Mentally I thanked the glamorous Eleanor. "It seems there is little more he can offer."

Dermot grinned. "But there is something else. Before we leave Aquitaine, Henry intends to present you with his favourite merlin which he had stuffed and which is studded with jewels. So that you will remember your visit to the royal mews."

On the morning we were leaving Poitiers, I went out through the painted door of the Maubergeon Tower to take a last look at the vista of sea and cliff and the castle town far below. I would miss the palace, and the golden hours I had spent there, the songs of the troubadours, the plays, the gardens, the wonderful walks, the peacocks, the fountains playing and above all the enchanting Queen who reigned over all. I stood on the ramparts a long time, gazing down at the rocky gullies and crevices where birds nested and gulls screamed and fought. In the morning light, the ocean sparkled green and blue, sun danced on the waves and far away ships carrying cargoes from distant ports made for the harbour. I saw a golden eagle soar over the heath-strewn cliffs, then drop like a stone in search of prey. And I thought of the golden eagle who ruled a kingdom that stretched from the Tweed to the Pyrenees. We had been so lucky, Dermot and I, in our fortuitous pause in the royal mews when Dermot's silly jingle had amused so great a king. And of course there was the Queen. She had kept her word. I sent her a note expressing my gratitude for her help. She didn't answer and I was never to meet her again. But all the days of my life I would remember her kindness to two people from a western island of which she knew little and cared less.

We covered the homeward journey in record time. Winter was fast approaching, the nights were long and the winds chilled the bones after the golden warmth of Aquitaine. On our way down we had seen the plenty of harvest, had been welcomed to weddings and wine feasts. But now it seemed that every door was closed and the hostels and abbeys where we managed to find lodgings were damp and cold. Roads were choked with beggars and lepers making their way to towns and cities before winter fully set in. Once we saw a crusade on their way to the Holy Land, but they were nothing like what I expected. A motley band of knights, banners waving in the sharp breeze. They were followed by an army of wagons and camp followers and scullions who had set out to pleasure the troops. How many would return to their homes? How many would find themselves prisoners in a Turkish brothel or slaves in an Eastern harem?

I felt tired and out of sorts and longed for the journey to be over and to be back in my beloved house on the strand. But then again I feared what awaited us when Dermot returned with his Norman mercenaries. I was sick and tired of war and intrigue and disease and death and longed for peace. But Dermot seemed driven by some demon that would give him no rest. He spoke constantly of how he would put Rory O'Connor and Tiernan O'Rourke to flight. He was sure to be acclaimed High King of Ireland before the next year was out. I marvelled at his mad optimism, I felt the struggle would be long and bitter and who could tell what the outcome would be?

Chapter 17

*I*t was more than twenty years since I had last set foot in London. Then I had been a young woman on the threshold of life. Little I guessed in those days that before my story was told, a civilisation that was old when the pyramids were young would be swept away in the winds of change. And all because on a fine autumn evening, at a civic reception in Dublin where there was wine and heather ale, laughter and music, a young girl had flirted with a young man and had tossed off airy lines from an old tale her nurse had told her. It was at that moment, Dermot confessed, he had fallen in love with me.

In the intervening years, London had changed. On my last visit the once great Roman highway leading into the city had been a death-trap of pot holes and boulders, enough to lame any horse, upturn any carriage and send an unwary traveller to his death. During the long years of civil war between Stephen of Blois and the Empress Matilda, houses and churches, hostels and roads had been destroyed. Now the King, known by the beloved name Henry FitzEmpress, had repaired what was ruined and brought peace and prosperity to his Norman and

Saxon subjects. Earls and barons rode their horses to the Palace of Westminster where they discussed the politics of the day; canny merchants busied themselves buying up land and building houses out in the suburbs so that year by year the city spread. Fashionable ladies, whose only interest lay in the cut of a new gown or in catching the eye of a handsome knight, took the air on their palfreys or were carried around on silken litters. Maids and street vendors and apprentices gossiped at doors as they had always done, engaged in the age-old game of mating; students in their clerical gowns gazed longingly at every pretty wench they met and wondered were priestly power and prestige worth the price of this new-fangled celibacy Rome was enforcing.

The only cloud in the sky over England was Henry's quarrel with Thomas à Beckett, a quarrel that seemed to drag on and on.

Dermot had heard that good lodgings were to be had in Cheapside. He intended to seek out the more influential barons and lords and recruit an army to take back to Ireland. With Henry's Letter Patent in his pocket and Norman gold in his purse, he felt confident of success.

The channel crossing had been vile and I had felt unwell since we landed in England. "I have made up my mind to pay a visit to my cousin Gwyneth who lives in the garden suburbs outside the walls of the city," I told Dermot, in a voice that brooked no opposition. "You will have no trouble finding someone who can speak Gaelic and other languages in this polyglot city. Besides, with all the practice you have had, you can speak Norman

French as well as the next."

I had not forgiven him for his cursory dismissal of my help in Poitiers, though I understood the reason. Anyhow I was tired. I had done all I could to help him since the fall of Ferns, put Nils and my ship at his disposal, made the long and wearisome journey to Aquitaine and back without complaint. Now all I wanted was a couple of weeks on my own, to relax beside a log fire with a glass of wine, to take a stroll down by the Thames, or to exchange gossip with my cousin Gwyneth about Dublin and London. I had had enough.

Dermot was outraged at what he saw as my abandonment of his cause. Why leave him in the lurch when he needed me more than ever? Was I tired of his company that I intended to bury myself with some cousin whose name I seldom mentioned?

I answered wearily that I needed a rest, beyond that I had given my future no thought. He could come to see me whenever he wished, but no doubt all his time would be taken up with the Norman warlords he hoped to engage. Nils and Beg were torn between us. They were both loyal to me, but they did not wish to spend their days with two women and a house full of servants when they could be more agreeably employed drinking in London taverns and inns, exchanging news of home with Norse traders from the Irish ports, and being party to Dermot's plans. Who could blame them for wishing to be where the action was?

Gwyneth was delighted to see me. Her husband, Rupert de Luci, was dead these ten years or more and she now lived the life of a wealthy widow, devoting herself to her gardens, her dogs, her church and her friends. We settled down well enough and if at times she was inclined to reminisce at too great length about her dead nephew, Gilbert de Breton, I bore with her gossip. When I tried to cast my mind back to that first time in London, all I could remember was the Empress Matilda arriving in the Palace of Westminster, and how a couple of days later my foolish young husband had ridden off without so much as a backward glance. He had been so young and so eager, like a puppy dog let off a leash and had died so unnecessarily.

Despite his Letter Patent from Henry and his offer of gold and land, Dermot found no takers for his proposed invasion of Ireland. There was trouble enough around the Welsh borders without getting bogged down in the wars of the even wilder Irish, Londoners said. They advised Dermot that he should either settle down in London or try to patch things up, make peace, with this Tiernan O'Rourke and the High King, Rory O'Connor. No woman was worth the loss of a night's sleep.

"I have decided to go back to Bristol." Dermot was planted in my cousin's sun room, his face heavy with gloom. "I have had no support in this city. Do you intend to come with me, Dervogilla, or shall you remain in London?" He ran his hands through his hair so that it stood up in tufts. I noticed new lines on his face, a bald patch on the top of his head, and my heart betrayed me.

"Shall you remain in London, Dervogilla?" Gwyneth said parrot-like.

She was a good woman and had made me very

welcome, but truth to tell I was growing bored with her company.

"I had better go with you," I said briskly. "It is time I returned home to Ireland. Bristol is on the way home."

"If you pack your boxes I can send Nils and Beg to collect them by river," Dermot said quickly, before Gwyneth could speak. "And now that is settled, I would be glad to drink that bumper of wine."

"Glad to drink that bumper of wine," Gwyneth repeated to herself and trotted off to do her duty as hostess.

I left soon after. Gwyneth promised she would come to Dublin to see me, but I knew her promise was empty. She murmured something to the effect that if Dublin was attacked by Tiernan O'Rourke and the men from Breifne, I should hurry back to London. I kissed her and promised I would. In many ways she was like a child, good-natured, emotional and living for the moment. I was glad she was in comfortable circumstances with a wide circle of friends and good Saxon servants who were devoted to her and whom in turn she spoiled.

When we reached Bristol after a tedious journey that took more than a week, we were received very courteously by Robert FitzHarding, who listened carefully to all we had to tell him and complimented Dermot on his success with King Henry.

"I should have no trouble recruiting an army," Dermot said cheerfully. "Tomorrow I shall have Henry's Letter Patent read out by the town crier."

The Norman magistrate rubbed his chin. I could guess what he was thinking. The men of Bristol, like the Londoners, were comfortable in their surroundings. King Henry's Letter would cause little if any stir. And such proved to be the case. Dermot went here, went there, spoke to this Norman and that, had Henry's words read out in the market place, in the Civic Centre, on the steps of Bristol's cathedral, down by the docks, to no avail.

He was listened to politely and everyone wished him well, but Henry was in France, England continued to prosper and there seemed no reason why a sensible man should go into exile and face possible death for a stake in a country in which he had no interest. Besides, their wives would object.

Then, when it seemed as if there was no hope, the wheel of fortune turned in Dermot's favour. One of the border lords of Wales, Richard FitzGilbert de Clare, came on a visit to Bristol and called to pay his respects to the Chief Magistrate.

"He might be a man who could help you," Robert FitzHarding told Dermot that night at supper. "His father was Earl of Pembroke and a knight of some standing. He was known as Strongbow, somehow the sobriquet has clung to his son."

"The nickname is all he has inherited," Beg piped up. He had picked up a smattering of Norman French and now there was no stopping him. He was seated at the end of the table, head cocked, ready to interrupt if he got a chance. He was like a precocious child whom no-one liked to put down. Certainly Robert FitzHarding was tolerant and Dermot let his jester say and do as he pleased.

"The De Clares are an old and distinguished Norman family, who were once the Earls of

Pembroke," our host continued blandly. "Strongbow's great grandfather came over with William the Conqueror and was given great tracts of lands in Wales. Then, as so often happens, the family backed the wrong horse. In the civil war they supported Stephen against the Empress Matilda. When Henry FitzEmpress came to the throne he stripped the family of much of their land and honours, though Strongbow retained the title of Earl of Striguil."

"A man whose past is brighter than his prospects, whose blood is better than his brains and whose claim to succession is larger than his lands," Beg put in and cackled with laughter.

"Be quiet, you little fool," Dermot growled, though it was plain he was amused. It pleased him to hear Strongbow put down, to realise that this Norman earl would come as a supplicant, glad of a chance to make his way in Ireland.

FitzHarding frowned. "Strongbow is a brave knight. You would be lucky, McMurrough, to have his help. He is a man of kindly disposition who is a good leader, what he cannot accomplish by force he effects by gentle speech. As a private individual he is more disposed to be led than to lead. As Lord Marcher of Striguil, he is still a power in the land, and has vast experience in fighting against light-armed, swift-footed impetuous Welsh tribes in a difficult border terrain." He rapped sharply for more wine, and as the servants scurried around filling the drinking horns, he said, almost in an aside, "I understand that the Irish and Welsh fight in a similar manner." I could see that Dermot was impressed by this, and for once even Beg was silent.

A couple of days later Strongbow called to pay his respects to our host and after the usual courtesies, the Norman magistrate left the room.

Strongbow looked the typical Norman earl, well-built, of middle-age, with reddish hair that was going grey, an aquiline nose, a thin face, a generous mouth and grey eyes; yet he lacked the Norman arrogance. He listened quietly to all Dermot had to say, readily admitting that he was out of favour with King Henry and anxious to recover his fortune. He spent some time examining the King's Letter Patent, then said it would be difficult and take time to recruit an army of men.

"I can offer you a large tract of land," Dermot said impatiently. "And sufficient money to pay a strong force. When you are settled in Ireland you can bring over your wife and children."

"My wife died some years ago, I have never re-married." Strongbow's voice was light against Dermot's bellow. I wasn't surprised to learn later that he had a fine tenor voice when he could be persuaded to sing.

"Ireland has many beautiful women," Dermot said airily. He chewed on his thumb and then came up with an astounding offer. "You could marry my daughter, Aoife, she is red-haired and handsome, as the Lady Dervogilla here will vouch."

I was appalled. "Aoife has probably fallen in love with some man of her own age," I said quickly.

"I have never thought of re-marriage." Strongbow gave a tentative smile. "I have little to offer any woman. As you will have heard, the King has stripped my family of land and titles."

"If you marry my daughter Aoife you could become King of Leinster after my death." Dermot seemed determined to raise the stakes. He was deliberately misleading this man Strongbow whom I rather liked. In disgust I got up and left the room.

A few weeks later we took our farewell of Bristol and crossed over the border into Wales. "Strongbow has told me of a family who may help," Dermot said. "They are cousins of his, FitzGeralds by name. He promises they are reckless young men always eager for a fight. Will you marry me when this is all over?" he asked suddenly.

My heart lurched and I thought how once I would have sold my soul to hear him say those words, but now it was too late. "And what about Mor?" I asked.

"Mor has gone back to her people in Wicklow, now that her sons are dead or destroyed she no longer cares."

"And what of Aoife?"

"You were always closer to Aoife than her own mother."

"Why did you promise her in marriage to Strongbow?"

Dermot smiled. "She always wanted to marry a Norman knight, he is an earl, she will be a countess. Besides he is a kind man, and FitzHarding declares he is the best soldier on the borders of Wales."

"Why did you mislead him about the kingship of Leinster? You know better than anyone else that under Irish law, kings and princes are elected from the ruling families and by popular vote."

Dermot winced. "Perhaps it is about time the Irish law was changed." He reined in his horse and we dismounted. "Well, what do you have to say, will you marry me, Dervogilla, and make me an honest man?"

I was in his arms, laughing and crying. He was kissing me and I was kissing him back, then I pushed him away. "It's too late, Dermot, and I am too old."

He pulled me to him again. "Too old to share my bed, old woman, too old to let the King of Leinster love you?"

"No, Dermot, I am too old to follow the road you have chosen. Too old for wars and death and destruction. I have come with you so far, I will support you until we get back to Ireland, then I shall go back to my house on the strand where I hope to find peace."

"And if the Ostmen fight, if there is no peace in Dublin, what then?"

"Then I think I might go to Clonmacnois or build a convent in Mellifont Abbey."

He groaned. "Oh Dervogilla, all I have done is for you."

I said sharply, "That is not so. You wanted to be High King of Ireland and bring peace. It was a worthy ambition, after a century of strife."

We had stopped in the shadow of a wood, the others had gone on before us and we were alone. He took me in his arms and laid me down on his cloak. "It will be dust and ashes in my mouth without you, my love. Oh Dervogilla, have pity. Let me love you, my darling."

And there in the darkling woods, with only the bright eyes of a squirrel, watching us, he took me. And I thought I had never loved him so much as I did on that spring evening.

Part VIII

Wales, 1167

Chapter 18

We took the coast route through South Wales to the stronghold of the FitzGeralds who were Norman knights and marcher lords. It was a clear day with good visibility. Away in the distance I could make out the coastline of Ireland, though at times it was difficult to distinguish between cloud and land. I had never longed for my own country as much as I did on on that bright morning, yet my joy at our imminent homecoming was soured by the thought of the forces Dermot might soon unleash. Would the Norman mercenaries help restore him to his kingdom and then, duty done, return to their own country? Or would they see themselves as settlers in a land worthy of their steel?

Strangely, it was meeting Richard de Clare, the man who would go down in history as Strongbow, that had brought home to me the seriousness of the undertaking. True, I had liked the little I saw of the man. He had been unfailingly courteous with nothing of the brutal soldier in his bearing or language. Robert FitzHarding, whose judgement I valued, saw Strongbow as a good commander, a man respected even by his enemies, the Welsh. Yet I guessed that this gentle-spoken man would be different on the field of battle and had his own dreams and ambitions. Why else would he have listened to Dermot? He had been stripped of land and titles by Henry and was determined to regain in Ireland something of what he had lost in Wales. To satisfy Strongbow's needs and those of the land-hungry Norman knights and adventurers, Irish men and women would be dispossessed, driven onto the roads. There would be death and destruction, sacking of cities, the overthrow of an ancient way of life. And I asked myself again, as I had asked myself many times before, was I the catalyst for this change? I tried to remember how Robert FitzHarding had counselled me, insisting that the bloody rule of the High Kings, the jealousy and insane rages of my husband Tiernan O'Rourke were none of my making. If I blamed myself at all it was for falling in love with Dermot, but who, least of all the lover, can fathom the workings of the human heart? Dermot had told me in one of our more tender passages that on the evening of our meeting in the Thingmote, he felt as if something from under his ribs had left his body and entered mine. He described it as a physical sensation. I laughed it off, said it must have been one of Cupid's darts. Yet our love had been strong enough to survive parting, abuse, the loss of his kingdom, the destruction of his sons.

Riding along that coast road, to journey's end, I tried to explain to Dermot something of what I was thinking but he brushed aside my fears. "The Normans would come sooner or later, King Henry is only biding his time. The world is changing,

Dervogilla, our tribal system is archaic, our Brehon Laws out of harmony with the times. We need a strong overlord like Henry FitzEmpress, even the Irish church is in need of reform. Archbishop Laurence O'Toole sent me his blessing before we left Bristol."

It was all too pat. "And what of your people in Leinster? How will they see your homecoming?" I said acidly.

Dermot smiled. "From ships trading with Ireland I was able to pick up good news of home. My brother is Acting King of Leinster. He will support me on my return. The Hy Kinsellas are ready and waiting."

"You told me nothing of this in Bristol."

He leaned across his horse to squeeze my arm. "You worry too much, Dervogilla. This is man's work. When we get back to Ferns you must relax and recover your courage. I want the men of Ireland to envy me when I am crowned High King and you are by my side."

I smiled bitterly and touched the scars on my face. "No man will envy you. Tiernan O'Rourke saw to that."

Dermot spun his horse around and, pulling me half off my horse, kissed me on the mouth. "To me you will always be the beautiful young girl I first met on that summer evening so long ago. I fell in love with you then, my darling. I have never for a moment been out of love with you since."

The FitzGerald stronghold was a slender fortress surrounded by an earthen rampart, a stockade and a palisade, but its splendid position on an immense rock, washed on three sides by arms of the sea, rendered it strong and almost impregnable. After the luxury that was Poitiers, the FitzGerald castle was spartan, almost comfortless at first glance.

Yet I was happy during the months I spent there. The weather was glorious, summer had come early that year and the air was perfumed with a hundred smells given off by wild flowers in crevices of rocks. Blue spirals of burning peat had their own peculiar flavour, a scent I have always loved, and this, mingled with the good salt tang of the sea, was heady stuff. I could have listened forever to the crash and thunder of water breaking on the rocks below, gazing hypnotised at the swirling sucking foam. Overhead, the sky was alive with the cries of guillemots, kittiwakes, razor bills, puffins and other sea birds I could not name.

Once when out walking I saw a golden eagle rise out of a gully and soar upwards. It is something I can never forget, the limitless blue of the sky, the silence and the glint of golden wings. I was reminded of the eagle of Aquitaine and of Eleanor, his queen. I wondered had she yet given birth to John Lackland, as she had called the bulge in her stomach, and would a day come when her sons would tear out their father's eyes, as she had foreseen. I never expected to see Henry again. "Except he follows his Norman lords to Ireland and adds our small green island to the rest of his vast domains," a voice in my head warned. And I thought of the island that had helped civilise the rest of Europe during her Golden Age. And how later she had tamed the savage Vikings. Perhaps the same would happen with the Normans who were being invited by Dermot to invade his country. I stood on the cliff top, gazing far into the future, and seemed to hear voices borne on the wind say: "And in time the Normans became more Irish than the Irish themselves."

It was only a dream, it could never happen. These men in armour, disciplined, arrogant, powerful, would despise our way of life, would reduce us to serfdom.

I have to admit that I warmed to the charm of the FitzGeralds at once; handsome, fair-haired, grey-eyed men and women, though here and there a dark-haired blue-eyed member might pass for Irish. They had all the arrogance of their Norman inheritance, yet they seemed carefree, quick-witted and laughter came readily to their lips. They made us welcome even before Dermot mentioned Strongbow's name or showed them King Henry's Letter Patent. Their halls and rooms were bare, but they spread great armfuls of rushes on floors, hung green wreaths on the walls and lit blazing fires. They had Welsh bards and harpists entertain us with music and song, and they were not sparing in food or drink.

The idea of going on an expedition to Ireland appealed to their sense of adventure, it was like a prank. They had no quarrel with the Irish, they liked those whom they had met. They immediately began planning what they would do when they arrived, which seemed to consist mainly of wiping up any pockets of resistance in a couple of days and then going hunting. They had heard great tales of Finn and the Fianna, and the open air barbecues the heroes of old had held, digging pits for roasting and boiling meats. Was our venison as sweet as theirs? Dermot boasted that ours was better and that our pork was the most flavoursome in the world, that our pigs fattened on mast, the fruit of the oak and beech.

He told a story he had read in an ancient manuscript in Clonmacnois about a certain oak wood on the western plains of Macha, of which the scribe said: *No mast was ever like its mast for size and fragrance. When the wind would blow, the odour could be smelt throughout the land, so that it was a heartbreak to the swine of Ireland when it reached them.*

The FitzGeralds loved this story and promised that when they reached Ireland they would make for Macha and feed the pigs all the mast they could eat.

Listening to them, it struck me that they could have been Irish. Like us, they had the gift of storytelling. We heard about ghosts and shipwrecks and legends of Merlin the Welsh magician and King Arthur and his knights waiting for the word that would free them from their enchanted slumber. They boasted of their prowess as lovers, but always their conversation returned to accounts of sorties and battles and hunts and hawking, and the outdoor life.

I spent much of my time with their womenfolk. They were kind and hospitable, eager to hear about the places I had visited and the sights I had seen. Most of them had never been outside the borders of Wales.

I described the Maubergeon Tower and told them the love story of Dangerosa and Duke William, and in return they told me about Nesta, who was the grandmother of all the FitzGeralds. Nesta was beautiful and had many lovers, including the powerful King Kenry I of England. When he tired of her, he married her off to one of his knights. It was from this Norman, Gerald de Barry, that the family name of FitzGerald had come.

Before we left for Ireland the FitzGeralds made us promise to visit their mother's brother who was Bishop of St David's, further up the coast. He had a son named Miles who loved a good fight and might be induced to join them. Oh yes, they intended to take Dermot up on his offer. He could expect them in spring. Never fear, they would put him back on his throne and then we could marry. It was a shame, a sweet lady like me forced to traipse around France looking for help. They would put paid to Tiernan O'Rourke's antics when they caught up with him in Breifne.

They stood at the drawbridge, thumping each other, waving to Dermot, calling out that it wouldn't be long now, to give the Bishop their respects and not to attempt to seduce his mistress He wasn't as hospitable as his nephews. Sure enough, Dermot had been offered his pick of their wives and sweethearts to warm his bed, but he was canny enough to say that I was a handful and all he could manage.

We came to the Bishop's castle at the end of a hot and exhausting July day. The little river Alun ran babbling past Menevia, which the locals called St David's. The castle was situated in a remote corner of Wales, jutting out into the Irish sea, a forbidding place of stony soil, barren fields and no trees to give shelter. Around the castle and courtyard the wind moaned constantly, gathering itself at times into gusts of fury.

Yet my heart lifted as I surveyed the rocky coast below with its dozens of little inlets, bays and natural havens. Ireland seemed only a stone's throw away across the water, and soon we would be returning home after more than a year of weary travelling.

The Bishop of St David's resembled his FitzGerald nephews. He greeted us warmly and introduced us to his mistress, Bronwyn, a pleasant middle-aged woman, and to their son of whom we had heard so much. Miles, or Milo as his mother called him, was a gangling lad with reckless eyes. He was eager to come to Ireland with his cousins. He was brave and foolhardy but would become the founding father of one of the most powerful families of Geraldines in Ireland.

I warmed to Bronwyn at once. She doted on Milo and managed the Bishop and his household with consummate skill. She resembled Grandmother. The Lady Deborah had after all been the daughter of a Welsh baron. When I told the story of how Ragnor had scooped her up on the beach at Anglesea and carried her back to Dublin in his long-prowed Viking ship but how her happiness had been short lived, Bronwyn wiped away a tear.

"Mother is soft-hearted," Milo said, passing her a goblet of mead to cheer her up.

The Bishop laughed and said it reminded him of how the Irish monk Madomnac had stolen away Welsh bees. Seemingly, Madomnac had come to visit St David whose oratory still stood after six hundred years. But when the time came for Madomnac to return home, the bees followed him across the Irish sea. "Monk and bees settled in a place called Fingal," the Bishop mused.

Dermot said Fingal was north of Dublin and great

hunting country and Milo promised that when he had won sword land in Ireland he would visit Fingal and reclaim their honey. It struck me that between searching for woodmast at Macha and honey at Fingal, the FitzGeralds were promised a busy time.

We stayed some time as guests of the Bishop. Then at the beginning of August on a day of lowering clouds, we set out from St David's for Glascarrig on the coast of Wexford. At the last moment we had been joined by a young Norman knight, mad for adventure. Richard FitzGodebert had heard of our visit and rounded up a force of a dozen. Beg was heard to mutter that an invasion force of that size wouldn't hold back a herd of cattle, let alone the army of the High King of Ireland, while Nils growled in his beard that the Ostmen would swallow the Normans down in one gulp. But I think Dermot was pleased. At least it would show his clan, the Hy Kinsellas, that he meant business. He worried that Strongbow and the FitzGeralds might not keep their word and arrive in the spring, while I worried they might. But it was good to be on the final stage of our journey home.

Chapter 19

When we reached Ferns Dermot was welcomed with loud cheers and clashing of swords by his clan, the Hy Kinsellas. His brother, Murrough, who had rebuilt part of the town, gladly handed over the kingship of Leinster. Aoife threw herself into her father's arms.

When Dermot enquired about his son, he was told that the boy had entered the monastery of Clonmacnois. It was hard to accept that the red-haired Conor, so like the strong-willed Aoife, with his zest for living, was condemned to a world of darkness. Even in an age when blindness was a common form of punishment, it seemed an obscenity to destroy a young man guilty of nothing more terrible than being his father's son. I could only pray that Conor would find some measure of happiness in the life he had been forced to embrace.

To cheer us up Murrough boasted that Conor was now the chief gardener at Clonmacnois. He had green fingers. Murrough was a frequent visitor to the monastery and described the flowers with which Conor decorated the high altar, a riot of colour and perfume. And as for the vegetables served up at meals, the herbs which decorated salads and egg dishes, why, they made eating a pleasure, even to an old sybarite like Murrough himself.

Aoife, not to be outdone, boasted that her brother had learnt to play the harp and flute, and that his voice soared above the rest of the community. She giggled. He had been asked by the Abbot to lower his voice unless he was soloist, which happened on Sundays and feast days, when the monastery rejoiced and gave thanks to God. She linked her arm though her father's and snuggled up beside him. "Tell me about your success," she commanded. "Did you meet King Henry and Queen Eleanor?"

She was excited and happy and yet I thought she had changed, had lost the trusting look that had once been her most endearing quality. Her green eyes were wary, and she was shabbily dressed. She seemed at once older and younger than her years. I remembered with a pang how she had come to my room as a child and listened wide-eyed to Beg's description of Henry's wedding to Eleanor of Aquitaine. She had boasted that one day she would wed a knight in shining armour. "Are the Normans coming to our rescue?" she demanded.

Dermot rubbed her hand. "I met King Henry in Poitiers and was given permission to recruit an army. I brought a sample with me."

She tossed her head scornfully. I was touched to see she still wore the gold balls. "A handful of boys. Rory O'Connor will quake in his shoes when he hears. Tell me about the great Norman lord, this Strongbow who is coming to save your kingdom."

Dermot looked uneasy. "What do you know

of Strongbow?"

She said carelessly, "Uncle Murrough has spies who bring him all the news."

Dermot got to his feet and moved around the room. "Richard FitzGilbert de Clare, Earl of Pembroke and Striguil, is a mighty warrior who has promised me his support. I have made him various promises."

Aoife wasn't listening to her father. She clutched my arm. "What is he like, Dervogilla?"

I said, slowly choosing my words, "I liked him. He is a widower of middle years. He has reddish hair, not as beautiful as yours, Aoife, even the loveliest hair fades with age. He has kind grey eyes and fine features."

She pulled a face and I went on quickly. "He is tall and well-built and when I met him I thought of the knight in shining armour that you used talk about when you were little."

She grimaced. "The dreams of youth. I expect he shouts like my father."

Dermot made to say something and I held up my hand for silence. "Richard de Clare has a musical voice and speaks softly. Though he is a great knight, he is kind and even tempered. They say in defeat he is as calm as in victory."

"A change from Father here, who bellows like a bull when things go wrong. You should have heard him when Ferns fell. If this Strongbow is all you say: rich, titled, well-liked, why is he coming to Ireland?"

I held my peace and Dermot said bluntly, "He fell out of favour with King Henry and hopes to gain in Ireland what he lost in Wales."

"Bully for Strongbow," Aoife said carelessly. It was evident she had lost interest in the Welsh earl. "I only hope he thumps Rory O'Connor and that madman Tiernan O'Rourke, after what they did to you, Father, and to Eanna and Conor." She bit back a sob.

"He will," Dermot said grimly. "But I had to offer him something I treasure more than anything else."

"The Cross of Cong?" Aoife said, knuckling her eyes.

I wondered how Dermot would handle what he had to say next. It was hard on him, it would be harder on Aoife. "Many years ago," he said, "I told Dervogilla here when she was little more than a child that kings and princesses cannot afford to marry for love. That is a pleasure reserved for their humble subjects. People like us marry for practical reasons, to cement a treaty, as a measure of goodwill, as a reward for services rendered."

Aoife drew back. Her face was suddenly gaunt. "What are you trying to say, Father?"

Dermot's neck reddened and he swallowed several times. "I promised Strongbow that on the day he conquers Leinster for me I shall give him your hand in marriage and that when I am dead he will inherit Leinster."

She broke into a storm of tears and turned to me. "It isn't true, Dervogilla. He cannot do that. Leinster is not his to give away like a toy. There is the heir." She bit back her sobs and looked distractedly around at her Uncle Murrough and the remainder of the Hy Kinsella clan.

"Well, what do you have to say to King Dermot's

promise to this – this Norman upstart? You know the Irish laws. He cannot give away the kingdom, nor his daughter, as if we were his to order."

Dermot said quickly, "Time enough to argue about Leinster when I am High King of Ireland and the Hy Kinsellas in line for the High Kingship after me. That is what I had in mind."

"And I am to be sacrificed," Aoife wailed. She turned blindly away and I followed her in the direction of the stables.

It was a fine autumn day, the air crisp and clear, a balm on flushed cheeks. A swift ride would do her good. An ostler helped us mount and in silence we galloped out of the courtyard, away from the town, as we used do in the past. The sky was cloudless, the leaves on the trees glorious, it was ages since I had ridden so hard and so fast. I was too old for this mad gallop, but speed was necessary. As we flashed past fields, rivers, banks, hedges of crimson berries, I saw the tenseness go out of the lonely figure before me. After a time she slowed to a trot and took a bridle path that led to a wood. She dismounted in a small glade and helped me down. "Sorry for riding so fast, Dervogilla," she panted.

Our horses wandered away in search of patches of clover and we seated ourselves on a broken log.

"What shall I do?" Her body was taut, she was like the strings of harp that would quiver at a touch.

"Are you in love with someone else?" It was a question I hated to ask, but felt I must.

She nodded miserably. "There is a young man, he is here at Ferns. He is one of Uncle Murrough's captains. I do not know if Fergal loves me, he hasn't declared himself, but sometimes we go riding together. He gave me a ring for my birthday, an amber ring. It isn't very valuable. I wear it around my neck. I think that if I were not a king's daughter . . . " She rubbed her eyes and swallowed. "There were times when Father was away that I hoped he would settle down in France or England. That you would never come back." She said passionately, "I love Father, I know what he has been through, but . . . "

"I understand," I comforted her.

"What shall I do?" she said and tears stained her cheeks.

I held her hand. "Have patience. Who knows when, or indeed if Strongbow will come?" I tried a joke. "Perhaps when he sees you he will not wish to marry you. If he is successful he will have the pick of all the women in Ireland."

She wiped her eyes. "If only it were true."

"Even if the worst happened would it be so bad?" I whispered. "Richard de Clare is a very honourable and kind knight who comes of an old and noble family. His people came over with William the Conqueror. His wife will be countess and one day may well be a queen."

I was spinning out the words, giving her time to recover herself, doubtful if what I was saying was reaching her.

She got to her feet and brushed down her gown. "Thank you for listening to me in patience." Her white skin seemed so translucent that the freckles stood out like ugly blobs of paint. Her mouth twisted. "I will not be parted from Fergal, I will follow him to the ends of the earth and beyond if he but asks me, no matter what promises my father has made. I am my own mistress and will do my own thing."

I let her ride away. Who could blame her? What advice could I give? I had been as stubborn, as self-willed at her age, but it had not brought me happiness.

Of course it wasn't long before Rory O'Connor and Tiernan O'Rourke heard we were back in Kinsealy, and marched south to give battle. Dermot gathered what forces he could, the handful of Normans who had come over to Ireland with him, his clan, his family. They would be no match for the forces they were meeting and he knew this, but his only hope was to play for time.

I warned him that Tiernan O'Rourke would demand that I leave Ferns, and that he was to agree to this. I was anxious, I said, to get back to Dublin to see if my house on the strand was still standing.

Dermot later gave me an account of what happened. his forces met the High King's army at Coill Dorcha, the black woods where previously he had been defeated. It was considered an unlucky spot for Leinstermen and was doubly unlucky that day. Dermot's army was hopelessly outnumbered, and after a brief encounter in which one hundred Leinstermen and five Norman soldiers were killed, he submitted. He gave cousins and sons of his captains as hostages and promised to send the few remaining Normans back to Wales where they would spread word of the Irish High King's victory. Tiernan O'Rourke, who wanted Dermot's head on a platter screamed like a mad woman, demanding that his lawful wife Dervogilla be restored to him and that Dermot give him the Cross of Cong as honour payment for the grievous loss he had suffered. Dermot said it was not in the power of any man to force a princess of Meath to return to a husband from whom she had been parted for more than fifteen years, nor would he commit sacrilege by taking the Cross of Cong from the high altar of Clonmacnois. He would pay O'Rourke one hundred gold pieces, blood money. If not, he would fight him in single combat, until one or the other of them fell.

O'Rourke refused and Rory O'Connor intervened and suggested that the Princess Dervogilla leave Ferns. She could return to Dublin where she had made her home.

Dermot agreed. Dublin was once more an independent city, and King Hasculf knew how to look after his own. Neither Rory O'Connor nor Tiernan O'Rourke, for all his madness, had any wish to come to grips with the Ostmen whose support they might need in the future and whom they hoped to keep sweet.

It was a sad homecoming for Dermot and the remnants of his army. Over the dead bodies of the Irish and the Norman soldiers who had come so adventurously to Ireland on what for them was no more than a lark, the women raised the Caoine na dTrí Muire – the lament of the three Marys at the Cross on Calvary.

Aoife was distraught. Amongst the slain was her sweetheart, Fergal, the captain to whom she had given her heart and more, if I was to judge by her passionate nature.

All the dead were buried in a single grave in the

cemetery of the Augustinian Church which was one of the few buildings which remained intact after the burning of Ferns. Solemnly the Hy Kinsella raised the cairn of stones and Beg played Brian Boru's lament for the dead.

When the last of the mourners had left, Aoife remained and I with her. She climbed on top of the cairn, her long red hair blowing out behind her. I shivered and crossed myself. There was something about her outstretched arms, something uncanny about the way she stood as if gazing at some distant spot visible only to herself. Then it came to me. She was one of the sibyls of old, the seers and visionaries of ancient Rome, who were possessed of powers of divination and prophecy.

"I curse Rory O'Connor, last High King of Ireland." Her words echoed and re-echoed around the stillness. "I curse Tiernan O'Rourke whose head will one day be nailed to the walls of Dublin. Leinster destroyed, my brothers destroyed, Fergal, the pulse of my heart, destroyed. He was closer to me than kin. We lay together and his body was sweet in mine."

Her voice rose to a shriek. "I see Strongbow with his knights and archers coming over the sea to conquer Ireland. I see myself wedding with Strongbow while the city burns and women and children weep."

Her voice dropped to a wail. "'Vengeance is mine, I will repay,' saith the Lord."

"Aoife," I called urgently. She blinked as if awakening from a long sleep and I held out my hand to help her down. She gave a great sigh.

"What happened me, Dervogilla? What was I saying?"

"That you would marry Strongbow."

"What else is there for me to do?" she said hopelessly.

I drew her close and kissed her forehead. "Come with me to Dublin, Aoife. You will be safe."

She pulled away. "Oh no. You do not understand. I must remain at Ferns. I must be ready when Strongbow sends for me. It is fated."

Chapter 20

*R*achel was waiting to greet me in Dublin, looking bonny and buxom with masses of dark hair which she caught up in curls, disdaining the coif worn by married women of her class. It was evident that marriage to her great bear of a Norwegian husband agreed with her. We hugged and kissed and she told me that she had engaged a cook and a couple of maids to look after my needs. When I reached the house on the strand I expected to see signs of neglect, but all the rooms were clean and fresh smelling, flowers everywhere and the good smell of baking bread wafting from the kitchen quarters. Rachel, who insisted on waiting on me, had ordered my favourite supper dish: roast chicken with herbs and mushrooms with a green salad and garlic bread, followed by a syllabub of cream curdled with wine and a ripe cheese. I persuaded her to pull up a chair and join me in a beaker of wine while we gossiped about family and friends. Her twin sons, Nils and Ragnor, had grown almost as tall as their father, the monks were teaching them their letters, but their only ambition was to go to sea, like their father. Millany, the comb maker's daughter, had made a spectacular match with the son and heir of King Hasculf and was now the leader of Dublin society. I would be shocked when I saw Christchurch Cathedral, the wooden structure was riddled with dry rot. Archbishop Laurence O'Toole was a saintly man, but, according to Nils, had no head for business. The restoration of the Cathedral had been discussed by the City Fathers but King Hasculf had little interest. It was rumoured he had reverted to the Old Religion, being descended on his mother's side from a pagan princess from the far north. It was a crying scandal. I was amused at her vehemence. For a girl brought up in another faith, she had embraced Christianity with fervour and zeal.

At first I had plenty to occupy my time. When I wasn't working in my neglected garden or at my tapestry frame, I took long rides over the strand when the tide was out and tried to put my worries behind me: Dermot cowering in Ferns; the threat of the Norman invasion; Aoife's pale distracted face. My heart went out to the girl I had known from childhood, but there was little help I could offer. She had wept when I was leaving Ferns and made me promise that I would be there when she married Strongbow. It was like being invited to attend her wake. I am not a religious woman but I prayed for my country and for Aoife's happiness when I went to hear Mass in Christchurch Cathedral. What Rachel said was true. The chancel was propped up and the thatch on the Archbishop's house sprouted green weeds.

"Hasculf doesn't care what happens the Cathedral," Mia said, standing to gaze at the damage.

She had waylaid me coming out of church, greeting me warmly. We had remained friends over the years since the days when she had married my one-time admirer, the brewer of the heather ale. I thought she looked dowdy, swathed in furs though the day was mild, but her skin was good and she seemed pleased with her state. "My husband has spoken out at the Thingmote about the neglect of the Cathedral," she confided, taking my arm. "He has even offered to contribute to the cost of a new building, as I am sure other merchants of the town would be glad to do, but the King has other worries. People think Rory O'Connor will attempt to take the city. They fear a sack."

I knew that Dublin was now an independent kingdom, but I thought that the danger might come not from the High King but from another quarter. I visualised the Norman soldiers waiting in Wales for a sign from Strongbow. My heart quailed at the prospect.

After that first meeting, Mia and my other girlhood friends frequently visited me and we exchanged gossip. Millany, who had been the plain one of our group, was now the most striking. She painted her face skilfully, wore her golden hair swept up and dressed in imported silks and fine jewels. She was eager to learn all she could about Aquitaine, and the description of Queen Eleanor's wardrobe, her gowns of cotton and muslin, fascinated her. The rest were just as eager as Millany and crowded in on me demanding to know of the luxuries the Queen had imported from the east, sighing with envy at the mention of tableware of gold, silver and faience, sunken baths, silken sheets, scented soaps, sugar, spices. Millany positively drooled when I gave an account of our meals: caviar served on fingers of toasted bread, marvellous chocolate and lemon cakes, oranges and pomegranates, grapes and persimmons. She complained bitterly that it was impossible to get fresh fruits in the markets of Dublin and that a diet of meat and pottage and bread and all the other fattening foods we were forced to eat was disastrous for the figure. I was aware of her problem, and the answer. She took absolutely no exercise.

Birgitta, who had been the prettiest of my friends, had married badly. Her husband was a penny-pinching innkeeper who constantly ranted about the cost of living, and the expense of a family, though this did not prevent him from giving his wife a child each year. "Dublin is going downhill," she said gloomily, "there are few visitors and even the traders who put into port do not linger. They are afraid of an invasion."

We were sitting in the sun room looking out over the strand where the sands were blown about by sudden gusts of wind. Dark clouds were rolling up over the mountains. Before nightfall a storm would blow out on the sea. I thought with longing of the long sun-drenched days we had spent travelling through Aquitaine, the harvest dinners, the wine festivals, the great Palace of Poitiers, the music, the laughter and the blue seas crashing on the rocks below.

"Hasculf thinks that the Normans will come one of these days," Millany was saying, protuberant eyes searching my face. At times, neither my veils nor hair hid my scars, but no-one passed any comment. Tiernan O'Rourke's name was never mentioned, though on occasions when I visited their homes and the discussions became serious, their husbands might mention Dermot McMurrough and what he planned to do. The wives were inclined to giggle and cast prurient glances in my direction. They were, I knew, both censorious and envious of my life, but as I was a princess and known to be wealthy, they were careful not to give offence.

Now they waited to hear what answer I would give Millany.

Dermot had cautioned me against idle gossip.

"A handful of Normans arrived in Ireland with Dermot McMurrough," I told their eager faces. "Half of them were killed at the battle of the Dark Woods in Kinsealy." This was common knowledge. "I met the FitzGeralds of Wales and quite liked the family," I rattled on. "Richard de Clare, who is Earl of Striguil and whom they call Strongbow, is experienced in border warfare, but whether anything will come of the meetings is anyone's guess. Personally I am all for peace." They echoed my hopes fervently, and drank a goblet of wine, spilling a few drops, a libation to the Unknown God.

Now and again Dermot made a sudden and unexpected appearance. I was never sure whether he came to Dublin to see me or Hasculf. Often he came in the disguise of a fisherman. Boats from around the east coast frequently put into the port of Dublin where they sold their catch. Dermot, clad in skins and with a cap pulled down over his face, could pass unnoticed in the crowd.

He would ride out at sundown across the strand, and my heart would leap at the sight of that still-straight figure, though he was no longer the fair-haired hazel-eyed boy of my youth. We would ride over miles of golden sand re-living the journeys we had made to Bristol, Wales, Normandy and down into Aquitaine. Sitting on a hillock in sight of the sea with the Dublin mountains rearing on one side and the Hill of Howth rising out of the waters on the other, we would recall days long past. Or we would sit for hours when supper was over, feeding apple wood to the flames, drinking wine and he would tell me how Leinster was rallying to his cause, and how each day more and more men pledged him their support. He lived for the day when the Normans would keep their promise and raise an army in Wales.

"What hinders Strongbow from coming is that Britain is uneasy. The trouble between Henry and Thomas à Beckett grows worse," he confided as we lay in bed. "All Beckett's followers, men, women, children, babies not yet old enough to walk, have been seized by the King's men and sent overseas, in leaky boats. Many have died on the journey. And meanwhile Beckett appeals to the Pope to excommunicate Henry and the King holds court at Angers with the Queen and threatens his former friend and Archbishop with exile and disgrace."

I shivered. "They go too far. Who will win out in the end, Church or crown?"

"I neither know nor care." Dermot ran his hands through his thinning hair. "All I think of is how soon will the Normans come. I cannot hold Rory O'Connor and Tiernan O'Rourke at bay forever."

"I wish we had peace," I said huskily.

"And so do I, sweetheart, but there will be no peace while Rory O'Connor continues as High King of Ireland." He kissed my scarred cheek. "Will you marry me, Dervogilla, when the day comes for me?"

I threaded my fingers through his. "I am too old, Dermot, too much water has flowed under the bridge. I often think of taking the veil. I have sent the Abbot of Mellifont gold to build a convent. I foresee a day when I may need a refuge."

He gathered me up in his arms. "Don't, Dervogilla. I cannot bear the thought of losing you. You have been my love since the first evening we met."

He was kissing me passionately and as I responded, the thought occurred to me that Aoife and other young things like her would never believe that her father and I could desire each other so ardently, would probably shudder at the thought. And after we had made love, I lay awake in the still darkness and wondered why it was that all the great love stories of the world told of the young and the beautiful. Dermot was old and grey and tired, and I who had once known beauty was marked and battered by time and events. Soon the cycle of my womanhood would be ended. Yet in many ways Dermot and I loved each other more deeply, more intensely and more tenderly, than in the days when the sap of youth flowed free in our veins. Maybe it was that the sands were running out. Or was it as the poet said the last drop of nectar in the goblet is the sweetest?

A year passed, a time when there was a nervy

feeling abroad, like the calm before the storm. Even the insouciant Dubliners were affected. They laughed too loudly, drank too deeply, quarrelled too easily and boasted of what they would do if attacked. And it seemed that the rest of Ireland was similarly affected. There were rumblings in Connaught, small outbreaks of war in Ulster, unease in Munster and something akin to panic in Leinster. It seemed that the centre could not hold much longer.

In desperation Dermot sent pleas for help to Wales. And then almost two years to the day after our return to Dublin the first contingent of Norman knights landed at Bannor Bay on the south coast of Wexford. The FitzGerald lords came and Milo, the bishop's son, and the FitzStephens with their horsemen and archers. Over seven hundred men in all. "The flower of Wales," they proudly boasted.

A couple of days later King Hasculf sent for me. He received me grimly in his palace. Spies had brought him word that the Norman contingent had landed on a sandy part of the coast and sent word to Ferns. Shortly after, Dermot arrived with five hundred men and the Normans and Leinstermen marched on Wexford.

Hasculf sketched out the scene for me. The Ostmen of Wexford streaming through the gates and being brought up short in their tracks. Instead of the motley gathering of scantily clad Irish warriors they had expected, they were faced with serried ranks of foot soldiers and grim-faced archers on either side of a squadron of horsemen. I could see the long lances, the kite-shaped shields, the Norman helmets and coats of mail, glittering in the morning sun.

Hasculf spat on the ground. "The citizens capitulated, what else was there for them to do, outnumbered as they were?"

I drew in a deep breath. "There was no blood shed."

Hasculf raised himself up to his full height of six feet four. Towering over me he shouted, "If they attack Dublin there will be bloodshed in plenty. We will not give in without a fight. Let Dermot of Leinster know what faces him."

Would Hasculf believe that I had had no word from Dermot since his last visit to Dublin, months before, no way of getting a message through to him, not that he would pay any attention if I could? The Normans had come, he was prepared to gamble his all on victory.

Beg it was who brought me news of the next move in the deadly game of knights and castles, kings and pawns. He came and went like a wisp blown hither and thither by the wind of change. He was thick with Nils. I think they patrolled the east coast in search of news. According to Beg, Strongbow had sent an advance party of ten knights and seventy archers under one of the FitzGeralds, Raymond Carew, known as Raymond le Gros because of his girth though it was said he ate sparingly.

"Carew landed his men on a rocky headland called Baginbun," Beg said, rubbing his nose. "They threw up an earthen rampart and collected a herd of cattle. Begod, it wasn't long before the Irish attacked, three thousand strong, men from the Decies, Ossory and Idrone aided by the Ostmen of Wexford, mad to get a blow back at their enemies. And do you know what the wily Normans did?"

"What?" I asked wearily.

"They let loose the cattle they had rounded up, poking sharp pointed sticks and knives up their rumps, driving them up the ramparts and into the path of the attackers. Picture the thundering, the galloping, the dust and the panic with Irish and Ostmen running madly in every direction to escape. Many were killed in the stampede. Behind the maddened beasts the Normans charged, taking seventy prisoners alive, then hurling them over the cliffs to their doom."

Beg gave a little dance and burst into a jingle: "At the creek of Baginbun, Ireland was lost and won." He grinned. "Begod, I must remember to tell that to King Dermot. He loves a good jingle."

I wanted to hear no more, even when news filtered through that Strongbow had landed at Passage in Waterford with an army of twelve hundred knights and archers. Running through my head was water music: three rivers meeting, the Nore, the Suir and the Barrow. Water tinkling, laughing, babbling, gushing. Soon the rivers would be drowned out by the clash of swords, the twang of archery, the hoarse commands given in Norman French, the screams of the dead and dying.

Part IX

Waterford, 1169

Chapter 21

"Lady Dervogilla." It was midnight and Nils was at my bedside. "Excuse my boldness in forcing my way into your room, but I have news. Strongbow is marching on Waterford city."

I sat up in the bed, pulling a shawl around my shoulders. "The hounds of war are let loose. Tell me no more."

He said firmly, "You must get up and dress at once. Aoife has sent for you. She said the time has come for her marriage. You promised you would be there."

I thought of that figure with the wild look and the red hair blowing in the wind behind her on the burial mound in Ferns. She had foreseen this. She needed me.

"How did you arrive in Dublin so soon?" I was scrambling into my clothes, not waiting for the arrival of my maid. Nils, bless him, was lacing my bodice. "I came by boat, the winds are fair. It is the quickest way. If you will hurry we can go out with the tide."

We rowed through the night, the wind was in our favour and the sails billowed out behind us. A new moon threw a glittering path across the waters and Venus shone unblinkingly beside her. As dawn broke we passed fishermen sweeping the seas with their nets. They shouted their news.

"Waterford has fallen after a bloody battle at Reginald's Tower!"

"Raymond le Gros breached the walls and the Normans poured through! The citizens put up a brave resistance but hundreds lie dead in the streets!"

"The city has burnt to the ground!"

It was early afternoon when we reached Waterford. Even before we entered the city we could see dark spirals of smoke, and get the horrible stench of smouldering buildings and burning flesh. It was deadly, eerie and the worst part was the silence. We went in through the western gate, blackened teeth in a gaping mouth. A townsman, his clothes in tatters, face streaked with blood and smuts, ran past. A soldier said that Strongbow had given orders to his men to draw back and allow the citizens attend to their dead. They were buried in mounds or in open graves. We came on a gang of wild dogs worrying human flesh, and a fox slunk past, a foot trailing from its mouth. I felt sick with fear and disgust at what had been done to a once-thriving city. A woman went by, bent under the weight of a handcart in which lay the bodies of two children. She was moaning, now and again pausing to utter a piercing shriek. With her hair streaming out, her blackened face, her ragged cloak, she was the embodiment of the banshee herself, that faery harbinger of death, whose terrible keening had been heard around Maolseachlain's castle on the night I was born.

On we went through the ruined city, picking our way over rubble and beams and thatch, past what had once been comfortable homesteads and were now no more than obscene ruins.

A crowd of weary Norman soldiers and some half-crazed citizens were gathered in front of the cathedral and we pushed our way through. Inside was dark, except for a few flickering candles. I saw the bishop in purple, Strongbow in his coat of chain mail but with his head bared and beside him the frail lovely girl with her red hair hanging loose. She had dressed for her wedding in a cream gown of some soft material. Around her head was a fillet of gold, and she wore golden slippers. Behind her knelt Dermot, face buried in his hands.

As the marriage ceremony finished and the couple turned to walk down the aisle, Beg emerged from the shadows playing his silver flute, music of such heartbreaking sadness that I was forced to fight back a lump in my throat. As they emerged into the light of day, the music changed to a merry trilling sound, bird music, water music, the laughter of children, and the far off flutter of angels' wings.

As if on cue, the sun burst through the clouds. Norman soldiers clashed their swords in salute, and even the ragged citizens raised a little cheer. I had never seen Aoife so pale, nor so beautiful. She looked around at the still smouldering city in shock. "It is terrible," she said in a voice so low that only those within earshot could hear. "I weep for the people of Waterford."

Strongbow put an arm around her. "Do not grieve, little one," he said. "There will be no more looting or taking of lives. The city will be rebuilt. This shall be my wedding gift to my bride."

Aoife gave him a tremulous smile and he bent and kissed her.

Dermot had come up beside me. He looked grave, yet triumphant. "It is the welding together of English feudalism with Celtic tribalism," he said. "It will be hard in the beginning but there will be peace in the end." I turned away. It was too soon, I could not yet take this long-sighted view, not when I looked around me at the devastated city, the dead.

Aoife had left Strongbow's side and had come to me. "It will be alright, Dervogilla," she said, touching my arm. "Strongbow will restore Waterford."

And I thought, she is comforting me. They have made their way to each other through blood and tears. No marriage like this has ever taken place before.

Chapter 22

Immediately after the wedding Strongbow and Dermot prepared to return to Ferns to hold a council of war. King Hasculf, that wily Ostman, had his spies in the Irish-Norman camp. Not that they were needed, everyone knew what the next move would be. Nils, usually a man of few words, made what was for him a small speech. "Wexford and Waterford have fallen, but the greatest of the Norse strongholds remains independent. If Dermot is to be High King he must win Dublin. It would be better, Lady Dervogilla, if you leave Waterford at once."

What he said was true. To my dying day I would never forget the sights and sounds I witnessed in that city. He stroked his great beard. "Where would you go?" I know he hoped I would return with Dermot to Ferns.

I patted his hand. "Dear Nils, where else should I go but back to my house on the strand?" I knew that if the worst happened, if Strongbow took Dublin, he would extend his protection to me. Not that I cared about my own safety, but I wanted to make sure that Rachel and Nils and their sons were safe. They could stay with me until all danger was past. Besides, I was finished with Ferns. It had never been my place, I could never end my days there. There were too many memories, too many ghosts.

We arrived back to a city gripped by fear. King Hasculf had sent word to the High King in Connaught that he needed help. Rory O'Connor was quick to respond, it was what he had hoped for.

Before a week had passed, the forces of Connaught, Breifne and Ulster had mustered and were setting out on the long march to Dublin. They gambled that the Leinster army would take the most direct route from Wexford to Dublin, which meant following the course of the Slaney to the west of the Wicklow Mountains, veering off at Nás na Ríogh, where the ancient kings of Ireland raced their chariots. Outside Clondalkin they would lie in wait to ambush the Hy Kinsella clan and their Norman allies.

I had not been privy to Leinster's plans, but I could have charted the route they would follow. In my mind's eye I saw again the secret paths Dermot and I had taken, the narrow defiles we had skirted on that never-to-be-forgotten journey from Dublin to Ferns so long ago. Once again I waded the pools, felt the pull of the rough paths we had climbed. We had been cunning, silent, leaving no trace behind us, wanting nothing more than to be alone. And Dermot would remember that journey, take his army that route, knowing that cunning and silence would spell the difference between success and failure, between life and death.

I was to be proved right. Dermot led his army from Ferns, through the Black Country, over the mountain ride to Glendalough, where the holy monk Kevin had once sought refuge and had hurled the lovely temptress Kathleen to a watery grave in the lake below.

I dreamt I followed the path they had taken. The moon shone down on Irish and Norman soldiers stumbling along the narrow rugged path, cursing their masters, trying to control their frightened horses. Then, like most dreamers, I was transported to another place, to the deep woods of Rathfarnham where the army rested to wolf down their iron rations of oatmeal mixed with butter. I was in their midst. I pressed on with them until we reached the banks of the Dartry river that would lead us to the sand banks and walls of the city. And I knew that before many seconds had passed I would wake in my bed, would sigh, stretch myself and comfort myself with the knowledge that the army of the High King was camped many miles from Dublin, and that they would wait in vain for the tramp of feet of the Leinster army, the thunder of horses' hooves and the flash of Norman steel and iron mail.

Dublin was shattered when Strongbow, at the head of his knights, rode up to the city walls, threatening to take the city by force. Archbishop Laurence O'Toole came out to make terms. The once proud Ostmen would have died sooner than sue for peace in the days when they had come sweeping down from the North Sea and around the Irish coast in their scarlet long-prowed ships. But times had changed. Since they no longer believed in the old gods of war, no longer believed the Valkyries were waiting to bring all who fell bravely in battle to

Odin's Hall, they had lost much of their dash and daring. Christianity with its message of peace had quenched their fires.

But even while Strongbow and Dermot parleyed with Laurence O'Toole and the leading Ostmen, trying to find a peaceful settlement, their efforts were set at naught by two young Norman firebrands, Raymond le Gros and Milo de Cogan, the bishop's wild son from Wales. With a handful of followers they rushed the city and cut down the guards. It was Nils who brought me word that Dublin had fallen, that King Hasculf and many of his kinsmen had fled to their ships and sailed away to Orkney, the Hebrides and the Isle of Man. Mia and Millany and Birgitta with their husbands and families had gone in the train of the Ostman King. I thought bitterly that Raymond le Gros and Milo de Cogan should be imprisoned in the deepest dungeon for breaking the hard-won peace and forcing into exile those very people whose ancestors had first built the city.

As the sun was setting over the mountains, Dermot came to the house on the strand. He was gaunt, unshaven, his skin crusted with dirt. I sent him out to the bath house and had the servants sluice him down with hot and cold water and then when he was clean and dried and changed, we ate supper beside a fire of apple wood and drank heather ale.

"The last you will get. The brewer you so much admired has fled with Hasculf and his sons and I have lost many of my oldest friends." My voice was grim.

Dermot smacked his lips. "The taking of Dublin was not worth the loss of such a brewer. It was badly done. Strongbow has promised Laurence O'Toole to rebuild Christchurch Cathedral in stone in reparation." He managed a smile, but I knew that his mind was on other things.

"Will you go back to Ferns?"

He rubbed his mouth with the back of his hand. "Pity about the brewer. You should have traded a night in his bed for the secret. Even I who love you so much would have forgiven you."

I smiled sourly. "You would trade me this moment, body and soul, for another beaker of heather ale. Well, what are your plans or are they secret?"

He took up my hand and kissed the palm. I wished he wouldn't. It made me feel helpless, yielding and I wanted to be strong, uncaring.

"I must pursue Tiernan O'Rourke. There will be no peace until he is dead. Rory O'Connor is witless, he can be handled by Strongbow. He is afraid of might, but Tiernan O'Rourke is mad. He is still obsessed with you."

"He was never in love with me," I protested.

"Maybe not but he will not rest until I am dead." Dermot sighed. "I wish it were not so, but if ever I am to claim the High Kingship I must put an end to him once and for all."

I was weary of talk of war and strategies and the Church suing for peace, and sick to the pit of my stomach of what I had been forced to witness in Waterford. "The Normans are here to stay," I said bleakly. "They will never go home."

Dermot came over and knelt beside my chair. I stroked his thinning hair, somehow it made me want to cry. "Would you not give up, Dermot?" I pleaded. "I will go back to Ferns with you. You can be strong there. Now that Dublin is yours, all Leinster will support you."

"And leave the Normans to conquer the rest of Ireland? Beside, there is Tiernan O'Rourke."

Always Tiernan O'Rourke, I thought tiredly.

"Come to bed, Dervogilla," Dermot said burying his head in my lap. "I haven't closed my eyes for more than a week."

He fell asleep the moment his head touched the pillows. He awoke in the early dawn and made love with such passion and tenderness that it was like the first time. I little knew that it would be the last time we would ever lie together. Had I known would I have held him close, refused to let him go? Would he have listened? I only know now that we, all of us, have our particular devil who rides our backs and who forces us to give battle in the end.

Dermot and the Leinster army, swollen by the ranks of the Normans, set out on the long march north. They met pockets of resistance on the way, plundering Clonard, burning Kells, laying waste the shores of the Boyne. Word filtered back that Tiernan O'Rourke had put to death the hostages he held from his last sortie into Ferns, the young princes and chieftains, the captains' sons, even the priest who had gone with them as proof of good faith. But by the time Dermot reached Breifne, Tiernan O'Rourke had fled into Connaught leaving the grisly bodies of his victims hanging upside down from the battlements.

I later heard that the Lady Sunnivea had set fire to the castle. She was the only one left in the place when Dermot and his army reached the drawbridge. She had been sighted on the battlements enveloped in flames. The people from the surrounding districts had fled to the hills. When Beg brought me the news I wept for what had happened and for the time I had gone booleying to the top of the Iron Mountains. I saw again sturdy men and boys with ash plants driving the cattle, dogs barking, carefree young girls carrying spinning wheels and wool combs. Old men and women, stepping it out, children running and sliding. And I saw my small son, Tiernan Óg riding on Rachel's back, his face creased in a fat smile and the poor foolish young man who had saved my darling's life. The thought was too painful and I put it away, remembering instead my first journey to Breifne, the cold wooded country we went through in that frosty dawn. Sparkling lakes, reeds beaded with icicles, glittering like diamonds. There is another picture I have: hedgerows of whitethorn, ash, green oak, holly, wild cherry, an inquisitive bushy-tailed fox and my small son gurgling with laughter, popping blue marly clay into his mouth.

Shortly after leaving Breifne, Dermot disbanded his army and retired to the Black Country. Winter set in. Then came the day that is etched in everyone's memory. Four days after the feast of Christmas in the year of Our Lord, 1170, Thomas à Beckett was done to death. Murdered on a day when there was darkness over England, when black rain came driven in great gusts across Canterbury, when thunder crashed and forked lightning uprooted trees and set fire to thatch. Afterwards people asked each other, "Do you remember where you were, what you were doing, when you heard the news?"

I was walking over the strand, the day was cold

and blowy but I was well wrapped up when Nils came riding across the sands. For a moment I thought it was Dermot, though they were not at all alike.

"Word has just come through that King Henry's knights have murdered the Archbishop in the sanctuary of Canterbury Cathedral." His voice was hoarse.

I clung to a rock for support. It was the end of the world as I knew it. "Thomas à Beckett, done to death in the cathedral."

Nils jumped down and supported me with his arm. "They came from Normandy, four Norman knights, Hugh de Morville, Reginald FitzUrse, William Tracy and Richard Brito."

The names meant nothing to me. "And where is Henry?"

"They say he held his winter court in Bures in Normandy."

As Nils described the scene I saw the Great Hall, a riot of colour, blazing fires, green boughs nailed to the walls, the parti-coloured robes of the courtiers, Eleanor all gold and crimson silk. The air, rich, scented, alive with lute and laughter and song. "They were enjoying the feast," Nils went on, "when word was brought to Henry that the Archbishop had gathered an army around him and was marching on London."

"And was it true?"

"A rabble," Nils said scornfully. "An army of the lame, the sick, beggars, the destitute, they followed the Archbishop wherever he went, even after six years of rebellion, and the authority of the church in England in tatters. They revered him as a saint."

"What did Henry do or say to cause such a terrible thing to happen?"

"He fell into one of his rages for which he is known, pounding his fists on those who were near him, falling onto the ground, writhing and screaming out for all to hear. 'Who will rid me of this troublesome priest?' And the four knights took him at his word."

Nils gave a wry smile. "They were only waiting for a signal. They left the castle at once, riding through the night to the channel port. When they came to Canterbury, the Archbishop put up no resistance. They hacked him to death in sight of the high altar. Already there is talk of miracles."

"And their fellow Normans have come into our country," I whispered. "Surely they are the cursed of God. What has Dermot brought upon us?"

Beg brought me news that Dermot was fading. On a spring day when the apple blossoms were a glory to see, Strongbow sent for me. He had taken up residence in Hasculf's mansion, overlooking Hogg's Green. I thought he looked old and worn.

Aoife was there and she put her arms around me. "Father is dying. We are going to Ferns. He has asked for you. Will you come with us?"

I could feel the icy fingers of death around my heart. This was the end. But I told myself I must gather together my courage, go to Dermot, give him what help I could on his journey into eternity.

We set out for Kinsealy at once. We travelled with a strong escort, taking the fastest route, following the course of the Slaney.

Ferns was bright with flowers and flags fluttering in the breeze. The castle had been rebuilt and the town looked prosperous and pretty. Aoife had held herself well during the journey, had been pleasant and even gave the occasional smile. But now as we came within sight of the castle she burst into wild lamentations.

"Dermot will hear you," Strongbow said, trying to quieten her. "He needs peace in his last hours."

She clung to me. "Will you come with me, Dervogilla?"

"Not yet," I said, kissing her cheek. "First let you and your husband make your farewells."

"He must name his heir before he dies," Strongbow said slowly and I remembered how Dermot had promised this man the kingship of Leinster one day in Bristol. Would he remember that promise in his last agony? Would Strongbow understand?

Aoife enquired for her mother but was told that Mor was ill with dropsy in Wicklow and unable to travel. Blind Conor had arrived from Clonmacnois and with Strongbow and Aoife he went into the dying king's chamber. Dermot's brother and nephew had already taken their farewells.

I paced the cloisters of the Augustinian monastery, my years with Dermot slipping before my eyes with the beads that slipped through my fingers. The Abbot took me into the Lady Chapel and we prayed together, the prayers for the dying. It was there Strongbow found me and led me into the castle and up to the chamber smelling of incense and flowers and death. A nun who was in attendance beckoned me to enter.

Dermot lay propped up on a heap of pillows, his eyes closed, his breathing laboured. I came softly forward and put my hands on his. He opened his eyes and smiled at me, and for a wild moment I saw the boy with whom I had fallen in love all those years before, riding up Cork Hill on his charger, straight-backed, cloak billowing out behind him, hair the colour of ripe corn, hazel eyes, deep trout pool eyes flecked with gold.

"Dervogilla," he whispered. "You came."

"Where else should I be but with you?"

He stirred in the bed. "I cannot die peacefully," he said. "I have done grievous wrong. I have been proud and ambitious and put my trust in the things of this world . . . " His voice died away and he coughed.

I wet his lips. "Hush, don't trouble yourself, Dermot. You did what you had to do."

The thread of his voice. "Tell me, Dervogilla, was I wrong?"

I uttered a prayer to the Holy Spirit to inspire me to say the right words. "There was no peace in Ireland," I said softly. "There had been no peace for more than a century. Had you been High King . . . but it was not to be."

He moved restlessly and I smoothed his pillows. "Dermot, do you remember Aquitaine, the red-roofed houses, the walled towns, the harvest festivals, the wine we drank? And the Maubergeon Tower where we were happy?"

He stared at me, then his face twisted in pain. The nun who was at the end of the bed started forward but I waved her away.

"I invited the Normans to Ireland," he whispered.

I wiped his forehead of beads of sweat. "With the approval of the Church. Archbishop Laurence O'Toole supported you all the way. It was Pope Adrian who gave Ireland to Henry."

He licked his lips and I gave him a drink. "And now Thomas à Beckett is dead and Henry will come and there will be more slaughter." His voice was a wail.

I bent over the bed. "There is not much time left but I must tell you of a dream I had. The first time I dreamt it was in St David's in Wales. Again last night it came to me. I saw far into the future, to a time when the Normans had settled down, intermarried, adopted our customs, our bards, our music and legends. And I heard the words: 'They have become more Irish than the Irish themselves.'"

Dermot's face grimaced in a smile. "And you think that will happen?"

"I know it will happen, darling. This dream will come true. I was vouchsafed a glimpse of a time to come. Now try to rest."

He raised himself up on his pillows. "I have always loved you, Dervogilla, ever since that evening in the Thingmote. What was it you said . . . *Pillars of gold and silver . . .*"

"*A ceiling of swans' feathers,*" I whispered, "*and a company of fair men and women with a handsome king presiding over all . . .*" There was a hurting lump in my throat, I bit back the tears. "Oh Dermot, I love you," I said. But it was too late, his spirit had fled.

I kissed his cold lips and closed his eyelids. I thought I had never seen Dermot look so peaceful in life as he did in death.

The nun at the end of the bed had come round and was shaking holy water, murmuring, "Out of the depths I have cried to thee, O Lord. Lord, hear my prayer."

The room was filling with people, Aoife and Strongbow and Conor were there, and Dermot's brother Murrough and his nephew who would one day be King of Leinster. Monks from the Augustinian monastery were filing in waving censers, chanting the office for the dead. And after them came the keening women in black who would raise the lament. Beg was perched on the end of the bed, his little face twisted in grief, and Nils was there trying to comfort the king's jester who would jest no more. Unnoticed I slipped away. It was the end of our story.

Epilogue

Dublin, 1176

To Robert Balmais, Clerk of Canterbury Cathedral, from the Princess Dervogilla of Meath. Written under her seal in the month of September, in the year of Our Lord, 1176.

Since last we met in Mellifont, I have decided that it is fitting that I set down the story of my life, not as an apologia for what happened, but for the sake of the records. It is my wish that you will keep this manuscript in a safe place until such time as I am called to a greater judgement to answer for my sins and omissions. When this happens, you are free to do as you wish with this manuscript. To add it to your account of the history of my country, to keep for another time, or to consign to the flames.

Today I stood under the High Cross of Dublin where public announcements are made, in the shadow of Christchurch Cathedral which has been rebuilt and where Strongbow, who died a month ago, lies in his tomb. It is four years now since the town crier announced the death of my husband, Tiernan O'Rourke. His body was brought to Dublin and his head raised over the door of the fortress. I did not dare look. I preferred to remember him in happier days – and there were a few. We are all a mixture of good and bad. Nothing in life is ever clear-cut. I have learnt to forgive him, as I hope for forgiveness. I pray for his soul.

Tiernan O'Rourke was slain in single combat by Hugh de Lacy, on the Hill of Ward near Athboy. He had made many enemies in his life, and many

Normans and Irish wished him dead. There would be no peace while he lived.

Dermot McMurrough once said: "In our beginning is our end." He was born to be High King of Ireland, had been nurtured on the dream, but fate had decreed otherwise. In the childhood of Tiernan O'Rourke, the seeds of his madness were sown. Donnell, son of Annadh O'Rourke of his own clan, betrayed him. Tiernan O'Rourke had seduced his chieftain's young wife, and then, in a fit of rage, branded the girl. Afterwards she drowned herself in the waters of Lough Erne.

King Henry has come and gone. He landed in Waterford, six months after Dermot's death and his journey to Dublin was a triumphal procession. Normans, Norse and Irish all bent the knee. He was received at Cashel by the bishops, headed by Laurence O'Toole. They gave him their blessing and paid him homage. The church was safe, that was all that mattered. I wonder if, as they swore fealty, they thought of that murder in the cathedral.

Beg and Nils went on pilgrimage to Canterbury and described the mortuary chapel where the body of Thomas à Beckett is buried, the altar all gold and marble and jewelled. A lavish tomb for a man who wore a hair shirt riddled with lice. This was not revealed until the Archbishop was dead. They travelled the roads with the blind, the lame, those afflicted in body and spirit, and those who, like themselves, suffered from nothing more serious than curiosity or itchy feet. They brought back stories of miraculous cures, as well as bawdy tales which Beg has repeated in every inn and hostel between Dublin and Ferns. Nils said that Henry swore on the saint's tomb, where he was whipped by the monks in penance, that he neither sought nor desired the archbishop's death. The Church may absolve Henry, but not Eleanor. She cared little for Beckett in life, but Henry's liaison with Rosamund Clifford bit deeply. She visited the love-nest in Woodstock and is said to have offered her rival a choice of deaths. A dagger or a cup of poison. Whatever the truth, the fair Rosamund is no more. Queen Eleanor is not a lady with whom it is wise to trifle as I sensed long ago in the Palace of Poitiers.

The Peace Treaty of Windsor has been signed by Henry, King of England and Lord of Aquitaine, and Rory O'Connor, High King of Ireland, in the presence of Laurence O'Toole, Archbishop of Dublin. Rory O'Connor has pledged to recognise Henry as his Overlord and to collect annual tribute for him from all parts of Ireland. Henry was heard to mutter that Rory would be the last Irish king to reign. It will take time and diplomacy but I foresee a day when there will be friendship and perhaps something even closer between Norman and Irish. Already the signs are there. Rory O'Connor has promised his daughter in marriage to a Norman lord, other kings and princes are following suit. Soon a new breed of Norman-Irish will be raised up and the vision I had will come true. I think that dream helped Dermot in the end.

Recently I went on a visit to Ferns. Grass grows between the stones that were raised on Dermot's cairn, but the common people still mourn him, laying their tributes of wild flowers on his grave. Only the scribes will allow him no rest. In the *Annals of Ulster* they have written his obituary:

Dermot McMurrough, King of Leinster, after spoiling numerous churches and territories, died at Ferns without the body of Christ, without penitence, without making a will, through the merits of Columcille and Finnen and all the other saints whose churches he spoiled.

They have chosen to forget the Dermot who founded the Cistercian Abbey at Baltinglass, the Priory of All Hallows in Dublin, the Convent of St Mary de Hogg, the Augustinian Monastery at Ferns. The Abbot, a saintly man, gave Dermot the last rites and his monks chanted the prayers for the dead.

I love Dublin, it is my city, my home, but I have decided to exile myself. I shall visit the convent at Clonmacnois within sight of the Shannon, where I hope to confess and be shriven. Then I shall take my final journey to the convent I have founded in Mellifont. Already the community of nuns have offered to make me their Abbess. There is much work to be done amongst the poor and afflicted; in the sanctuary for lepers, the hospice for the dying, and, dear to my heart, the refuge for battered wives and orphaned children. I shall give comfort and cheer. If one's heart is totally hollow, no one seems to notice the difference.

I shall put the past behind me, knowing there is no going back. Yet sometimes I may be seduced by a chance word, a smell, a chord of music, the sound of running water, a drifting cloud, the flash of an eagle's wing. Then I shall walk in imagination the gardens of

the golden Palace of Poitiers, revisit the Maubergeon
Tower, reach over the ramparts to the sea far below,
or enter the FitzGerald Castle in Wales where there
was laughter and music and song.

But there is one place I know I dare not stray. It is
the Great Hall of the Thingmote in Dublin and I am
fifteen years of age. I am showing off, recounting to a
young man with hazel eyes and hair the colour of ripe
corn the opening lines of a legend we both know and
love . . .

*Pillars of gold and silver, a ceiling of swans' feathers
and a company of fair men and women with a handsome
king presiding over all.*